"I love the way this man writes! I adore his style. There is something about it that makes me feel as if I'm someplace I'm not supposed to be, seeing things I'm not supposed to see and that is so delicious."
REBECCA FORESTER, USA Today Bestselling Author

This book "is creative and captivating. It features bold characters, witty dialogue, exotic locations, and non-stop action. The pacing is spot-on, a solid combination of intrigue, suspense, and eroticism. A first-rate thriller, this book is damnably hard to put down. It's a tremendous read."
FOREWORD REVIEWS

"A terrifying, gripping cross between James Patterson and John Grisham. Jagger has created a truly killer thriller."
J.A. KONRATH, International Bestselling Author

"As engaging as the debut, this exciting blend of police procedural and legal thriller recalls the early works of Scott Turow and Lisa Scottoline."
LIBRARY JOURNAL

"The well-crafted storyline makes this a worthwhile read. Stuffed with gratuitous sex and over-the-top violence, this novel has a riveting plot."
KIRKUS REVIEWS

"Verdict: The pacing is relentless in this debut, a hard-boiled novel with a shocking ending. The supershort chapters will please those who enjoy a James Patterson–style page-turner"
LIBRARY JOURNAL

A "clever and engrossing mystery tale involving gorgeous women, lustful men and scintillating suspense."
FOREWORD MAGAZINE

"Part of what makes this thriller thrilling is that you sense there to be connections among all the various subplots; the anticipation of their coming together keeps the pages turning."
BOOKLIST

"This is one of the best thrillers I've read yet."
NEW MYSTERY READER MAGAZINE

"A superb thriller and an exceptional read."
MIDWEST BOOK REVIEW

"Verdict: This fast-paced book offers fans of commercial thrillers a twisty, action-packed thrill ride."
LIBRARY JOURNAL

"Another masterpiece of action and suspense."
NEW MYSTERY READER MAGAZINE

"Fast paced and well plotted . . . While comparisons will be made with Turow, Grisham and Connelly, Jagger is a new voice on the legal/thriller scene. I recommend you check out this debut book, but be warned . . . you are not going to be able to put it down."
CRIMESPREE MAGAZINE

"A chilling story well told. The pace never slows in this noir thriller, taking readers on a stark trail of fear."
CAROLYN G. HART, N.Y. Times and USA Today Bestselling Author

KILLER
MAYBE

Thriller Publishing Group, Inc.

KILLER
MAYBE

R.J. JAGGER

Thriller Publishing Group, Inc.

KILLER MAYBE

Thriller Publishing Group, Inc.
Golden, Colorado 80401

Copyright©2020 RJ Jagger

Library of Congress Control Number: Available

ISBN 978-1-937888-72-5 (Hardcover)

10 9 8 7 6 5 4 3 2 1

Printed in the United States of America

For Eileen

ACKNOWLEDGEMENTS

Special appreciation goes out to Esperanza Marcia for doing brave editorial battle against tenacious typos and all shapes and sizes of hidden little errors.

DAY
ONE

July 18
Monday

1

Sophia Phair got pulled out of a cavernous sleep Monday morning by a painful drumming inside her head. She opened her eyes just enough to see daylight squirting around the window coverings. The clock said 9:02, long past what it should. She was supposed to have been at the law firm more than an hour ago.

Her heart raced.

She yanked the covers off and maneuvered her naked body to the bathroom. In the mirror she saw blood in her hair, lots of blood, dried now but from a vicious wound. It was caked on, thick and messy.

What happened to her?

She couldn't remember.

She turned the shower on, got the water up to temperature and stepped in. Gently, she eased her head under the spray in short motions. Blood washed down her chest and stomach and thighs and pooled briefly at her feet before moving to the drain. She kept her raven-black hair under the spray until the water turned clear and then took shampoo to it.

She got out, pat-dried her hair with a towel and slipped into a robe. The wound was visible now, about four inches long, cresting over a large lump, raw but not bleeding. She checked the bedroom and found no blood that would indicate she'd fallen.

She went downstairs.

A trail of blood droppings started at the front door and led up the stairs, as if she'd come into the house already bleeding. She turned the knob and found it was unlocked.

Outside on the front steps were more drops.

She checked the inside of her car. Blood was on the headrest and the front seat, meaning she'd driven home with the wound.

Where had she been?

Her memory was blank.

Aspirin; she needed aspirin, not in ten seconds, now, this second. Back up in the bathroom she popped two and washed them down with a full glass of water.

She wasn't drunk.

She wasn't hung over.

She didn't feel like she'd been drugged.

Her body was as it should be, taut, strong, in its prime. Her face was unmarked, as hypnotic and beautiful as ever. Her eyes were green and focused without blurring. She remembered everything that happened since she got up this morning. She remembered yesterday afternoon, taking a grueling bike ride up Lookout Mountain. She remembered yesterday evening, paying bills and washing laundry with the TV on. She remembered something with her phone, getting a call or a text.

She couldn't remember who it was from.

That's all she could remember.

Everything about last night was a blank, a scary, confusing blank.

According to her phone she received a text at 4:38 p.m. yesterday from Jackie Lake:

Need UR help. I developed a conflict for Monday morning and need someone to cover the Anderson sta-

tus conference in the AM, Denver District Court, Courtroom 18, 8:30. Make my day and say you can do it. I have
the file at home. My flight gets in at 9. I should be home
by 10. Thx GF! Owe you 1!

Sophia texted back:

Can do. See you tonight.

She must have gone to Jackie's last night.

If that's what happened, she didn't remember it.

She didn't remember getting in the car, or driving over, or
talking to her, or anything else for that matter.

The Anderson file wasn't on the kitchen counter or on the
desk or on a chair or anywhere else in the house. It wasn't in
the car either.

She called Jackie's cell phone.

No one answered.

She got dumped into voicemail.

"Jackie, it's me, Sophia. Call me as soon as you can. We may
have a problem."

She hung up.

The aspirin wasn't working, or if it was, not anywhere near
where it needed to. She opened the bottle, tapped two into her
palm, then thought better of it and put one back in the bottle.

The other one went into her mouth with a large swallow
of water.

She called Courtroom 18 and got the division clerk. "This is
Sophia Phair with Beacher, Condor & Lee. We had a status
conference set for 8:30 this morning in *Anderson v. Delta Financial Group*. We might have had a mix-up in our office. Did
Jackie Lake or anyone else from our firm show up there this
morning?"

"No."

"No?"

"No."

"I can be there in twenty minutes. Is it too late to come down?"

Yes, it was.

She should reschedule.

"Thanks."

She placed a fingertip gently on her wound. When she pulled it off there was a wet drop of blood. She patted the cut with a towel then blow-dried, got dressed in a gray pinstriped skirt and crisp white blouse, and headed downtown.

Traffic was thick.

On the way, something unexpected happened.

She couldn't remember how old she was.

She pulled her license out.

According to it she was twenty-eight.

Seeing it didn't refresh her memory.

The information didn't exist inside her head.

She flashed back to Saturday.

For that, her memory was clear.

She woke Saturday morning after ten still partially drunk, in a bed that didn't belong to her. Next to her was a naked man sound asleep, a man with a model's face and a gladiator's body and a wild mane of thick black hair that went halfway down his back. She didn't know his name but it wasn't because she didn't remember, it was because she pressed her finger to his lips when they first met earlier that night and said, "No names."

"Okay."

He bought her liquor.

He brought her to his loft.

He took her like an animal.

He took her every bit as good as she hoped he would.

For a brief moment she even considered checking his wallet

and getting his name.

Instead she got silently dressed and wrote *Thanks* in lipstick on the bathroom mirror.

Then she gave him a peck on the cheek, took one last look and slipped out.

The sky was cerulean blue.

The sunshine went straight to her brain.

That was Saturday morning.

It seemed like a century ago.

2

Nick Teffinger, the 34-year-old head of Denver's homicide department, got up before dawn Monday morning, took a three-mile jog, showered, and filled a thermos with coffee. Then, with a bowl of cereal in his lap and a cup of coffee in his left hand, he pointed the front end of the Tundra east on the 6th Avenue freeway, primarily steering with his knees. The sun lifted off the horizon and blinded him as best it could. Even with the visor down, the glare ricocheted off the hood with an evil intent. He hunted around for his sunglass for a few heartbeats before remembering he sat on them last week.

Traffic was already thick but not insane.

He punched the radio buttons, hoping to get a Beatles song or, if not that, maybe something by the Beach Boys, although fat chance of that. What he got was a bunch of DJs who started drinking coffee two hours before him. He decided if they were dogs they'd be French Poodles and punched them off.

The victim lived in a nice standalone house on the east edge of the city, just west of Colorado Boulevard. Teffinger pulled up in front of her house, killed the engine and stepped out.

It was already hot.

It would probably break a hundred again today.

If that happened, it would be the tenth day in a row.

If there were any blades of grass still alive somewhere in the city, today would be their last.

He got halfway up the victim's cobblestone driveway, then went back to the car, got the thermos and continued to the front door.

It was crisscrossed with yellow crime-scene tape.

He took a sip of coffee, tore the tape off and opened the door with a key.

Inside it was quiet.

It was the complete opposite of the chaos and movement and buzz and lights and questions and anxiety and tension and detail work of last night. He stood there for a moment listening to the nothingness.

It felt like cool water.

The victim was a lawyer named Jackie Lake, age 32, physically fit, single, with strawberry-blond hair. Last night someone tied her wrists to the headboard, removed her pants and panties, and strangled her to death while he raped her. From the marks on her neck, he removed his thumbs from her windpipe several times, taking her to the edge and bringing her back time after time after time.

When he was done he took a souvenir; her left ear.

Teffinger sipped coffee and headed for the bedroom. The bed was still there but the sheets and pillows had been taken as evidence.

He set the cup and thermos on the nightstand next to the alarm clock.

Then he did what he couldn't do last night when the room was full of people.

He laid down on the bed.

He put his arms up as if they were tied to the frame.

Then he held his breath for as long as he could.

He didn't breathe in.

He didn't breathe out.

He kept his lungs immobile as if they had been separated from the world by thumbs pressing into his throat. He imaged the weight of someone straddling his stomach, someone heavy, someone stronger than him. He imagined looking into that person's eyes and seeing no mercy, and instead seeing only a sick joy of finally doing what he'd dreamed about in his twisted little mind over and over and over.

He exhaled.

He inhaled.

Then the thumbs came again, just that fast. He thrashed his body but could hardly get it to move an inch. The movement barely registered on the person above. It didn't come within 1% of throwing him off balance. He pulled wildly at the ropes.

They dug into his flesh.

He could feel the skin ripping.

He didn't care.

He didn't care if his whole hands ripped off.

He needed air.

Air.

Air.

Air.

The pain was terrible.

His mind got foggy.

He was dying.

He was slipping away.

It was almost over.

He sat bolt upright in a cold sweat.

His lungs screamed for air as if he'd just broken the surface of the water.

He inhaled deeply and quickly, again and again and again.

Oxygen rushed into his blood.

Blood rushed through his veins.

His body responded by not shutting down.

He would live.

He would live.

He would live.

He swung his legs over the side of the bed and dipped his head into his hands. He stayed like that until he got his composure back. Then he stood up, looked at the empty bed and said, "I promise."

Suddenly the doorbell rang.

Teffinger opened it to find a man he recognized, the guy who lived across the street. What was his name? Rosenfield or Rosenberg, something like that; it was in the notes. Teffinger talked to him briefly last night. The man hadn't seen anything.

"I saw you come in," the man said.

"Right."

"I said something last night that wasn't quite true," he said. "I said I didn't see anything. Actually, I did. I was afraid to get involved."

Teffinger nodded.

"That happens," he said. "Personally, I think it's all those flashing lights. I've seen them a hundred times and they still creep me out, especially at night."

"You're messing with me."

Teffinger raked his hair back with his fingers.

It immediately flopped back down over his forehead.

"I wish I was," he said. "So what'd you see last night?"

"Come on outside and I'll show you."

"Hold on, let me grab my thermos."

3

Yardley White took one last look at her hotter-than-sin reflection, blew herself a kiss, and strutted her perfect five-foot-five body across the plush beige carpet and out the front door of the loft, making sure it was locked behind her. She took the granite-walled elevator down eight floors to ground level, walked through a vaulted contemporary lobby and got deposited into the trendy heart of LoDo on the north edge of downtown Denver.

The sun was bright.

The air was already warm.

She wore a short 20s skirt, stockings with a seam up the back attached to a garter belt, and black high heels. Up top was a white blouse tucked at a slim waist and cinched with a wide black belt. Her thick blond hair was pulled up. Her lips were soft and red.

She slipped designer sunglasses on, pulled a pack of Marlboros out of her purse, tapped one out and dangled it in her lips. She dug around for a book of matches and felt two. She pulled one out. It was black with a red M. Inside was writing, not hers, a male scroll that said, "Aaron," followed by a (303) number.

She remembered him.

He wasn't bad.

Maybe she'd call him someday.

She lit the smoke and stuffed the matches back in her purse. The nicotine was magic in her lungs. She held it in then pointed her 25-year-old body west, towards the less trendy areas farther away from downtown and Coors Field.

Three blocks later she came to Wazee and turned right.

Real estate was cheaper there.

Old warehouses were home to small restaurants, not-so-good art galleries and small offices, mostly architects and lawyers who were more interested in the ambiance and texture and parking availability than they were about a fancy 17th Street address.

A block down she came to a brick standalone building with a worn patina that included a dozen different shades of mortar patching. While the building was old, the door was new, pure oak and heavy. The trim around it had been painted burnt-red. Matching awnings hung over the two front windows, one on either side of the door. Stenciled on the left window were the words, *Extraordinary Books.*

She pushed the front door open and walked in.

The air had an old parchment aroma to it. Weaving through that air was a scratchy record coming from a turntable over in the corner. A female was singing. A band, a big band—too big in fact—was playing behind her, something from the 40s. Surprising, as poor as the quality of sound was, the melody was catchy, even within just a few bars.

The place was crammed with bookshelves.

On those shelves were old books.

Lots of them were leather bound and hand stitched.

They looked like they had been carefully hand collected one at a time over a number of years.

They looked expensive.

They looked rare.

They looked collectable.

Deven Devenshire emerged from the back room looking yummy but slightly hung over.

"I heard you got a lead on a new Steinbeck manuscript," she said.

"I wouldn't call it a manuscript," Yardley said. "It's more of an outline."

"For which book?"

"Cannery Row."

"Has it been authenticated?"

"No, it's underground."

"You're going to get burned."

"Haven't yet."

"Maybe not but the day's coming."

"Not today it isn't."

She headed into the back room which had a small kitchen and an old roll top desk inundated with papers. On the north side she opened another door, which looked like it led to the outside. Immediately behind it was a second door, a thick steel one with a tumbler. Yardley worked the numbers to the right and left five times, pushed down on the handle and swung the door open.

Inside was a small room with steel walls, a steel floor and a steel ceiling. A thick, textured oriental rug covered the floor. In the middle of the room was a contemporary table with a green banker's lamp.

Three of the walls were inundated with bookshelves.

Yardley pulled a worn leather briefcase out from under the table and set it on top. She opened it just to be sure everything was inside and undisturbed even though there was no reason to think otherwise.

Everything was there.

She closed it, grabbed the handle and locked the vault behind her.

Deven was at the counter reading 5280.

Yardley approached her from behind, wrapped her arms around the woman's stomach and nibbled her neck.

"Did you get screwed this weekend?"

Deven turned and grinned.

"You can't even believe."

"Oh, really? By who?"

"Someone named Brittany."

"You going to see her again?"

"Don't know," Deven said. "She has a powerful little tongue though, I'll tell you that much. Are you jealous?"

"I'm always jealous," Yardley said.

"No you're not. Brittany was a kinky little thing. She had toys I didn't even know existed."

Yardley cocked her head and said, "Remind me again why I employ you—"

"Because you're secretly in love with me."

"Trust me, that's not it."

"Okay, lust then. Not love, lust."

Yardley shook her head.

"Keep an eye on things. I'll be back some time this afternoon."

A hour later she was in a Grob Aerospace SP jet, the only passenger, heading west over the Rockies with the briefcase on the seat next to her. Three hours later she touched down at LAX where she rented a black 5-Series BMW.

She punched the home address of disbarred attorney Richard Blank into the GPS and studied the map.

Then she merged into traffic.

4

Beacher, Condor & Lee, LLC occupied floors 40, 41 and 42 of the cash register building on 17th Street in the heart of Denver's financial district. For years it was the city's second largest law firm. This year it muscled into the top dog position as a result of the continuing decline of Holland, Roberts & Northway, thanks to the Michael Northway fiasco last year.

Sophia scurried through the reception area intent on making up the lost part of the day to the extent possible. Before she got past the glass walled conference rooms and into the hallways, the receptionist waved her over.

"Did you hear?"

'No. Hear what?"

"Jackie Lake got murdered last night."

Sophia studied the woman's face, waiting for the punch line. Then her chest pounded.

"You're serious," she said.

"It's so freaky."

"What happened?"

The woman shrugged.

"No one knows yet other than it happened and it's being investigated as a murder, not an accident or a suicide."

"Is it on the news?"

"It started to break an hour ago," she said. "I'll bet dollars to donuts that the cops will be around here today asking questions. Condor's already put out a global email telling everyone to be around as much as possible."

"I'll be here," Sophia said.

"We're having lunch catered," she said. "The big conference room at noon."

"Okay."

In her office, Sophia closed the door and locked it. She left the lights off and slumped into her chair. She had one thought and one thought only, namely that she was the one who killed Jackie.

That's how she got the wound.

They must have had a fight.

It must have been traumatic.

That's why she couldn't remember.

Her brain was trying to protect her.

The cops could be here any second.

Sooner or later, probably sooner, they'd get their hands on Jackie's cell phone records. They'd have the text messages and know that Sophia went to Jackie's house last night. That plus the head wound would be all they'd need to hold her as a prime suspect. Then the forensics would start to get matched up. She unquestionably left prints, DNA, fibers and who knows what else.

Think.

Think.

Think.

As wrong as what she did was, she didn't want to get carted out of the firm in handcuffs. She couldn't take the stares and the whispers and the wide-eyed looks of surprise. She couldn't take watching the news tomorrow from a jail cell and hearing one of her co-workers tell a reporter, "It really doesn't surprise me. There were rumors that she had a secret side."

"What kind of secret side?"

"I don't know, it was just gossip."

"Gossip about what?"

"I've already said too much."

Taylor Sutton was a good defense attorney and her office was close, just a couple of blocks down the 16th Street Mall. Maybe Sophia should go over there right now and tell her what happened. If nothing else, the woman could negotiate her surrender and get it done privately.

What to do?

What to do?

What to do?

Her head pounded.

The Aspirin was working but only halfway.

Suddenly a knock came at the door.

Sophia stared at the sound, frozen, and said nothing.

The knob jiggled but didn't turn.

"Sophia are you in there?"

She recognized the voice.

It belonged to Renn-Jaa Tan, the associate next door.

5

Teffinger parked the Tundra in the underground lot, bypassed the elevators, took the stairs to the third floor and pushed into the homicide department. His desk was over by the windows, a cubical, open and exposed. His predecessor had an enclosed office down the hall; quiet enough to sleep in. Teffinger could have it if he wanted but elected to stay right where he was when he got promoted to head of the department three years ago.

"Closer to the coffee," he said.

Actually that wasn't true.

Three people paced it off to prove it.

He dialed the cell phone of Dr. Leigh Sandt, the FBI profiler from Quantico, Virginia, and pulled up an image of a classy, 50-year-old woman with Tina Turner legs.

She actually answered.

"Your caller ID must not be working," Teffinger said.

She laughed.

"Long time," she said.

"Too long. I have a situation."

"An angry husband?"

"Not funny," he said. "I have a victim of last night, an attorney, single, attractive, repeatedly choked while being raped. Her wrists were tied to the headboard. Here's the unique thing.

The guy cut off her left ear."

"Did he take it with him or leave it there?"

"Took it."

He let the words hang.

He knew that she knew what he wanted, namely to check and see if any similar murders had taken place across the country over the years.

"Personally it doesn't ring a bell but I'll check," she said.

"How soon?"

She exhaled.

"You know what your problem is, Nick? You never stop being you."

He smiled.

"I'm writing something down," he said. "It says, Send Leigh flowers."

"Nick, you're the cheapest guy on the face of the earth. It's never going to happen. You know it and I know it."

"That's why I told you I was writing it down," he said. "That way you at least know I thought about it." A beat then, "Remember when you stayed at my house? The towel malfunction—"

"Stop. I'm still in therapy over that."

"Good."

He hung up and found Sydney Heatherwood sitting in one of the two worn chairs in front of his desk. She was the newbie to the department, stolen out of vice personally by Teffinger last year. She wore a pink sleeveless blouse that showcased strong arms and contrasted nicely against her mocha African American skin.

"Do you want me to send Leigh flowers for you?"

He pictured it.

"Yes," he said. "That will totally flip her out."

She held her hand out.

"Give me thirty bucks."

He checked his wallet.

There was a five and three ones.

He picked up a pencil, wrote Send Leigh Flowers on a piece of paper, and handed it to Sydney. "Tell you what," he said. "Just fax her this."

Sydney gave him a look.

Then she pushed a stapled set of paper across the desk.

"That's the victim's cell phone records," she said. "Just came in."

"That was quick. I'm impressed."

He studied them starting with the most recent and going back three days.

Sydney pointed to the most recent pair, which was a text from the victim asking someone to cover a court hearing in the morning

"That was to a number registered to Sophia Phair," Sydney said. "She's an attorney in the same firm as Jackie Lake."

"Okay."

The entry before that was a phone connection, not a text, lasting about two minutes. Sydney pointed to it and said, "That call was to Grayson Condor. He's an uppity-up in the firm."

Those were the only entries from yesterday, the day she got murdered.

Teffinger stuffed the records in a manila envelope and said, "You feel like taking a ride?"

"To where? The law firm?"

"I'll give you a hint. I'm either thinking of that or the flower shop."

"Well it's not the flower shop."

"Bingo."

6

The disbarred lawyer, Richard Blank, lived in a contemporary mansion in Beverly Hills. Yardley pulled the BMW through the wrought iron gate past the stone lions, up the cobblestone driveway and next to the water feature, where she killed the engine and stepped out.

The air was more humid than she expected.

Cotton-ball clouds swept overhead.

When she knocked on the door, a man answered. It was him. She recognized him from the pictures and, seeing him in the flesh for the first time, began to work on how to best change his face.

"Yes?" he said.

"How would you like to be a lawyer again?" Yardley said.

The man wrinkled his brow.

He was 45, six-one, with blond surfer hair and a manly face with a dimple in his chin, the epitome of what a good trial lawyer should look like.

"Who are you?"

"I'm someone who can change your life," she said. "Before I say more, I need your assurance that our conversation will remain personal."

He sized her up.

Then he swung the door open and said, "Come in."

They ended up in the back by the pool in the shade of a cabana with a pitcher of iced tea.

"This is nice but it's not a courtroom," she said. "You're bored here." She looked around. "I would be too. There's no fight, no action, no conflict. There's no one hanging on your every word." She looked him in the eyes. "You miss that. That's not the question. The question is, how much do you miss it? Do you miss it enough to do what it takes to get it back?"

He cocked his head.

"What's your game?"

"No game," she said. "I'm someone who can get your license back. It's that simple."

"No one can do that."

"I can."

"How?"

"I'll explain," she said. "But first answer my question. Do you miss it enough to do what it takes to get it back? The reason I ask is that if we go forward, you're going to have to do things, some extreme things. So, here it is again, do you miss it enough to do what it takes to get it back?"

A pause.

His face got serious.

"Yes."

"Good," she said. "In that case we may be able to do business together. Let's find out."

He took a sip of tea.

"Let's."

She studied the pool.

"The water looks nice," she said. "Is it warm?"

"Warm enough."

She walked over, scooted down and felt it with her hand. It was almost the temperature of a hot tub. The sun reflected into her eyes.

It felt nice.

"Have you ever been to New York?"

Blank shook his head.

"No."

"That's where you'll be practicing," she said. "New York. It's nice there. You're going to like it. You're going to be a freaking rock star again. You won't have a pool though. No one in New York has a pool."

7

S ophia waited until Renn-Jaa stopped knocking, then opened the door a crack, stuck her head out and looked up and down the hall. No one was in sight. Her plan was to slip out of the firm but that changed just before she got to the elevators. Instead, she took the spiral staircase up to 41 and went to Jackie Lake's office. The door was closed but not locked. She slipped in and closed it behind her.

She sat down in the woman's chair and shut her eyes. Her head spun as if she'd just chugged a glass of wine.

What happened last night?

What got so important that it escalated to murder?

Something grabbed her attention on the floor under the desk. It turned out to be a picture of Jackie straddling a man's lap as if giving him a lap dance.

It was jagged but sensual.

The man was enjoying it.

So was Jackie.

Sophia stuffed it in her bra next to her heart and closed her eyes.

The darkness was a drug.

She needed more.

Suddenly the door opened and Xavier Zarra walked in, one of the senior partners from the top floor. The shock on her face was palpable.

"What are you doing in here?"

"I don't know. Saying goodbye, I guess."

"This office is off limits," she said. "There was a global email sent this morning to that effect."

"I'm sorry, I—"

"Did you touch anything?"

"No."

"Are you sure?"

"Yes."

The woman gave a mean look, then let it transition to a smile.

"We're all upset," she said. "Let's just try to handle it."

"Okay."

She walked back down to 40 and headed for the elevators, only to spot a man and woman in the reception area. The man was about thirty-four, six-two, with a solid body and a drop-dead gorgeous face that belonged on the cover of GQ. He had long-ish brown hair that tended to flop over his eyes. He wore jeans, black leather shoes, a blue cotton shirt and loose blue tie. He was engrossed with one of the oil paintings on the wall, the Delano.

The woman was younger, African American, with a gym build.

The man turned to Sophia as she crossed.

Their eyes met.

There was something wrong with his, no, not wrong, *different*. It took a heartbeat before she figured it out. One was blue and one was green.

He looked at her, first as one stranger looking at another, then as something more.

"Hi," he said.

"Hi."

She continued.

He grabbed her arm.

"Hold it a second," he said.

"What's the problem?"

He brought his face close to hers and whispered, "I looked for you, after that night. I went back to that bar six different times."

She pulled her arm free.

"You have the wrong person."

"No I don't."

"I've never seen you before in my life," she said.

"Why are you saying that?"

"Because it's true."

He wrinkled his forehead.

"You really don't remember me?"

"You can't remember someone you've never met," she said.

"If we never met, then tell me one thing," he said.

"And what's that?"

"How come I know you have a yin-yang tattoo on your right cheek?"

The words startled her.

They were true.

"I have to go," she said.

"Then nothing's changed," he said. "That's too bad."

She headed for the elevators. Halfway there she turned and came back.

"I'm sorry I don't remember you," she said.

He shrugged.

"It's okay. I'm a pretty forgettable guy."

She paused, not sure if she was actually going to say what she was thinking of saying, and then said, "Not really." A beat then, "When was it that we knew each other?"

"Last summer, late August," the man said. "For two days."

"Two? Are you sure?"

He nodded.

"I'm sure. Well, let me take that back. Friday night to Sunday morning, whatever that calculates to be."

"That's a long time," she said. "You must have made an impression."

"I do what I can."

She smiled and walked away.

"Hey, wait."

She turned.

"Yes?"

"What's your name?"

She shook her head.

"No names."

8

When the raven-haired beauty left, Sydney got in Teffinger's face and said, "You never told me about that one. Why not?"

"You want the truth or lies?"

"Whichever you have handy."

"That would be the latter," he said. "She picked me up in a bar one night. We spent some time together. She left while I was sleeping. That's it."

Sydney made a face.

"No, that's not it, because if that was it you would have told me about it back when it happened," she said. "You kept her from me." Her face brightened. "You actually liked her."

He shrugged.

"Maybe."

She punched his arm.

"You dog," she said. "You're in love."

"*Was,*" he said. "A little bit, maybe."

She studied him.

"No *was* about it, Teffinger. I know that look. It's the same one a wolf has when it sees a rabbit."

"Nice comparison."

"So what are you going to do now that you know who she is?"

"Nothing."

She shook her head.

"The day you do nothing is the day I start liking the Beach Boys."

A woman approached and announced that Mr. Condor was free now. "Would you like to take the stairs or the elevator up to his office?"

"Stairs," Teffinger said.

Five minutes later they were on 42 in an unoccupied corner office that was bigger than Teffinger's house. Two of the walls were glass, not windows, glass—floor to ceiling. Teffinger walked over, keeping his distance, and took a timid look down. Denver unfolded beneath his feet and fifteen miles to the west the mountains jutted out of the flatlands with a jagged force.

Against one of the interior walls was as old jukebox.

Teffinger went over and checked the playlist, then punched K5. The machine jumped to life, a 45 got placed on a turntable and a needle set down. A scratching sound came from the speakers.

Then the music came.

Geraldine, oh Geraldine,
Get your big old tits off my back.
Geraldine, oh Geraldine,
Get your big old tits off my back.
It's sugar in your tea baby,
But it's giving me a heart attack.

Suddenly the door opened and three people walked in, two men and a woman, each wearing clothes that cost more than Teffinger's first car. The front man extended his hand. "I'm Grayson Condor, the managing partner. These are two of my partners, Tom Fondell and Xavier Zarra."

Condor was almost Teffinger's height with a solid build and a python-strong handshake. His face was tanned and his hair was slightly disheveled, as if it would be more at home on a sailboat than in a boardroom. His teeth were white and his smile was big. Tom Fondell wasn't even a candle compared to Condor. In fact, as soon as Teffinger looked away, he forgot what the man looked like. The woman, Xavier Zarra, reminded Teffinger a lot of Leigh Sandt, classy with shapely legs encased in nylons.

They ended up seated at a small but expensive conference table with fancy coffee cups and coasters. Teffinger looked at Condor and got to the point.

"Jackie Lake made a few phone calls yesterday. One of them was to you."

Condor nodded.

"That's true."

"What was that conversation about?"

"Jackie was in San Francisco taking depositions," he said. "On Saturday she deposed a woman named Blanch Wethersfield, the assistant CFO of Hedgley Management Group, which is a party that our client, Daniel Dexter, is suing. On Sunday Jackie deposed Johnnie Squares, the CFO of Hedgley. Jackie called me on Sunday to brief me on the depositions. I'm the primary attorney on the case. Jackie and two other attorneys—Peter Slide and Jesse Jones—are working the case with me, under my direction. All four of us have formally entered our appearance in court as counsel of record."

Teffinger nodded.

"So how'd they go?"

"The depositions?"

"Right."

"Well, I can't get into specifics because of attorney-client confidentiality and all that, but I'm probably at liberty to say they went well."

"What was Jackie's demeanor?"

"Normal."

"Did you detect anything wrong or off? Was she agitated or afraid or stressed or anything like that?"

Condor shook his head.

"She was glad the depositions were over," he said. "Taking a deposition is stressful work if you do it right. There's a lot to keep organized and remember. You have to think on your feet. It requires a hundred percent concentration."

"I wouldn't know. I rarely get above fifty and that's with full coffee. Did she mention anything about having a court conflict this morning?"

Condor wrinkled his forehead.

"No, what are you talking about?"

"The Anderson case."

Condor looked at the other two lawyers who had blank faces.

"I'm not personally familiar with that case," he said.

"She didn't mention it?"

"No."

"Okay," Teffinger said. "Let me show you something." Sydney pulled an envelope out of her purse and handed it to Teffinger. He opened it, pulled out a stapled set of papers and flipped to the last page. "This is a text that Jackie sent after she talked to you. The phone number belongs to Sophia Phair."

"She's one of our lawyers," Condor said.

"Right, we're going to want to talk to her."

"No problem."

Condor set the papers down and said, "I have no idea what kind of conflict she developed. She didn't mention it when she talked to me."

"So it developed after she talked to you," Teffinger said.

Condor shook his head.

"Not necessarily," he said. "She could have had it earlier. There'd be no reason for her to mention it to me. I'm not the person who would cover for her or arrange for it to be covered. That would fall in the purview of her secretary or another attorney who was working the case with her. I'm guessing that if we check the file we'll find that Sophia was a co-attorney on the case."

Teffinger nodded.

That made sense.

"So who killed her? Do you have any idea?"

No.

He didn't.

The woman had no enemies, no conflicts, and no drama that any of them were aware of. She was a good lawyer doing a good job for her clients and living a normal life. She'd be up for partner in four years and was right on track.

"I don't know what your resources are," Condor said. "We're here though in full force. We'll hire private investigators and do anything and everything we can to help."

"I'll keep that in mind," Teffinger said. "I'd like to see her office."

"Sure. No problem."

9

En route back to Denver flying in calm skies, Yardley called the law office of Baxter & Green, P.C. in Seattle, Washington and asked for Johnnie Axil, Esq. He was on the phone and she said she'd wait. Five minutes later his voice came through, "Hello?"

"It's me," she said.

"How are you?"

"I'm good," she said. "It's time to decide if you really want to go through with this."

Silence.

"Yes," he said.

"Let me be clear," she said. "You can't be 99 percent sure. You need to be a hundred. If we go forward, a lot of things are going to happen. Lives are going to change, yours not the least of them. This is the kind of thing that can't be unwound once it starts."

"I know that."

"I know you know that," Yardley said. "But what I need to know is that you're at a hundred, not 99. I don't ever want to get a call from you in the future to the effect that you've changed your mind and want to go back to square one. Square one forever disappears the second we move forward."

"I understand," he said.

"Are you sure?"

"Positive," he said. "I've given it a lot of thought. This isn't a flippant decision."

"Let me remind you that you'll be breaking the law," she said.

"Trust me, I understand all the implications, probably better than you; no offense."

"None taken."

"So, what's the next step?"

"Hold on."

Yardley pulled the Marlboros out of her purse, tapped one out and lit up.

"Your new name's going to be Johnnie Preston."

"Same first name," he said. "I like that. I kept having a vision of not responding when someone calls it."

"Now for the big question. Where's Johnnie Preston going to live?"

"I was thinking about Santa Fe."

Yardley chewed on it.

It was big enough to get lost in but not by much.

"Have you ever been there?"

"Once on vacation."

"Does anyone there know you?"

"No."

"Does your firm have any business going on in New Mexico?"

"No, we're pretty local."

"Do you speak Spanish?"

"Some. Not fluently but enough to get by."

"Well, that's good."

"Yeah, I know."

"What are you going to do when you get there?"

"Open a PI office."

"Bad choice."

"Why?"

"It's boring," she said. "You spend all your time with documents running down crap little things for crap little clients who stiff you on the bill. It's not filled with shadows and dangerous dames like what you see in the old black-and-white movies."

He chuckled.

"I'll be fine, don't worry."

"Your decision," she said. "PIs are regulated by the state. You're going to need good papers."

"That's your job."

"Right, that's my job."

"You can do it, I suppose."

"I can do it, don't worry." She blew smoke. "I'll be in touch tomorrow with more details. I'm going to give you one last chance to change your mind. When we hang up, we're in motion. That's the bright line. That's when there will be no turning back. This is it."

"In that case, if you're ready to hang up, then so am I."

She smiled.

"I'll call you tomorrow, Mr. Preston."

"I'll be waiting."

She hung up.

10

The 16th Street Mall in the heart of downtown Denver was busy midmorning but not as insane as it would be at noon when all the suits and skirts dumped out. Sophia walked past a hot dog vendor set up on the shady side of the street, sitting on a folding director's chair, reading the Rocky Mountain News. Ten steps later, the light caught her at California. In another block or two, she'd be at Taylor Sutton's office.

Her phone rang.

She checked the number.

It was Condor.

Damn it.

She answered.

"Where are you?"

"I have a coffee meeting with a client," she said.

A pause.

"Cut it short and get back here," he said. "There's a detective who wants to talk to you."

"About what?"

"About the text Jackie sent to you yesterday."

"I'll be there as soon as I can."

The light turned green.

She dropped the phone into her purse and walked forward.

What to do?

What to do?

What to do?

She didn't want to get carted out of the firm in handcuffs. She called Condor back and said, "See if that detective can meet me at Marlowe's. I don't want to push the client off."

A pause.

"He can," Condor said. "About half an hour."

"I'll break away when he gets here."

Marlowe's was the place to see and be seen in downtown Denver, but right now, in the dead zone, there wasn't much of either going on. Sophia took a booth near the back and sipped coffee as she watched the front door.

Half an hour later, a man walked in.

He was the man with the one blue eye and the one green one; a former lover, apparently.

He spotted her.

The corner of his mouth turned up ever so slightly.

He headed back and slid in next to her on the same side of the booth.

"I guess I have a name now," he said.

"It looks that way," she said.

A waitress showed up with coffee and wanted to know if Teffinger wanted anything.

"How are your pancakes, on a scale of one to ten?"

She lowered her voice. "Honestly, about a six."

He smiled.

"Can you stick some strawberries and whipped cream on top and get 'em up to a seven?"

"I think that can be arranged."

Teffinger looked at Sophia.

"Anything for you?"

A pause, then she said, "Same."

"Two seven's coming up."

Sophia put her hand on Teffinger's. "I have a favor to ask you," she said.

"Shoot."

"I don't want to go out of here in handcuffs," she said. "I'll go peacefully. I won't be any trouble. You don't need to put me in anything."

Teffinger nodded.

Then he put his hand lightly on her head, bent it towards him and pulled her hair back. He looked at the wound for a moment then took a sip of coffee.

"I pictured it as worse," he said.

Sophia narrowed her eyes.

"I don't get it."

"Tell me what happened last night," he said. "You went over to Jackie's to pick up a file, right?"

"I don't know."

"You're not in any trouble," Teffinger said. "All I want to know is what happened."

"I don't remember."

"You don't remember?"

"No."

"Are you sure?"

"Trust me, I'm sure," she said.

"You don't remember anything?"

"I woke up this morning with blood in my hair," she said. "That's all I remember. I don't know what happened last night. I'm pretty sure I killed her but I don't know why. It's all blocked out."

"You didn't kill her," Teffinger said.

"I didn't?"

"No," he said. "You went over there."

She nodded.

"Okay."

"What I think happened is that you interrupted the murder in progress or shortly after," Teffinger said. "The neighbor across the street saw a black-haired woman run out of the house being chased by a man. That black-haired woman, in hindsight, was you."

"I don't remember being chased."

"Do you remember a man?"

"No."

Teffinger exhaled.

"He was closing in on you. Another man was coming up the street, a man with black, shoulder length hair. You screamed out, *Help me! Help me! Help me!* Do you remember doing that?"

"No."

"The guy chasing you hit you from behind. You slammed headfirst into a fire hydrant. Do you remember that?"

"No."

"The two men fought," Teffinger said. "The one chasing you broke away and ran up the street. The one with the long hair ran after him but lost ground."

"So the guy got away?"

Teffinger nodded.

"What happened to the other guy, the one with the long hair?"

"We don't know."

"He didn't come back?"

"If he did, the neighbor didn't see him," Teffinger said. "What he did see is you lying on the ground for a minute or two, then stagger to your feet, get in a car and drive off."

Sophia processed it.

"So I didn't kill Jackie," she said.

"No. In fact—and this is just between you and me—she was raped," he said.

Sophia pictured it.

48

Her chest pounded.

"Here's the problem," Teffinger said. "You saw the guy's face."

"If I did, I don't remember it. I can't help you."

"That's not what I'm getting at," Teffinger said. "What I'm getting at is that the guy is going to be a whole lot better off if there wasn't a witness around."

The words landed with the force of a sledgehammer.

"Are you saying he's going to come after me?"

"I'm saying it's a possibility."

11

Teffinger dropped Sophia off at Denver General to get her head and memory checked, in spite of her initial resistance, then headed back to the law firm where Sydney was just finishing going through the victim's office and emails. As they walked down the stairwell forty-one floors to ground level, he told her about his meeting with Sophia and, particularly, her loss of memory.

"Here's the problem," he said. "If her memory comes back at some point—and I assume it will—she'll be a material witness. Technically, I'm in a conflict position because I've had a relationship with her, albeit only for a couple of days. If I follow the rules like I'm supposed to, I should bow out of the case."

"Why?"

"Because if this ever goes to trial, Sophia's credibility will be at issue, just like every other witness in a trial," Teffinger said. "The defense will argue that she's lying to support her lover, who happens to be the lead detective on the case."

"*Former* lover," Sydney said.

"No, *lover.*"

She gave him a look.

"You're going to make a move on her?"

"No, she's going to make one on me."

"You should leave her alone Nick. She's vulnerable. Take the little guy and let him play in someone else's back yard, if he absolutely has to play somewhere."

He smiled.

"*The little guy?*"

"You know what I mean."

He did.

He did indeed.

"Mr. Magic," he said.

She winced.

"That's more information than I need," she said. "You probably should bow out of the case. That's my point."

"I can't."

"Why not?"

"Because someone needs to protect her."

"Other people can do that."

"Not the way I can."

"Look," she said. "I'm not going to tell anyone about your past with her. If I were you though, I'd think long and hard about where you're heading."

"Long and hard? Are you talking about the little guy again?"

She punched his arm.

"I should get double pay for having to be around you all day."

"Put in for it," he said. "You never know."

Forty-one floors was a long way, even going down. By the time they reached the lobby Teffinger's legs were on fire and his chest pounded for air. He wiped sweat off his brow with the back of his hand.

Then his phone rang and the voice of Leigh Sandt came through.

"Your victim out there in Denver is number six," she said. "At least number six. Before her there's Brooklyn Winnfield,

Ashley Gibson, Rikki Amberdeck, Abby Night and Kimberly Johnson, in that order. They were all killed the exact same way, namely repeatedly strangled while they were being raped, and then got their left ear cut off."

Teffinger exhaled.

"What cities?"

"All over," she said. "Are you at the office?"

"I will be in ten minutes."

"Check your email when you get there," she said. "I'm gong to start sending the files over."

"Come to Denver," he said.

"I can't," she said. "It's not my case plus I'm swamped."

"Whose case is it?"

"A newbie by the name of Dale Radcliff."

"Did you tell him about the Denver victim?"

"I did," she said. "His reaction was, I knew there'd be another one. Conspicuously absent was any mention that he wanted to jump on a plane and head to where the fresh blood was."

"So you come then."

"Read my lips Teffinger, *I'm swamped.* I would if I could, you know that, but I can't."

"Not even for me?"

She laughed.

"Especially for you."

"Come on, when's your schedule going to clear up?"

"I don't know, when I'm sixty."

"That's thirty years," he said.

She exhaled.

"Nice try. Look, I'll see if I can rearrange something, but don't hold your breath," she said. "In the meantime, check your emails."

He hung up just as they got outside.

The sun was bright.

The air was downright hot.

It was definitely going to hit a hundred again today.

He filled Sydney in on the serial aspect of the case as they headed for the car and said, "Hopefully there's something in one of those files that's going to get us pointed in the right direction. That's not where I want to spend our time today, though. Today I want to track down that guy with the long hair."

"The one who saved Sophia?"

"Right," Teffinger said. "He must have gotten a pretty good look at the guy."

Sydney wasn't convinced.

"I don't know, they were fighting at the time," she said. "It was after dark."

"You might be right but he's the best thing we have right now," he said. "My guess is that he lives in the neighborhood somewhere."

They headed up the street.

Sydney grunted.

"Finding him won't do any good," she said. "He doesn't want to get involved. If he did, he would have come forward by now of his own volition."

"One step at a time," Teffinger said. "Let's just find him first."

"Maybe he hasn't come forward because the guy killed him."

"There'd be a body."

"Not if the guy shoved it in a trunk and dumped it in the mountains."

Teffinger looked at her sideways.

"Whose side are you on today?"

"I'm just being the devil's advocate."

"The devil doesn't need an advocate," Teffinger said. "I do."

"I know," she said. "That's why I said I'm being your advocate."

He thought about it.

Then he smiled.

"Good one."

"I didn't think you'd get it."

"I'm smarter than I look," he said. "In fact, between me and my brother, we can answer every single question in the world. Go one, ask me one, anything you want."

"Okay, what the square root of 534?"

"That's one my brother knows," he said. "Go on, ask me another one."

She punched him on the arm.

"Like I said, double time."

12

Flying en route back to Denver, over Vail pass, Yardley called her boss and said, "Our new little L.A. attorney frined Blank is on board."

"Do you see any problems with him?"

"Not really," she said. "He's hungry, he's good with the financial part of it and he understands the risks. I called Johnnie Axil in Seattle, too. He's a hundred percent committed. He's going to become Johnnie Preston and move to Santa Fe. Everything's a go from my end."

A pause.

"Okay, let me call New York."

Yardley hung up.

Twenty minutes later her phone rang and a woman's voice came through.

"New York's good with it," the woman said. "Blank will be going to Wells & Whitter. It's a 300-plus firm in Manhattan. His contact is Randolph Zander. He's expecting Blank's call. Be sure Blank uses the name Johnnie Axil when he calls."

"Done."

Thirty minutes later Yardley touched down at DIA.

In the back room of the bookstore, behind closed doors, she began the detail-oriented process of manufacturing the basic papers for Johnnie Preston, namely a social security card, a birth certificate and a Washington driver's license, which he'd surrender for a New Mexico one after getting to Santa Fe.

The door opened and Deven walked in.

"Who are you giving birth to?"

"Someone named Johnnie Preston."

"Teach me."

Yardley tilted her head.

Then she said something she didn't expect.

"Okay, go lock the front door and stick the closed sign up."

Deven's face lit up.

"Are you serious?"

"Why not? It's going to happen sooner or later. It may as well be today."

Deven reached under Yardley's dress, moved her hand up and rubbed her between the legs.

"Thanks."

13

Denver General closed Sophia's head wound with six stitches and conducted a number of tests to determine the cause of her memory loss, ruling out a brain tumor, oxygen deprivation, infection, drugs, or a psychiatric disorder. Although her impact with the fire hydrant didn't result in a concussion, it was nevertheless severe and located directly over the memory area of the brain. "Our best guess is that your amnesia is the product of physical trauma to the brain."

"How long will it last?"

The doctor shrugged.

"You never know with these things. The brain is a complicated organ. Cases like this can arise from being in the vicinity of an exploding bomb or from being in a car crash. Some people in those situations find their memory coming back fairly quickly, within months or even weeks. Other people never regain what they lost, or regain it only partially."

"Are you saying it could be permanent?"

"It's possible both ways. All we can do is wait and see. I treated a patient two summers ago. He was on a motorcycle trip to Sturgis, the last rider in a pack of eleven. He went down and ended up in a Flight for Life. Afterwards, he couldn't remember anything about what happened. He remembered cruising down the road and then he woke up in a hospital. To this day he still has no recollection of crashing or being in the helicopter or anything else about the day in question."

Sophia swallowed.

The hospital also conducted tests to determine the extent of the memory loss. It was a total loss from early Sunday evening until this morning when Sophia woke up. From that point on, it seemed to be working fine. There was, however, a larger problem. Her long-term memory had been affected. Events more that six months old were sketchy at best. She could remember almost nothing that happened more than a year ago.

"The best thing you can do at this point is get plenty of rest and eat healthy. Avoid alcohol, smoke, drugs and stress. You might be able to help the return of your long-term memory by reviewing things that happened in your past—photos, diaries, emails, things like that. Even talking to someone who can tell you about your past might help. There are no guarantees but it certainly won't hurt."

The law firm was a mile away. Rather than calling a cab she set out on foot, needing time to process things. The sun beat down and tried to strangle the life out of every human and dog and weed and bug in the city.

She kept her pace up.

Almost all of her cases were big, meaning they were more than a half-year old, also meaning that she'd forgotten a good deal of what happened in them. The only way to handle it would be to refresh her recollection when she needed to by reviewing the file. It wouldn't be fair to the client to bill for that time, so she'd need to do it on the side. Getting 40 billables in a week would take 60 in the chair.

She'd do it and keep her mouth shut.

The important thing was not to let anyone know she was having brain problems. If the firm put her on leave of absence it would take her off partnership track. She'd worked too hard for too long to let that happen.

She needed to get drunk.

Two blocks away from the law firm an image flashed in her brain, a terrible image, an image of Jackie Lake lying flat on her back with her wrists tied to the bed frame and a horrific look of betrayal on her face. Sophia was between her legs, ramming her with a cucumber that had a rubber stretched over it.

Beside her on the bed was a box cutter.

She kept it in her peripheral vision.

She'd use it to cut the woman's ear off after she strangled her to death.

The image didn't last longer than a heartbeat and then it was gone. It was as if she'd been in the dark and someone flipped a light switch up for a half-second, just long enough to show a monster.

Her heart pounded.

She stopped and leaned against the exterior of a building.

It was rough.

"Hey lady, are you okay?"

The words came from a man in a business suit, still walking past but slowing and looking over his shoulder.

She looked at him.

"Yeah."

The suit stopped.

"You don't look okay."

"I'm okay."

She forced herself to walk away.

Whatever was happening, she couldn't let anyone know.

She needed to appear normal.

14

Based on the files Leigh Sandt emailed over, all the victims before Jackie Lake had two things in common: one, they were drop-dead gorgeous and two, they had raven-black hair. "Jackie Lake doesn't fit the profile," Teffinger said, "but it's pretty obvious who does."

Sydney cocked her head.

"Me?"

Teffinger took a sip of coffee.

"Right, you; you and Sophia. I'm beginning to wonder if she was the target all along."

"If that's the case, why would the guy do it at someone else's house, with that someone else actually home?"

Teffinger shrugged.

"I don't know," he said. "Maybe he was looking for his first two-fur."

"Two-fur?"

"Right."

"You ever had one?"

"I've had two of 'em," Teffinger said. "Two two-furs are different that one four-fur though, just for the record."

"Maybe not," Sydney said. "You'd have to have a four-fur first before you could say that with authority."

"And what makes you think I haven't?"

"Had a four-fur?"

He nodded.

"Right."

"Well, have you?"

He nodded.

"Two of 'em," he said. "Two four-furs are different than one eight-fur though, just for the record."

Sydney punched him on the arm.

Teffinger stood up, drained what was left in the cup and said, "Come on. Let's go find our longhaired friend."

He filled a thermos.

Then they were gone.

Teffinger was pretty sure the guy lived somewhere in the neighborhood and had been out taking an innocent walk last night when he ended up in the wrong place at the right time. If that was the case, someone should know who he was.

They split up.

Teffinger took the west side and Sydney took the non-west side.

The sidewalks were ovens.

The lawns were brown.

An hour of motion went by.

None of it turned out to be forward.

Sydney called and said, "Cowboy, I'm starved. Feed me."

"As in me pay?"

"Yes. Shock my heart."

They ate at McDonald's then re-hit the pavement, intent on getting a witness. Teffinger had visions of landing a composite sketch of the killer on the evening news.

That didn't happen.

The afternoon slipped down a never-ending slippery slope of nothingness before they finally resigned themselves to the fact that only more slips were to be had.

Teffinger looked at his watch.

It was 5:02.

He called Sophia.

"Are you still at the law firm?"

"Yes, why?"

"I'm going to pick you up."

"Why?"

"Because I'm not going to let you be alone tonight," he said. "What time do you want me there?"

A pause.

"How about six?"

"Six it is."

On the way back to the office he asked Sydney if she had any energy left.

"I do if you want me to," she said.

"Are you sure?"

She was.

"Okay then, go into my emails and get the files Leigh sent me," he said. "Email 'em over to yourself and pull 'em up wherever you want, on your iPad or Mac or whatever. Go through 'em and find the common denominators."

She nodded.

"Okay."

"Somehow he picks his victims out beforehand," Teffinger said. "Figure out where he hunts. Then we'll trace Jackie Lake's footsteps and see if we can spot him on a surveillance tape."

"Okay."

"Thanks."

She cocked her head.

"What are you going to be doing while I do all the work? Repeat, *all* the work."

"You want the honest answer or lies?"

"Lies, like always."

"I'll be protecting Sophia."

Sydney gave him a look.

"You'll be protecting her from having a night without an orgasm," she said. "That's what you'll be protecting her from."

15

Deven's magic fingers were rubbing Yardley between the legs, on the outside of her panties, when the phone rang. Deven pushed the cotton to the side, inserted a finger and said, "Don't answer it."

Yardley hesitated.

Then she grabbed it and said, "Hello?"

The voice of her boss came through. She listened intently, memorizing the words, feeling the muscles in her neck grow tighter and tighter, all the while being worked between the thighs by Deven.

The massaging was starting to slow.

Yardley grabbed Deven's hand and held it in place.

"Don't stop."

The woman didn't.

Yardley hung up.

Then she said, "Hold it a minute."

She flipped the light switch off.

The room fell into total blackness.

She got down on the floor flat on her back and spread her legs. Deven rubbed her on the outside of the cotton, slowly, gently, the ultimate tease.

Yardley's hips responded.

"I'm going to teach you something," Deven said.

"What?"

"How to lick a pussy."

Yardley hesitated.

She'd had visions.

She'd had thoughts.

She'd never done it.

"Yes or no," Deven said.

A beat.

"Yes."

"Stay where you are."

Deven stood up. There was a rustling of clothes as she removed her pants and panties. Then she straddled Yardley's chest, grabbed her wrists and pinned her arms up over her head.

"You're my slut," she said.

Yardley's heart pounded.

"Say it!"

"I'm your slut."

"That's better," Deven said. "Now prove it."

She inched up until her pussy was on Yardley's mouth. "You're going to get what you give so make it as good or as bad as you want," she said.

Yardley stuck her tongue out.

It touched flesh.

The flesh pushed back, increasing the contact.

It was moist.

It felt like a deep kiss.

Sanders Cave was a private investigator with a second-floor office on Larimer Street between 14th Street and 15th Street in downtown Denver. Yardley pushed into his office at 4:45 p.m., set a briefcase on his desk and said, "I need to have a man investigated."

Cave opened the briefcase and took a quick look.

Inside was money, flat and green.

He closed the lid.

He wasn't overly big, five-nine or ten, but that didn't mean he couldn't hold his own. His 29-year-old waist was non-existent, his abs were rippled, and his arms, while not overly bulky, could do pull-ups and push-ups until dawn. Even though he smoked he could still run a mile under five minutes, three or four of them if he got motivated enough.

Face wise, he was the closest anyone could look like James Dean without actually being James Dean.

He wore a gray summer-weight suit with the jacket hanging on a rack over in the corner. Next to it was a Fedora.

At feet level he wore spit-shined wingtips, almost impossible to find nowadays but worth the hunt. He had four more pairs just like them in his closet back home.

He looked at Yardley.

"How thorough of an investigation are you looking for?"

"As thorough as you can make it."

He pulled a pack of Marlboros out of his shirt pocket, tapped two out, lit them from a match and handed one to Yardley.

"You look liked you just got screwed," he said. "Who do you want investigated?"

"His name's Peter Smyth. He lives in Miami."

Cave blew smoke.

"How soon do you want a report?"

"Yesterday."

He cocked his head.

"I'll leave tonight."

16

Sophia's thoughts were fatigued and losing focus, which wasn't unusual for this late in the day. On her credenza was a photograph of her and another young woman with their arms around each other, tanned, wearing summer attire, on a beach with a crashing surf in the background, smiling and facing whoever it was that was snapping the lens. Wind was blowing their hair. Their eyes twinkled.

Clearly they were good friends.

Sophia was three or four years younger then.

She had no memory of the person she was standing with.

She had no memory of where they were.

She removed the photo from the glass to see if there was an inscription on the back.

There was.

It said, *London and Chiara, Big Sur.*

It was dated four years ago.

The handwriting wasn't hers.

The other woman had dark features, possibly Italian. Chiara sounded like an Italian name. That name must refer to the friend, meaning London referred to her. She studied her face to see if it was a twin sister she had no memory of. If the woman was a twin, she was an identical one.

No.

That was Sophia.

It wasn't someone else, even if identical.

So why did the inscription say London instead of Sophia?

Was London a nickname?

She stuffed the photo in her purse and the frame in the credenza.

The Noblia on her wrist said 5:55.

It was time to meet Teffinger.

Suddenly a figure appeared in the doorway, Renn-Jaa Tan, the Hong Kong flower from next door. She was stylishly dressed in expensive threads tapered to show off a tight little waist. Her hair was thick and black, parted in the middle and cascading halfway down her back. At five-two she wasn't big and had a chest to match. Her face had a hypnotically erotic edge. Sophia doubted that there was a guy in the firm who wouldn't lay down a twenty just to give it a good lick.

"Knock, knock," she said. "You okay?"

Sophia nodded.

"Yeah, I'm fine."

"What are you up to tonight?"

"The detective's going to pick me up."

"What for?"

"Ostensibly to protect me."

Renn-Jaa stepped closer and put a devious look on her face. "You better lay him like you own him because if you don't I will."

Sophia smiled.

"You're such a poet."

"I'm serious."

"Hey, let me ask you something," she said. "Does the name London mean anything to you?"

"Yeah, it's a big city in England."

Sophia rolled her eyes.

"Get serious for a minute," she said. "Does anyone around here ever call me that?"

"No, lots of other things, but not that. Why?"

"No reason, I guess."

She headed for the door.

"Remember what I said about that detective," Renn-Jaa said.

"Don't worry. It's indelibly imprinted in my brain."

17

Monday night after dark a heavy thunderstorm swept out of the mountains and rolled over Denver with an evil intent. Teffinger grabbed a fresh Bud Light from the fridge, topped off Sophia's wine, and said, "Follow me." He took her to the garage and rolled up the door. Thick bullets of water shot down on the driveway.

The sound was like music.

The wetness of the air tasted like candy.

Backed into the garage, facing outward, was a 1967 Corvette convertible, red over black, a driver more than a trailer-queen, with one headlight stuck in the up position. There was supposedly a way to manually wind it down but Teffinger hadn't figured it out yet. Under the hood was the standard 327, not the insane big-block by any means, but not exactly a sleeper either. The numbers matched and the wheels were the original knock-offs.

Teffinger held the passenger door open for Sophia, then scooted behind the wheel and took a long swallow of beer. Watching the storm from this vantage point in the world was the equivalent of a Brian de Palma movie, say "Body Double."

"This is my favorite thing in the world," he said. "Don't tell anyone. It clears your head."

"So does slamming into a fire hydrant," Sophia said.

Teffinger smiled.

Sophia exhaled and put her hand on Teffinger's arm.

"I need to tell you something," she said.

Her voice was serious.

"What?"

"I think I'm the one who killed Jackie," she said. "I had a memory of doing it. It was just a flash but it was so real."

Teffinger wasn't impressed.

"That was just a trick of the brain," he said.

"No, it was more."

Lightning flashed.

Thunder rolled over Green Mountain, bounced off Teffinger's roof and shot towards Denver, fifteen miles to the east.

"I'll make you a wager," Teffinger said. "If I can prove to you that you didn't kill Jackie, you have to be my sex slave for a night."

She laughed.

"Your sex slave?"

"Right."

"So what does that job entail, exactly?"

"Whatever I want it to."

She clinked her glass against his beer can and said, "You're on, only because there's no way in the world you could ever prove it."

"So it's a deal."

"Sure."

He took a swallow of beer.

"I'm not supposed to tell you this so don't repeat it," he said. "Jackie Lake was number six. Before her, there were five more just like her, killed exactly the same way across the country over the last three years."

"No."

"Yes," he said. "They were all drop-dead gorgeous, they all

got strangled to death while they were being raped, they all had their left ear cut off. Someone has a jar of formaldehyde sitting on a mantelpiece somewhere with six ears in it. I'm assuming you've never seen anything like that sitting around your house."

No she hadn't.

"That's my proof," Teffinger said. "If that's not good enough then here's what we can do. I can give you the exact dates and locations where those murders took place. You can compare that to your billing records, which will show you were in Denver when those murders happened. So, there's only one thing left to determine."

"What's that?"

"Are you going to concede to my proof now or are you going to make me wait until tomorrow?"

She ran a finger up the back of his hand.

"I may as well surrender now," she said.

"Good."

He clinked his can against her glass.

Then he got serious.

"Jackie Lake was an attractive woman," he said. "I'm not trying to disparage her or anything, but she wasn't in the same class as the women who preceded her. You on the other hand are."

Sophia wrinkled her forehead.

"Is that a backwards way of saying that I was the intended victim?"

Teffinger shrugged.

"Let's put it this way," he said. "It's a thought that keeps growing in my mind even though, I have to admit, I can't quite make it fit. If you were the intended victim, why wouldn't he just do it to you at your place? Even if we assume that Jackie got dragged into it because the guy was looking for his first two-fur, how would he know that you'd be going over there that night?"

"He couldn't."

"That's what has me hung up," Teffinger said. "Only you knew you'd be going over."

"Maybe he followed me," Sophia said.

"That's possible. Maybe he's been tailing you, looking for an opportunity to get you and another woman alone together at the same time. Stranger things have happened. Maybe he made you watch Jackie die so he could see the fear on your face knowing you were next. You don't remember anything?"

"The only thing I remember is that flashback I told you about," she said. "I had Jackie's arms tied. I was raping her with a cucumber that had a rubber on it. Next to me was a box cutter that I was going to use to cut her ear off with."

Teffinger swallowed.

"Box cutter," he said.

"Right."

"That's what was used," he said. "That or some other kind of razor. Something sharper than a knife." He took a swallow of beer and said, "There was no cucumber at the scene."

"Maybe I flushed it."

"Look, I already proved you didn't do it," he said. "You're not going to get out of the deal."

"I'm not trying to."

"Good."

"I'm actually looking forward to it," she said. "Don't tell anyone."

The storm pummeled down.

Teffinger finished his beer, got another from the fridge and brought it back, together with the wine bottle. He topped off Sophia's glass.

"I'm thinking of all kinds of nasty things to do to you," he said.

"I'm sure you are."

She put her hand on his knee.

She wore white shorts, a pink tank and had tanned legs. Her hair was loose and slightly disheveled from running her fingers through it.

"Have you ever been tied up?" Teffinger asked.

"I don't remember."

"Then let me refresh your recollection," he said. "You have."

"By you?"

He nodded.

"You really don't remember?"

"No."

"Follow me."

He took her to the bedroom but didn't turn on the lights. The only illumination came from a soft streetlight that wove through the rain and cast a pale glow on the wall. Ropes were tied to the four corners of the bed. "The first time you came here you wanted to be tied up," he said.

She walked over to one of the ropes and tugged on it.

"You left these here? The whole time?"

He nodded.

"Why?"

"I don't know."

"Have you used them on anyone else?"

"No."

She set her glass down.

Then she wiggled her shorts off, pulled the tank over her head, unsnapped her bra and dropped it to the floor. She wore a white thong, nothing more. She laid down on the bed and spread her arms and legs towards the corners, then wiggled her stomach.

"Show me how these work," she said. "Do to me what you did before. Make me remember."

Teffinger stretched her tight and tested the ropes.

"See if you can escape?"

She wiggled and pulled.

Her body barely moved.

"I can't."

"Good."

"I just had a thought," she said. "Maybe the guy didn't follow me to Jackie's. Maybe he's the one who sent the text. Maybe he got a hold of her phone somehow and sent the text without her even knowing about it."

Teffinger ran a fingertip in a circle around her bellybutton.

"The text came while she was in San Francisco," he said. "He would have had to be there to do it."

"Maybe he was," she said. "Maybe he even flew back on the same plane as her."

Teffinger licked her stomach.

"I'll check the passenger list tomorrow," he said. "Right now I don't want you to think about anything except what I'm about to do to you."

"Yes master."

18

Miami after dark was smothered under a layer of thick humid clouds. The target—Peter Smyth—lived on the west side of the city, just south of Blue Lagoon, where the houses were five feet apart and jet engines rattled the skies. Sanders Cave drove past Smyth's house in a black Camry rental.

It was 1:30 in the morning.

A few dogs barked, an occasional TV flickered against a smoky wall, but otherwise it was dead.

The lights in Smyth's house were off; same for the neighbors on each side, plus across the street. An older model Mustang squatted in Smyth's driveway.

Cave parked a block away and killed the engine.

From under the seat he pulled an 8-inch serrated knife that he purchased for cash earlier this evening. He attached the nylon sheath to his belt, unsnapped the snap and pulled the blade out.

He ran the edge over his thumb, just to get a feel for the sharpness, then slipped the weapon back in the sheath.

He stepped out of the car and silently closed the door, leaving it unlocked.

Nothing moved.

No dogs barked.

No lights went on.

He headed up the street towards Smyth's house.

He didn't understand why anyone would want the man dead. The guy hardly existed. He was just someone who lived in a crap house and drove a crap car. In just this one night, Cave was probably getting more to kill the guy than the guy had made in his entire lifetime.

He must have seen something he shouldn't have.

It didn't matter.

Whoever Smyth was, Cave was getting paid.

Unlike Denver where the thin mile-high air turned to a refrigerator at night, here it was still in the 80's, and oppressive.

A mosquito bit Cave's arm.

He smashed it and flicked it off.

Lots of windows were open.

He would need to be quiet.

He'd sneak in and kill the man in his sleep.

The only sound would be metal sinking into flesh, possibly followed by an exhale of air from dead lungs.

Cave moved swiftly, a sliver of shadow in the night.

Suddenly a dog barked.

He turned.

A dark silhouette was behind him, closing the gap with a straight silent run, not more than two steps behind. It was a man, a large man, a large man with a nylon mask stretched taut over his face. He raised his arm. In it was a knife. A reflection bounced off the blade, then the reflection disappeared and the weapon swung with a fast fury directly at Cave's face.

DAY TWO

July 9
Tuesday

19

Sophia got dropped off at her house Tuesday morning before sunrise. The storm of last night was gone, leaving smoky remnants of clouds up top and puddles down below. Teffinger checked the house, made sure everything was safe, then asked if he could borrow her lipstick. When she handed it to him, he wrote *Thanks* on her bathroom mirror, gave her a kiss and said, "I'll call you later."

"Okay."

"Don't have sex with anyone until I get there."

She smiled.

Then she got serious.

"Email me the dates and places of those other murders. I need to be sure."

"You're wasting your time but fine."

Then he was gone.

Sophia pulled the Big Sur photo out of her purse, flipped it over and looked at the subscription on the back.

London.

London.

London.

Who are you?

There had to be something around here somewhere that would answer the question.

There were only a few boxes in the attic.

They contained things, not papers; same for the garage.

She had no photo albums.

On reflection, that was strange.

The master bedroom had a walk-in closet that could best be described as a dumping ground. She went through it for ten minutes before coming to an old shoebox buried on the top shelf in the back.

It was taped shut and covered with dust.

She opened it.

Inside she found a California driver's license with her photo on it and the name London Winger.

Her chest pounded.

There was also a passport in the name of London Winger with her photo on it. It was stamped for England, France and Italy, all in June four years ago.

There were twenty or thirty photos.

She was in a lot of them with friends, others she wasn't in at all. She recognized one of the friends as the same one from the photo on her office credenza. The other friends she didn't recognize at all. She read the backs, looking for names. She found the one she already knew, namely Chiara, except this time there was a last name, Chiara de Correggio. She found a few new names.

Michelle.

Sepia.

Alexis.

There were no men in any of the photos.

She stuck everything back in and put the box on the nightstand next to the bed, then headed for the shower.

The water was hot.

The room was dark.

One thing was clear.

Sophia Phair wasn't her real name.

Her real name was London Winger.

At some point in the last three of four years, it got changed and she relocated from California to Colorado.

Why?

Was she on the run?

Had she done something similar to Jackie Lake back in California?

Was she the serial killer Teffinger was looking for?

Teffinger.

He had his hooks in her, he knew it and she knew it. If she didn't break loose by the end of the day it would be forever too late.

He was a drug.

20

Getting to work Tuesday morning before anyone else, Teffinger flicked on the fluorescents, kick-started the coffee and worked up a warrant to get the passenger lists into Denver from San Francisco on Sunday, just in case Sophia was right and someone other than Jackie Lake sent the text.

Sophia.

Sophia.

Sophia.

Teffinger couldn't get her out of his brain. He kept pulling up a visual of her tied spread-eagle on the bed last night while the storm beat on the windows.

Her body was so damned perfect.

Her lust was so absolute.

Her passion was so free.

Her breath was so alive.

Best of all was that she was still there when Teffinger woke up this morning.

She was the one.

He knew it the first night they met but knew it even better now.

It was wrong to have sex with her last night. He knew that. But how do you stop a freight train when it's running through your blood? How do you not do something when all you can think about is doing it?

Sydney showed up at seven wearing a sleepy, pre-caffeine face. "There wasn't much in any of the victim's files about their social lives," she said. "It was interesting though that the file pictures for each and every one of them showed liquor or wine in the cupboards. They were drinkers. If they drank at home they probably drank at bars too. My guess is that's where this guy does his hunting, at bars or clubs."

Teffinger dumped what was left in his cup in the snake plant over by the window and then refilled.

"That makes sense," he said. "Sit back with a beer and look for that perfect lickable face." He took a sip. "So now the question is, what bars did Jackie Lake go to? That's one of the things I want you to figure out today."

Sydney tilted her head.

"Did you say likable or lickable?"

"Lickable."

She rolled her eyes.

"You're getting worse."

"It's not easy," he said. "I have to work at it. I've been thinking about Sophia's memory problems. Maybe they're not from that fire hydrant encounter at all. Maybe they're from that first encounter with me."

Sydney smiled.

"You've been known to have that effect on people."

"That I have." He took a sip of coffee, wrinkled his brow and said, "We need to find our friend with the long hair. It's making my teeth hurt knowing there's someone out there who can potentially wrap this whole thing up."

Sydney frowned.

"It's going to bust a hundred again today. I need to be in air conditioning."

Teffinger looked out the window. Across the street were old houses converted into bail bond joints painted in cartoon colors.

"You know what? You deserve air-conditioning," he said. "Go to the law firm. Keep an eye on Sophia today. I'm sure they'll let you set up in a conference room or something. If she goes out to lunch, go with her. Keep reviewing the other files. Call the detectives in charge. Get your brain wrapped around all the details."

"Are you serious?"

He nodded.

"I am," he said. "Most of all be accessible. Be sure everyone knows you're there. Maybe one of the attorneys will wander in and whisper something in your ear. Let's see if Jackie Lake had a deeper, more secret side."

21

Yardley woke Tuesday morning from the ringing of her phone. She opened her eyes and found a golden patina of sunlight awash on the walls. The clock said 10:32.

She answered.

"Hello?"

A voice said, "That was a big mistake. A very big mistake."

The voice belonged to Sanders Cave.

She sat up.

"What was?"

The line went dead.

She called her boss and said, "I just got a call from Cave. He said, *That was a big mistake,* then hung up. He sounded insane."

Silence.

Then, "Meet me at the bookstore at 11:30."

"Okay."

Thirty minutes later Yardley was out the door, showered and dressed. She swung into Starbucks long enough to get a carryout, then sipped it from her left hand and smoked with her right as she negotiated the downtown buzz over to Wazee. When she got to the bookstore the door was locked and the lights were out.

That was wrong.

Deven was supposed to open at ten.

It was 11:22.

Yardley opened the door, stepped inside and saw something she didn't expect. The reception desk lamp was on the floor, shattered. Next to it was a stapler lying quietly on its side.

"Deven?"

Silence.

Yardley headed into the back.

To her shock, the back door was wide open. Something reddish-brown was on the floor, shaped in drops, looking like blood. Yardley ran a finger over it. It was dry but definitely blood.

Behind the store was an alley.

Someone could have pulled a car back there, dumped Deven into a trunk and taken off without anyone seeing them.

Cave.

It had to be Cave.

The thought was simultaneously comforting and frightening; comforting in that at least she knew who she was dealing with, frightening in that she knew what Cave was capable of.

At exactly 11:30 the door opened and Yardley's boss walked in dressed exactly like what she was, an expensive lawyer.

"Cave took Deven," Yardley said. "What the hell's going on?"

The lawyer exhaled.

"The Miami deal was a set up," the woman said.

"What do you mean?"

"It was orchestrated to eliminate Cave."

"Eliminate Cave?"

"There are reasons," the woman said.

Yardley took a step back.

"You had no right to involve me without my knowledge," she said.

The woman said nothing.

Her face didn't move.

"You never told Cave who I am, correct?"

Yardley nodded.

"No, I haven't."

"He's smart enough to know that it was orchestrated by me, not you," the woman said. "If he thought you were responsible, you'd already be dead. He took Deven to force you to tell him who I am. You're not going to do that. We need to get that clear, right here, right now."

Yardley shook her head.

"I'd never do that."

"Yes you would," the woman said. "If you do though, I'll have a plan in motion to take Deven out—first her, then you. So be assured you won't be advancing your cause by giving me up."

"I already said I wouldn't."

The woman pulled a pack of smokes out of her purse, tapped two out and handed one to Yardley.

She lit them both up from a fancy gold lighter.

"We need to get Deven back and kill Cave," she said. "That's our only option." She blew smoke. "Either you're in or you're out."

Yardley paused.

Then she said, "I'm in."

The woman nodded.

"Hold on." She pulled her phone out, dialed a number and said, "It's me. I have an assignment for you. If I die at any time within the next month, and I don't care what the cause is—I don't care if I get hit by a bus or get a bullet in the head, either way—you're to kill two women, one's named Deven Devenshire and the other's named Yardley White. Money will be in your account within the hour."

She closed the phone and looked at Yardley.

"Do we have an understanding?"

Yardley nodded.

"When this is over, though, I'm done with you."

The woman blew smoke.

"One step at a time," she said. "I'm being a businesswoman and you know it. Right now my goal, just like yours, is to get Deven back. That call I made was just an insurance policy, nothing personal against you."

22

Sophia was besieged with work when she got to the law firm Tuesday morning. The echo of Jackie Lake's murder still resonated up and down the halls but the day-to-day operations of the firm were back to normal. Luckily no one talked to her about anything in the too distant past. She was able to hold her own memory-wise.

Sydney showed up to keep an eye on her.

Sophia got her set up in a conference room, poured two cups of coffee and settled into a leather chair. "So what's the deal with Teffinger?"

"What do you mean?"

"What I mean is, should I worry about getting in too deep with him?"

Sydney patted her hand.

"Girlfriend, you're already in too deep with him."

Sophia shrugged.

"You're probably right," she said.

"No probably about it," Sydney said. "I'm big-time jealous, just for the record."

"Did you ever—you know—do it with him?"

Sydney reflected.

"You mean have sweaty edgy sex in the back of his pickup down by the BNSF switchyard under a pitch-black night?"

"Right, that."

"No, nothing like that ever happened. I'll admit, though, there were a few drunken nights when I wore a short dress and let my panties flash more than they should have," she said. "His excuse is that we're partners. He doesn't want to cross the line." A beat then, "So, is he any good in bed?"

Sophia shook her head.

"No, you're not missing a thing."

Sydney punched her on the arm.

"You liar."

"Did you just call me an attorney?"

"I guess I did."

It was midmorning before Sophia got enough clear space around her to do what she'd been aching to do all morning, namely close the door and see if the internet had any information on Chiara de Correggio. The woman would be able to tell Sophia about her past.

Google had nothing on her.

It had hits on "London Winger," but on deeper investigation they weren't Sophia; they were separate people.

She got a listing of private investigators in Malibu and called the only female on the list, a woman named Aspen Gonzales, who had a soft Hispanic accent.

"I'm trying to get information on two people who lived in or around Malibu three or four years ago," she said.

"Hold on, let me get a pencil." A beat, then, "Okay, go on."

"The first is London Winger, 3883 Three Seagulls Drive, Malibu. The second is Chiara de Correggio. I don't have an address on her. She was a friend of London Winger's."

"What's your interest in these women?"

"It's personal."

Silence.

"I'm sort of in a hurry, too," Sophia said.

"Okay, I'm willing to see what I can do. I'll need a retainer, five thousand. That's standard. There are no guarantees. I'll do my best but that doesn't mean I'll necessarily find anything."

Sophia swallowed.

Five thousand.

That was a lot of money.

"Do you take credit cards?"

"As long as it goes up to five-K, sure."

"Hold on a second, let me get my purse."

She gave her the digits.

"All this is confidential, right?"

"Absolutely."

23

Most people along the front-range knew Jena as the Channel 8 TV roving reporter, the charismatic blond with the big blue eyes who wasn't afraid to get in the middle of the mess. Teffinger knew her from the old high school days in Fort Collins when she was the ticklish tomboy down the street, three years younger than him.

He called her midmorning and said, "I want to buy you lunch."

"Who is this?"

"Me, Teffinger."

"It can't be," she said. "The Teffinger I know doesn't use the word *buy*."

He smiled.

"Are you free?"

"No."

"Good. Wong's? Noon?"

"Let me see if I have this right. If I somehow do an incredible amount of work to rearrange my schedule and actually go, you're the one who's going to pay. Not me, you."

"Right," he said.

"Okay then, Wong's at noon."

"When I say right, that means we'll flip for it."

"So now I have to flip for it?"

"That's fair," he said. "That way you have a 25 percent chance."

"Fifty," she said.

"Twenty-five," he said. "If you win the first one, we flip again. That one will definitely count though."

"I'll tell you what," she said. "I'll just pay."

"Fine, if that's what you want."

Wong's at noon was a study in motion, fast, crowded and energetic to the point that it was a mystery why no one got trampled to death. Teffinger got there ten minutes early and managed to grab Daisy, who in turn grabbed a corner booth for him.

She leaned in.

"I'm on the menu today," she said. "For you only."

"In that case I'll take an extra large helping," he said.

"Would you like that with or without screaming?"

"With, please."

"Good choice."

Jena showed up five minutes late, looked around frantically, then scurried over and slipped in next to him on the same side of the booth.

"Last time we were here you promised to take me out and get me drunk," she said.

"I did?"

She punched his arm.

"Why am I hearing from you today? It's been three months—"

He narrowed his eyes.

"You're familiar with the murder of the lawyer, Jackie Lake, right?"

"Of course."

"This is between you and me," he said. "A guy actually ended up in a fight with the killer outside the house, a guy with long hair. I need to find him. That's where you come in."

"You want me to get something on the air?"

He nodded.

"There's more just between you and me," he said. "Another lawyer in the same firm as Jackie Lake is in the guy's cross-hairs."

"Why?"

He shook his head.

"I don't want to go there," he said. "Let me just say this. At first, I didn't want to go on the news to look for the guy with the long hair. I wanted the killer to think that the guy was already in contact with us. That would hopefully suppress him, to a point, and make it less likely that he'd make a move on this other lawyer. Unfortunately, now it looks like I'm not going to find the longhair without help. I already talked to the chief and the public information officer about getting something on the air. I have the green light. What I need you to do is help me figure out exactly how to frame it and then get it done. I want it on tonight's news."

She studied him.

"And what do I get in return?"

"What do you want?"

"Remember when we used to go way down the tracks by the bridge and you and Bobby Ray would tickle me to death?"

Teffinger nodded.

"I want that," she said. "But first you have to take me to a bar and get me good and drunk."

24

When the lawyer left Yardley got a Colt 45 from the safe and slipped it in her purse, then cleaned Deven's blood off the floor. Cave could pop out of the shadows at any second. Yardley had to let it happen. It was a necessary step in getting Deven back.

She waited.

Cave didn't show.

He was making her sweat.

He was emphasizing the fact that Deven was gone and would continue to be gone until he decided otherwise.

Yardley got the coffee pot going and drank a cup at the desk with the gun in the top drawer. Twenty minutes went by, then an hour, and then lunch came and went. In the afternoon a nicely dressed woman walked in, looked timidly around and said, "I've seen this place a hundred times and always wanted to stop in." She had short brown hair in a contemporary style, 2-inch heels, nylons and a sleeveless white blouse. Her arms were tanned and firm. She pulled sunglasses off. "This is embarrassing but do you have a restroom?"

She did.

"In the back."

"Thanks."

Two minutes later the woman returned and said, "I had to

be sure we were alone. I'm here about Cave."

"About Cave?"

"Right, Cave. I've been brought in to take care of him. Sooner or later he's going to contact you. When he does, play hard to get but eventually tell him that your contact is a woman named Madison Elmblade. Tell him she lives at 1775 Marion. Write it down."

Yardley obeyed.

"Describe me," the woman said. "When you talk to him, try to get him to tell you where Deven is."

The woman stopped.

The silence hung.

"Then what?" Yardley said.

"Then Cave will end up dead. If the police ever question you about it, this conversation between you and me never happened. That's important. Do you understand?"

Yardley nodded.

"What about Deven?"

"Getting her back safe and sound is the goal," she said. "Whether that goal gets met or not, only time can tell. There are no guarantees in something like this and we both know it."

Yardley exhaled.

"Can I ask you one thing?"

"Sure."

"Are you the one who just got the call about killing me and Deven if the lawyer ended up dead?"

The woman looked confused.

"No, that wasn't me."

"Okay."

"Then we're done."

Yardley cocked her head.

"You don't look like the type to be involved in something like this," she said.

The woman put her sunglasses on and nodded towards the

bookshelves.

"Don't judge them by the covers," she said.

"You should turn this assignment down," Yardley said. "Cave's dangerous."

"Cave's nothing. He's an hour of work."

Yardley pulled an old book off the shelf and handed it to the woman.

Moby Dick.

"Have you ever read this?"

The woman opened it up and flipped the pages.

They were heavily yellowed at the edges but white and clean inside.

"No."

"Read it," Yardley said. "It's about a man who goes after something he shouldn't. It ends up killing him. Take it, my compliments."

The woman set the book on the desk.

"Thanks but I don't have time to read."

Then she was gone.

25

S ophia was knee-deep in researching jury instructions for a case that Condor and she would be trying together in September when Renn-Jaa stepped inside and closed the door. "You really have this place buzzing with this detective here guarding you," she said. "Over half the money's bet on the fact that you're going to end up dead."

Sophia leaned back in her chair.

"Where's your money?"

"I know you too well to take the stupid side of the bet," she said. "Here's the thing and this is just between you and me so don't repeat it."

"I won't."

"I have a gun," Renn-Jaa said. "It's totally legal. I bought it from a store, it's registered and the whole bit. What I'm thinking is that you shouldn't be alone when you're outside the law firm. Tonight, I think it would be a good idea if you slept over at my place or I slept over at yours." She exhaled and added, "I've been researching the law on self defense. If you're in your house and someone comes in, it's okay to shoot them as long as you have a reasonable belief that your life is in jeopardy."

"Thanks but I'm not going to drag you into my problems," Sophia said.

"But—"

"No buts," she said. "This isn't amateur hour, no offense. If you got hurt or killed I'd never be able to forgive myself."

"You wouldn't need to," Renn-Jaa said. "I understand the risks. It's my decision to make. I'm a big girl."

"No. That's final."

Sophia's phone rang.

"Let me take this," she said.

The voice of the California investigator, Aspen Gonzales, came though. "I thought it would be best to touch base with you. It's about Chiara de Correggio."

"What about her?"

"Look, I don't know if you were a friend of hers or what, so I'm sorry if this is bad news."

Sophia stood up.

Forty floors below, the people looked like ants and the cars moved like toys.

"Go on."

"She's dead."

The words registered, not because Sophia had been friends with the woman and should feel something, but because it was yet another dark thing in her life.

"What happened?"

"She got murdered, actually," Gonzales said.

"By who?"

"It's an open case."

"So they never caught anyone?"

A pause.

"No. Here's the thing," Gonzales said. "There isn't much that's public about the murder. About the best I can tell you so far is what I already told you. Now, there are ways to go deeper."

"Do you need more money?"

"I will if I go that route but that's not the issue," Gonzales said. "The issue is that the case is dormant right now. If an investigator such as myself starts prying into it, someone on the other end is going to scratch their head and wonder who I'm working for and what their interest is in all this."

"You said you'd be confidential."

"I will, you don't have to worry about that," she said. "Here's what I'm getting at. I don't know if you or someone you know, a sister or friend or something, had anything to do with the woman's death. I'm not going to ask you and I don't want you to tell me if that's the case. What I'm saying though is that if that's the case, I'd let sleeping dogs lie. I'd just walk away from it right now. I don't need an answer this second. You can think about it and call me later."

Sirens came from below.

Sophia looked out the window.

A cop car was weaving in and out of traffic at high speed with the lights flashing.

"I'll call you later," she said. "Is that okay?"

"Yes, it's fine. I haven't done anything yet in connection with the other part of the assignment, London Winger. I'll start on that as soon as we hang up."

"Call me when you get something."

"I will."

She hung up.

Renn-Jaa looked at her and said, "What was that all about?"

Sophia studied her.

"I might need a friend," she said.

"You have one. Tell me what's going on."

26

Midafternoon Teffinger received a strange phone call from a female voice. "I may have information relating to Jackie Lake. I have to stay anonymous though."

"Don't worry, I won't—"

"Totally anonymous," the voice said, "even from you. Go to the 16th Street mall. There are back-to-back benches at 16th and California. Sit in the one facing towards Broadway. Don't look at the bench behind you. Face straight ahead. After you're situated, I'm going to come and sit in the other bench at your back. Don't turn around. We're going to talk. When we're done, you're going to get up and walk away. You're not going to turn back. You're not going to try to see who I am."

"This is a joke, right?"

"Those are the conditions," the voice said. "They're not negotiable."

Teffinger looked at his watch.

"When?"

"Right now."

"This better be something real," he said.

"Don't worry, it's real."

The destination was a fifteen-minute walk from homicide. Teffinger did it in twelve and sat down. An old couple occupied the bench at his back. Teffinger flashed his badge and said, "I'm sorry but you're going to have to leave. I need that bench for business."

The woman wasn't impressed.

"What kind of business?"

"Detective business."

"Don't you have an office?"

"No."

"That's not true."

"It's being painted."

The woman pointed to an empty bench thirty yards down. "Use that one," she said.

"Look, don't turn this into an incident," Teffinger said. "I need you to vacate that bench and I need you to do it now. Please and thank you."

"You just don't like old people," she said. "Just because we're not as strong as you, that doesn't give you the right to boss us around."

Teffinger exhaled.

"Look—"

"That's not even a real badge," she said. "I've seen real badges. That one's not real. Even your eyes aren't real. They're two different colors. Who has two different color eyes? No one, that's who."

Teffinger smelled alcohol on her breath.

He pulled a ten out of his pocket, dangled it in front of her and said, "Do you want this?"

A pause.

The woman snatched it.

"Take your stupid old bench."

Then she was gone, the man too.

Teffinger faced the way he was supposed to and kept pointed in that direction. The bench was in the sun. Heat radiated off every building in the stinking city. He wiped sweat off his forehead with the back of his hand. Five minutes later the weight of a body sank into the bench behind him and a female voice said, "Don't turn around."

"Next time pick a place in the shade," Teffinger said. "You didn't bring a cold Bud Light with you by an chance, did you?"

The woman chuckled.

"No."

"I didn't think so," he said. "Tell me why I'm here."

The woman cleared her throat.

"I'm an attorney," she said. "What I'm about to do is violate the oath I took when I became an attorney. I'm going to violate my client's confidentiality."

"Are you sure you want to do that?"

"Trust me, I don't *want* to," she said. "You need to promise me that you'll never tell anyone about this conversation, not today, not tomorrow, not ten years from tomorrow."

"I won't."

"If you ever tell anyone about it, I'll deny it," she said. "I'll deny it with a vengeance. Then I'll sue you for defamation to prove I'm right."

"You won't get anything," Teffinger said. "All I have is a '67 Corvette and the bank owns most of that. Do you like old Corvettes?"

"No. I'm a Porsche girl."

"Do you have one?"

"Maybe."

"I hope it's '89 or earlier," Teffinger said. "Those were the keepers, with the headlights sticking out like torpedoes. The new ones don't do anything for me."

"Me either," she said. "Mine's an '86."

"When did they put in the synchronized clutch?"

"Eighty-seven."

"Ouch. So you have to come to a complete stop to downshift into first?"

"Right."

"That makes for tough driving."

"There are worse things," she said. "The guy you're looking for refers to himself as Van Gogh. He was a client of mine. He never had an actual case with me, he just retained me and then told me about the killings."

"Why?"

"Who knows," she said. "Maybe he just needed to talk about it and knew I couldn't repeat anything because of attorney-client confidentiality. Maybe he just liked to put me on edge. Either way it was pretty sick. He's been doing them for years."

"What's his name?"

"Van Gogh, that's all I have," she said. "He never told me his real name."

"Do you have an address, phone number, anything?"

"No."

"You're not being much help," he said.

"He picks them out in bars," she said. "He follows them for a week or two or three, then he strikes. He ties their wrists to the headboard and then chokes them to death while he's raping them. That's how Jackie Lake died, right?"

"How'd you know that?"

"I'm an attorney," she said. "It's a small town."

"Has he called you about Jackie Lake?"

"Not yet."

"When he does I want you to record it."

"We'll see."

"What else can you tell me about him?"

"A little part of his left ear got shot off once. He's pretty proud of that," she said. "That was his inspiration for cutting off the left ear of his victims."

"Who shot him? The police?"

"He never said." She lowered her voice. "Every time he talked to me, he always finished the conversation the same way. He always said that if I ever told anyone anything about what he was telling me, he'd do the same thing to me that he was doing to the other women, only more slowly. That's why you're going to get up now and walk away, and you're not going to turn around, like you promised. Goodbye."

"What you just did took a lot of guts. Thank you."

"You're welcome."

Teffinger stood up.

He took a step and stopped.

He didn't turn around.

"Was Jackie Lake a friend of yours? Is that why you're coming forward?"

No one answered.

She was gone.

Teffinger walked away.

He didn't turn around.

On the walk back to the office he called Sydney and said, "See if you can find the name of a female attorney in town who owns an '86 Porsche 911."

"Who is this?"

Teffinger smiled.

"Thanks."

He was almost at the office when the phone rang and Sydney's voice came though.

"The attorney in question is someone named September Tadge."

"September?"

"Right."

"As in the month?"

"Right. July, August, *September.*"

"Her parents must have been hippies," Teffinger said.

"I wouldn't know," Sydney said. "That's a white infliction. You don't find any black girls called September. What's your interest in her, anyway?"

"She may have done something to make herself a target," he said. "Don't mention this to anyone. I'm serious, not a word."

"Okay."

"It's important."

"I understand," she said. "Not a word."

Teffinger almost hung up and said, "Are you still there?"

She was.

"Do me a favor," he said. "Cross-reference September to Jackie Lake. See if there's any connection."

"As in what? Common cases? Common clients?"

"As in anything at all."

"Teffinger, that would be a three week project."

"Don't let anyone know you're doing it," he said. "Love you."

He hung up.

Bars.

Bars.

Bars.

That's where the guy did his hunting.

That's where Teffinger needed to do his.

27

Yardley was pacing with a cigarette in hand when a chill ran up her spine. Maybe Madison Elmblade actually worked for Cave. Maybe she was trying to draw Yardley into a trap. Maybe she'd call later, after dark, and say they needed to meet and come up with a better plan. That's when the woman would club her on the back of the head and drive her to whatever sick little place Cave had picked out.

She called her contact, got dumped into voicemail and didn't leave a message.

If Madison worked for Cave, they might meet up sooner than later, as in now.

It was a long-shot, and probably a waste of time, but Yardley swung the sign from Open to Closed, stepped outside and locked the door behind her. Then she followed Elmblade up Wazee towards downtown.

The sun was fierce.

She felt like a moth making its way into the flame.

28

L ate afternoon Sophia closed her door and called the California PI, Aspen Gonzales. "If we go deeper into Chiara's murder, what exactly is the risk? They couldn't get a subpoena for your files, could they?"

"Unlikely," Aspen said. "The main risk is that the case won't necessarily stay cold. If we shake it up someone might want to dust it off and take a fresh look. They might see something they didn't see before. It might be the first slip of a slippery slope, meaning it might not end well for the killer, or killers or people who aided or abetted them, whoever that may be."

Sophia gave it one last thought.

"Go deeper," she said.

"Are you sure?"

"No but do it anyway. I assume you'll try to stay as discrete as you can."

"Of course," Aspen said. "There will be costs."

"How much?"

"Let me think . . . okay, let me see what I can do for two thousand. That's a straight pass-through by the way. I don't mark it up."

"I appreciate it. What do you have on London Winger?"

"Nothing yet."

As soon as she hung up, the phone rang and Teffinger's voice came through. "What bars have you gone to in the last three or four weeks?"

"Why?"

"Because that's where the guy does his hunting. He picks his victim out in a bar and follows her around for one or two or three weeks," he said. "Then he strikes. So, what bars have you been in?"

She hesitated.

"Can we talk about this in person, away from the firm?"

"Why?"

"It's a little embarrassing."

A beat then, "We're going to be barhopping tonight so if you have anything planned in the office for early tomorrow morning you may want to push it back. Oh, one more thing. Do you know anyone with a small piece of their left ear missing?"

"Not offhand."

"Okay."

"Where do you get this stuff?"

"I detect it. That's what detective's do. By the way, don't tell anyone what I just told you."

"I won't."

"Oh, I almost forgot, one more thing. Do you know anyone who goes by the name Van Gogh?"

"Is that his name? The killer's?"

"Maybe."

"It doesn't ring any bells."

"Okay, don't repeat it. You never heard it."

She hung up and headed to the kitchen for a cup of decaf. Renn-Jaa was lifting the top of a Krispy Kreme box. "There's one left," she said. "I'll split it with you."

"I have to stay away from those things."

The woman held it up.

"Chocolate frosting."

Sophia hesitated.

"Come on," Renn-Jaa said. "Don't make me eat the whole thing." She broke it in half and handed the smaller piece to Sophia.

"You're evil."

She took a bite while she poured coffee.

Suddenly a vision flashed in her brain. She was in Jackie Lake's bedroom, straddling her helpless victim. The fear on the woman's face was so real, so honest, so perfect. Sophia let her right hand drift to the side until it found the box cutter. She pushed the blade out until it locked. Then she bent her face close to Jackie's and said, "I usually do this after they're dead but in your case I'm going to make an exception."

Then she did it.

She sliced the woman's ear off with one quick motion.

The mug dropped out of her hand and shattered on the floor.

She looked around.

She was in the law firm's kitchen.

Someone was there with her.

Renn-Jaa.

The woman's forehead was tensed and her eyes were narrowed.

"Are you okay?"

29

For the first time in his professional life, Teffinger let a dark, illegal thought work its way into his brain. The lawyer, September Tadge, no doubt took notes of her conversations with Van Gogh. There would be a wealth of information in those notes over and beyond what September already told him. What time of day did he call? How long did he wait after the killing before calling? How long did the conversations last? Did he specifically name any of the bars where he picked out his victim? Were they biker bars, country bars, discos, fashion clubs, fancy hotels or what? What facts did he emphasize? Were the facts more about the woman and why he picked her or more about the act of killing?

One option would be to approach September and ask for the files point-blank.

If she said no, she might hide or destroy them.

She might feel like she'd gotten herself in deeper than she envisioned and try to pull out.

If she said yes, she'd be the one committing the wrongful act. What right did Teffinger have to have her do the dirty work instead of him?

The best option would be to break into her office, copy the files and put them back exactly like they were.

Okay, play it out.

Suppose she found out after the fact.

Would she turn him in?

That would be doubtful.

She'd have too much fear that the story could unravel to the point of origin, namely her communication with Teffinger on the 16th Street mall.

She'd end up disbarred.

She'd also officially elevate herself to being a target.

No, she wouldn't tell.

With a disposable cup of coffee in his left hand, Teffinger walked north on Bannock, past the courthouse, and then two more blocks.

September Tadge practiced out of an old two-story house that had been converted to an office. Teffinger walked past on the opposite side of the street with his face pointed forward.

In the front was a postage stamp yard with dead brown grass and a fancy wooden sign that said, "September Tadge – Attorney At Law." The structure was kept up, the paint was fresh and the old single-pane windows had been replaced with sliders. They were all up meaning the place probably didn't have air conditioning.

It sat deep in the shade of a 25-story luxury hotel.

Across the street was a parking lot.

Behind the house was an alley looking into the backside of restaurants and old brick structures.

Teffinger walked an additional half block then found a planter in the shade. He sat on the edge and called Dr. Leigh Sandt, the FBI profiler.

"I have some possible information on our guy," he said. "It's unverified but I have reason to suspect that it's reliable. One, the guy picks his victims out at bars then stalks them for one or two or three weeks. Two, he has a small part of his left ear missing, compliments of a bullet. Three, he refers to himself as Van Gogh. Spread the word and see if it loosens anything up."

"Who is this?"

He smiled.

"Funny."

"You sound stressed."

He exhaled.

"Between you and me, I'm thinking about bending a few rules."

"Don't."

"We'll see."

"I'm serious Nick," she said. "You're good enough to get him the right way."

"We'll see."

He hung up and took a long hard look at September's place.

"Just leave one of those windows up tonight," he said.

Then he headed back to the office.

30

Yardley followed Madison Elmblade into the financial district where the woman disappeared into the revolving doors of a high-rise.

Someone tapped on her shoulder.

She turned to find the James Dean face of Sanders Cave staring at her with a serious fix.

"Hot today," he said.

"I want Deven."

"Did you know that Miami was a set up?"

"No."

"No?"

"No."

"I'll be honest," he said. "I'm half tempted to believe you."

"In that case get fully tempted because it's the truth," she said. "I'm just a middleman. You know that as well as I do. I don't make decisions, I don't call the shots. I just do what I'm paid to do. In your case I was paid to give you an assignment. I don't know anything about it, not a single thing."

Cave ran his fingers through her hair.

"Why is it that you and I never fucked?" he said.

Yardley exhaled.

"Deven has nothing to do with anything," she said. "Just let her go."

He ran a fingertip down her arm.

"Who set me up?"

"I don't know. I just take orders."

"Who hired you to hire me?"

"Come on, Cave, you know I can't tell you that. I'll end up dead. Whatever's going on is between you and her. You both need to leave me out of it."

"*Her?*"

"Don't act surprised. I'm sure you already knew that much."

He nodded.

"You referred to her as a her once, a long time back," he said. "I don't even think you realized it at the time."

"Look, right now I'm not against you," she said. "If you hurt Deven though everything's going to change and it's going to change fast."

"If I go down you go down," he said.

"I'll do it from a distance," she said. "I'll already be gone."

"That sounds like a threat."

"Good, take it as one," she said. "I'm going to say it one more time. Let Deven go and leave us out of it."

Cave shook his head.

No.

No.

No.

No.

"This is your one and only chance," he said. "If I have to walk away, I'm going straight to Deven and drag her into the deepest hell she could ever imagine. Once I start there won't be any turning back."

He kissed her on the forehead.

"Now, I'm going to ask you one more time," he said. "You're going to give me an answer and then I'm going to walk away. That will be the end of our conversation. There won't be any more. This is it. Understand that all the way deep into your bones. Are you following me?"

She nodded.

"Say it."

"I understand," she said.

"Good. Now, last time. Who hired you to hire me?"

Yardley looked at the ground.

She shifted her feet.

Then she locked eyes with Cave.

"Her name's Madison Elmblade," she said. "She lives at 1775 Marian."

He nodded.

"Is that the woman who came to your store this morning?"

"Yes."

"What did you two talk about?"

"About how she would kill me if I ever told you what I just told you," she said.

"You were following her just now," he said. "Why?"

"I wanted to talk to her again."

"About what?"

She opened her purse and tilted it so Cave could see a gun inside.

"About how she needed to back off," she said.

"You were going to kill her?"

"Not right this second," she said. "I was just going to warn her. Now I don't have to bother, do I? Because you're going to kill her."

He smiled.

"That was my plan," he said. "That plan just changed."

Yardley wrinkled her forehead.

"I don't understand."

"Now I is we," he said. "Instead of me doing it by myself we'll both do it."

"I'm not interested," Yardley said.

"That's strange because I thought you wanted Deven back," he said.

"That wasn't the deal," she said. "The deal was that I give you the name and you let Deven go. That was the deal."

"The deal just changed," he said. "But I'll tell you what. I'll meet you halfway. I'll take you to Deven. You can tell her everything's going to be all right. That will calm her down."

"When?"

Cave put his arm around her shoulders.

"Right now."

31

Tuesday night after dark a thick blanket of clouds swept out of the mountains and let loose on Denver with a cool drizzle. Ordinarily, Teffinger didn't take the '67 out of the garage if there was even a one percent chance of rain anywhere within a three state radius. Tonight, however, he'd be with Sophia, and adding the '67 to the mix seemed like the absolute right thing to do.

The plan was simple.

They were going to drop into the bars Sophia frequented in the last three weeks or so. They were going to talk to the bartenders and see if they remembered anyone picking her out. Either way, they were going to grab whatever security tapes existed, if any, from the night she was there.

Teffinger picked Sophia up at her LoDo loft just after dark. She hopped in, shut the door and said, "How come this seat's all wet?"

"It is?"

"Yeah, feel."

He did.

She was right.

The ragtop was leaking.

She pulled Kleenex out of her purse, dried it off and said, "No biggie. It's just a few drops."

She wore a short slinky white dress that showcased her tanned little body to perfection. Down below were black high heels. Her hair was soft. Her perfume smelled like sex. "You said to wear what I usually wear when I go out," she said. "So don't complain."

"Trust me, I'm the last guy on earth complaining. What was the last bar you were at?"

"That would be Tequila Rose."

"Really?"

"Yeah, you know it?"

He did.

He did indeed.

It was Denver's largest country bar, south on I-25 to 50th, where the beer flowed hard and the women rode their cowboys even harder. "I have a story about that place that's not very flattering," he said.

"Tell."

"I was a fixture there in my mid-twenties," he said. "It was there on a drunken Friday night that I broke a hundred."

Silence.

The wipers swept back and forth.

Teffinger worked through the city over to the freeway.

Once he got on it would only be a ten or fifteen minute drive.

"Broke a hundred?"

"Right."

"A hundred what?"

"A hundred nights of pleasure, let's say."

"You bagged your hundredth woman there. That's what you're saying."

"Bagged isn't a word I use."

"You did back then."

He nodded. "I was different back then though. Now I'm older—"

He must have had a look on his face because Sophia said, "What?"

"I almost said older and wiser," he said. "But I caught myself."

Sophia patted his knee.

"Good catch. So what's the number now?"

"I don't know."

"Yes you do."

"Honestly—"

"Teffinger, no one counts to a hundred and then stops. So what is it? Two hundred? Three?"

"It's not important," he said. "What's important is who's there in the bed with you when you look at her and realize you've just hit your last number. You don't need any more."

"Have you hit that number yet?"

He smiled.

"Five or six times."

She punched his arm.

"I should get paid to be around you."

Teffinger didn't know if Tequila-R would be hopping or dead on a Tuesday. Judging by the sardine parking lot it was the former.

Inside the place hadn't changed much.

Bodies were everywhere.

No one was feeling any pain.

A good band cranked out a catchy song that had the dance floor packed. Teffinger leaned into Sophia and said, "Three chords and the truth. That's what country music is."

They wedged towards the bar.

Sophia tugged on Teffinger's arm and pointed to a bartender. "That guy there should remember me."

They headed over and got his attention.

"I was here Friday night," she said. "Do you remember

me?"

"Yes."

"Did you notice anyone stalking me?"

"You're kidding, right?"

"No, I'm serious."

"Every guy in here is stalking every woman in here," he said.

Teffinger smiled.

It was true.

He leaned in.

"Does the fat man still run the place?"

Yes.

He did.

"Is he here tonight?"

"Yeah."

They made their way through a thousand bodies to the far back corner where Teffinger knocked on a black door. "The fat man's sued everyone in town," he told Sophia. "That's how you know if you're someone or not, by whether he's sued you."

The door opened.

A six-four cowboy appeared.

Teffinger looked around him and saw the fat man hunched behind a desk tapping cigar ashes into an ashtray. There was enough smoke in the room to outdo a forest fire.

"I need to talk to the fat man."

The cowboy stepped aside so the fat man could see.

"I'll be damned," he said. "Let him in."

"This needs to be private."

"Private, huh?" To the cowboy, "Give us five."

The room had no windows. When the door closed, Teffinger would have given his whole paycheck just to double the space.

"This is Sophia Phair," Teffinger said.

"Whoa, whoa, whoa."

"What?"

"The fat man," the fat man said. "You're the one who started that name. It stuck. Did you know that? I'm not complaining, I'm just saying that next time you pick out a nickname for someone, you know, keep in mind that it might stick."

"It's a good name for you," Teffinger said. "It fits."

The man shrugged.

"I don't mind it actually," he said "I even got a license plate, Fat Man. So why are you here wanting to talk to me in *private*?"

"My friend Sophia was here Friday night," he said. "Someone may have been stalking her. What I need is all your surveillance tapes from that night."

"All of 'em?"

Teffinger nodded.

"Parking lots too?"

"Everything you have," Teffinger said.

The fat man sucked on the cigar and blew a ring.

"Sometimes the liquor board gets on my case," he said. "Some of the cowboys piss in the parking lot once in a while. Sometimes an underage sneaks in, that kind of thing. It would sure be nice if you could put in a good word."

Teffinger pulled out his phone, punched numbers and said, "Hey, it's me, Teffinger. I need a favor. Next time you're down at the Tequila-R, extend your blinders a little bit. Don't go crazy, just cut 'em a little slack." He hung up, looked at the fat man and said, "Done deal."

"You're a good man."

32

The dark illegal spark of a thought that worked its way into Teffinger's brain this afternoon was now an all-consuming wildfire. He needed to break into September Tadge's law office and get the files on Van Gogh, he needed to do it tonight, and he needed to do it before he changed his mind. He dropped Sophia off at the house of a coworker named Renn-Jaa, where she should be safe for the night. Then he drove over to September's, parked two blocks away and headed nonchalantly up the street at a quarter to midnight with his head down and his hands in his pockets, to all intents and purposes just one more lost soul adrift in the middle of a lonely Denver night.

Four beers were in his gut.

The buzz was gone, now replaced with leaden eyelids.

He should be home.

He should be screwing Sophia into oblivion then rolling over and bringing those lids down tight and hard.

Tomorrow.

He'd do that tomorrow.

The rain had stopped.

The sidewalks were littered with puddles.

Light from the hotel next door to September's office sprayed onto the front of the structure and onto the dead flat lawn in front of it. A woman came out of the hotel and walked towards the one and only cab out front. She wore a short expensive skirt, nylons and a truckload of face paint.

Escort, Teffinger thought.

Bought and paid for.

He turned left into the darkness at the side of September's office. The tires of the taxi squashed through puddles up the street and the taillights disappeared around the corner.

Teffinger exhaled.

He'd never crossed the line before, not once.

If he did it now, he couldn't erase it.

It would be with him forever.

It would define him in a new way.

It would also be a secret he'd have to carry. The weight would increase over time.

Was he actually stupid enough to do it?

He could feel the files just beyond those walls. Getting them might help keep Sophia alive. Not getting them would keep Teffinger clean. Was he so interested in his own pathetic little existence that he'd leave Sophia at risk to preserve it?

No.

He wasn't that guy.

He wasn't the coward.

It was time to get what he needed.

He made his way to the rear of the structure and found to his amazement that one of the windows had been left halfway up.

He silently climbed through and touched down in a conference room.

It was small.

There was a rectangular wooden table and four chairs. A hotplate for a coffee pot sat on top of a credenza.

He was in.

He'd broken and entered.

The dirt was on him.

Surprisingly he didn't care.

In fact he felt strong.

The sounds of the city trickled through the air—the changing gears of a motorcycle, the wavelike wash of a siren, the drone of cars pulling away at a green light.

Teffinger headed deeper into the structure.

The files would probably be in a filing cabinet.

They'd be arranged alphabetically.

What would they be called?

Van Gogh?

The conference room opened up to a reception area with a desk and a winding stairway to the upper floor. Teffinger walked past the stairway and entered a larger room with a number of plants, a large contemporary desk with a computer monitor on top and a fancy wooden filing cabinet in the corner.

Teffinger pulled a small flashlight out of his pocket.

In the top two drawers of the cabinet was an eclectic mix of non-client files—billing records, bank statements and the like. The bottom two drawers were equally useless. The main filing cabinets must be upstairs.

He silently headed up.

It turned out he was right.

A large room held a number of mismatched metal filing cabinets, brown, gray, tall, short, flea market purchases. They were labeled with magic marker on pieces of paper taped to the top drawer, A-C, D-J, K-P, Q-T, U-Z. Teffinger headed for U-Z. In the second drawer down he found an expandable file labeled Van Gogh.

Inside were several manila folders, each labeled with a date. He flipped one open. Inside were two pieces of paper with handwritten notes.

The others were similar.

He copied every single piece of paper, being careful to keep them in the proper order and in the proper folders, then put the originals back in U-Z exactly where he found them.

He slipped into the night.

No one saw him.

No one knew.

DAY THREE

July 20
Wednesday

33

Yardley woke up to find herself in the driver's seat of a rented Ford parked in a dark neighborhood in the middle of the night. The air was coffin quiet. It was 1:32 a.m., meaning she must have dozed off for at least half an hour. Madison Elmblade's house, two doors down and across the street, looked the same as before. Yardley stretched, worked a cramp out of her neck and pulled the house in closer with a pair of binoculars. Everything was the same. There were no open doors or windows or anything else to indicate that Cave had struck.

Cave.

Cave.

Cave.

The guy was gifted with that James Dean face but inside he was an oak that had grown hard and twisted. Yardley still wasn't sure whether he was just screwing with her earlier when he said they'd kill Elmblade together or whether he was serious about it and then changed his mind. All she knew for sure is that two blocks down the street he sent her packing with a warning; "Stay out of everything and keep your mouth shut. If the dust settles the way it's supposed to you'll get your precious little Deven back. If it doesn't then it doesn't."

She took the gun out of her purse and weighed it in her hand. The steel was cold and hard. Headlights appeared from around the corner and came slowly up the street. Yardley dropped down as they passed then brought an eye up just far enough to see the taillights move down the street.

It was Cave's car.

He was making his move on Madison.

Thunder rolled through Yardley's blood.

The taillights disappeared around a corner.

A few minutes later headlights came back up the street, not passing this time but pulling into a street slot right behind Yardley.

She ducked down.

The car was a Ford rental.

Cave wouldn't recognize it as hers.

He'd have no reason to look inside.

Even if he did, Yardley had an explanation ready: she'd anticipated that he'd show up tonight, she was there to help him. That's what she'd say. There'd be no reason for him to not believe it. He'd probably smile and slap her ass. "Prove it," he'd say.

A car door opened and then closed.

A horn didn't beep.

Cave hadn't used the remote to lock the doors.

He was leaving them open in case he needed to make a quick getaway.

Yardley dug deeper into the seat.

A distant dog barked, once and again, possibly a warning to Cave, then it stopped. No other sounds cut the air. Cave should be past Yardley by now. She brought her head up and checked.

She was right.

There he was, sneaking through the side shadows of Madison's house into the deeper darkness behind.

With the gun in hand, Yardley opened the door quieter than quiet and hugged the shadows back to Cave's car. The door was opened as she suspected. She got all the way in to kill the overhead light as quickly as possible and fumbled around under the dash until she found the trunk latch.

She pulled it.

A movement came from the rear of the vehicle.

She got out, stayed low and headed to the back. A dog barked, the same as before. Her heart raced. The trunk lid was unlatched, a few inches up. She pulled it up higher and confirmed there was an emergency release inside.

Then she got in.

There was room for her body but not by much.

The claustrophobia was already climbing up her throat.

She swallowed it down.

She pointed the gun at Madison's house. It was time to scare Cave enough into getting the hell out of there, before Elmblade killed him and Deven was lost forever.

This was it.

Bam!

Bam!

Bam!

Glass shattered.

She pulled the lid shut and curled up in a fetal position. Thirty seconds later Cave bounded into the car and squealed away. The violence of the turn at the corner pushed Yardley's head into something sharp.

She didn't care.

Hold on Deven.

I'm coming.

34

Wednesday morning Sophia got a couple of billable hours under her belt then closed the door and watched one of the Tequila Rose surveillance tapes. What she saw sent ice up her spine.

The gladiator she picked up Friday night was there in all his glory.

What became clear, however, was that Sophia was only half right in thinking that she was the one who picked him up. At every move, he was watching her from a distance, then eventually positioning himself so they'd meet.

There were no names exchanged.

She didn't know his.

That didn't mean he didn't know hers. She'd been in the bathroom a couple of times that night at his loft. That would have given him time to rummage through her wallet, replete with not only her driver's license but also a half-dozen business cards.

A knock came at the door.

The knob turned and Renn-Jaa walked in.

"Something's wrong," she said.

"Close the door."

Sophia showed her the tape.

Renn-Jaa wasn't impressed.

"He had you for free Friday night," she said. "Why would he go off on some crazy elaborate scheme on Sunday to rape you? It doesn't make sense. Plus, look at the guy. He can get laid three times before noon without even trying."

"Yeah, but he can't strangle them while he's doing it," Sophia said.

Renn-Jaa cocked her head.

"Close your eyes," she said.

"Why?"

"Just do it."

Sophia did.

"Now, think back to Sunday night," she said. "Do you see this guy there anywhere? Does he spark even the faintest recollection?"

Sophia opened her eyes.

"No but that doesn't mean anything."

"I think it does," Renn-Jaa said.

"My memory's gone."

"It can't be gone a hundred percent."

"Trust me, it is."

She stood up and grabbed her purse.

"Where are you going?"

"To find out who he is."

"You don't know his name?"

"No," Sophia said. "I have this thing. I pick guys up, I get screwed like crazy and I leave. There are no names involved. There, I said it. It's out. I don't know his name but I know where he lives."

She headed for the door.

"Hold on," Renn-Jaa said. "I'm coming with you."

"No, you have billables to worry about."

"Screw the billables. I never knew you were such a slut."

They ended up in Renn-Jaa's car with the air on full and the radio on hip-hop, parking over on Bannock and then heading out on foot in search of a red brick "not very fancy" building. After ten minutes Sophia pointed and said, "That's it."

Renn-Jaa made a face.

"You screwed a guy who lives in that?"

"Not funny."

"Does it have running water?"

She ignored it.

"He's a photographer," Sophia said. "He has the top floor."

The lobby was an empty space with an elevator that looked like it hadn't had a code inspection since the caveman days. Next to it was a stairwell with a steel door propped-open with a brick. The light was dim, provided by under-wattage bulbs screwed into minimal ceiling fixtures.

There was no directory or listing of names.

"Stay here," Renn-Jaa said. "I'm going up."

"No."

"I'm just going to see if there's a name on the door. I'm not going to knock or anything."

"No, don't."

"Does he use the elevator or the stairs?"

"What do you mean?"

"When you came here Friday, how did you get up, the elevator or the stairs?"

"Neither," Sophia said. "We used an outside fire escape."

Renn-Jaa exhaled.

"Okay, I'm taking the stairs," she said. "Keep a lookout. If you see him coming, get the hell out of here. Don't worry about me. He doesn't know me. For all he knows I'm here to see someone else."

The woman disappeared into the stairwell and headed up, keeping her heels quiet.

Sophia shifted her feet.

Then she followed.

At the top level was a steel door with a painted number 701 but no name. The stairs continued up past a sign—Roof Access.

Sophia put her ear to the door.

No sounds came from behind it.

No TV.

No radio.

No nothing.

Then she put her hand on the knob and twisted, expecting to find it locked.

It turned.

She looked at Renn-Jaa, then pushed the door open an inch. No signs of life came from within.

35

Teffinger pitched and flipped all night in some kind of not-quite-sleep netherworld before finally giving up at 4:48 in the morning and heading outside for a jog. The exuberance of walking out of September's law office last night with the Van Gogh notes in his pocket was gone. In its place was a dull realization that he'd actually let himself get dirty and there was nothing in the world he could ever do to undo it.

The dirt was his.

He owned it.

The notes were on his kitchen counter next to his keys.

He hadn't read them yet.

Nestled into the side of Green Mountain fifteen miles west of Denver, Teffinger's street went down and that's the way he was forced to go outside his front door, meaning at the end of his run when he was dog-tired he'd be coming up. The gravity always started him out too fast and this morning was no exception. Two blocks later he regulated and got into a sustainable pace. The world was dark, broken only by streetlights and the occasional bathroom light.

The air was crisp.

He sucked it deep into his lungs.

A fox bounded out from behind a car, stopping long enough to turn a startled head in Teffinger's direction before trotting across the street and disappearing into the shadows.

The dirt was serious.

A homicide unit couldn't have a rogue running around doing illegal things all in the name of the end game. There could be lawsuits. There could be evidence thrown out. The Constitution required fair play.

The Constitution was bigger than Teffinger.

If he got caught, he would be discharged.

There wouldn't be another option.

His record, his personality and his excuses however noble wouldn't save him.

Nor should they.

Damn it.

Damn it.

Damn it.

How did he get so stupid?

The four beers didn't help but he couldn't blame them. He'd drunk four beers plenty of times before without going out afterwards and trampling all over the law.

He hadn't read the notes yet.

What if he just went home and burned them to ashes and then flushed those ashes down the toilet? That would get him about as close back to square one as he could ever hope at this point.

But what if Sophia ended up dead and then he found out afterwards that the notes had information that would have prevented it?

Which was more important, him staying clean or Sophia staying alive?

It was the same question as last night.

Three miles clicked by.

"One more."

He did two.

When he got home the notes were sitting on the counter exactly where they should be. Teffinger gave them a sideways glance as he got the coffee pot going. Then he headed for the shower.

Decide before you get out, he said.

Read them or burn them.

Do one or the other by the time the first cup of coffee is done.

Be done with it.

36

Yardley's dark ride in Cave's claustrophobic trunk was marked with hip-hop pounding with such an amped-up, overdrive blare that the metal vibrated. Cave's voice rose over the speakers, violently, and his fist drummed on the console. Halfway through a song he'd punch to a different station, swear when he got a crap song, then punch to the next, ten or fifteen times if he had to.

Yardley kept the gun in her hand until her fingers got tired and then stuffed it under her body where she could feel it.

Her back was cramped.

Her legs were cramped.

The muscles on the right side of her neck were on fire from constantly being stretched to the left.

She fought the urge to open the trunk and stick her legs out. Someone might see them and flag Cave down.

Songs came and went.

After a long time the vehicle turned right and the smoothness of pavement gave way to gravel and ruts. The terrain rose gently but steadily then dropped steeply with a number of switchbacks.

The tires stopped rolling.

The engine didn't shut off.

The vehicle rocked slightly as Cave got out. The door didn't slam shut. What was he doing? Opening a gate?

He got back in, pulled the car up a short distance, then got out again.

That must be it.

He was going through a gate.

The vehicle drove for another couple of minutes and then came to a stop. The engine shut off. Cave got out and slammed the door.

Yardley got the gun into her hand and pointed it at the lid of the trunk.

There was no need.

Wherever Cave went it was somewhere else.

Yardley waited for a full minute, maybe two, to let Cave get situated, then she silently felt around in the darkness until she found the release latch. When she pulled it the lid popped and caught, barely audible but with a slight sound nonetheless.

Cool air worked its way through the crack.

Crickets punctuated the night.

Yardley pushed the lid open far enough to get her body through, then eased her way out and gently pushed the lid down.

She stayed low.

The dark silhouette of a building of some sort took shape. No lights or sounds came from it. With the gun in hand, she headed towards it one silent step at a time.

The building was a metal structure with ribbed sides. In the front was an overhead rolling door, currently down but letting a sliver of light from inside define its perimeter. Next to it was a man door.

Yardley worked her way down the side of the structure and found no windows.

At the far backside, however, she located one.

It was high.

The lower edge was six feet off the ground.

The glass wasn't clear, it had some kind of rippled texture. It was cracked, though, as if it had been hit by a rock. Maybe there was a sliver wide enough to see through if she could get her eye up to it.

She looked around for something to stand on.

There was nothing.

She headed around to the other side of the building and walked into a stack of chopped logs. She grabbed the biggest one she could carry and silently wedged it against the metal under the window.

Her right foot went onto the top of the log.

Then with one quick motion she boosted herself up.

As she was bringing her eye to the glass, a sound came from behind her.

37

When no sign of life came from inside the gladiator's loft, Sophia pushed the door open farther and stuck her head in. The bed was at the far end of the space, empty. The gladiator was nowhere to be seen.

Sophia swallowed and said in a soft friendly voice, "Hello? Anyone home?"

No one answered.

She looked at Renn-Jaa.

"Are we really going to do this?"

The woman nodded.

"We have to. We'll never get this chance again."

They stepped inside and locked the door behind them.

The space was just that, free flowing space, uninterrupted by walls except for the bathroom in the far right corner and another room next to it. The floors were wooden, stained from some prior industrial life and periodically pockmarked with screw holes and indentations from heavy things that had dropped. The windows were a floor-to-ceiling mesh of single pane glass. Several were cracked and patched with gray tape. At ceiling level the ductwork, water lines and electrical wires were exposed but not dusty.

On the wall to the left was a door to the fire escape.

Sophia opened it and looked down to find no gladiators on

the way up.

"One of us should stand guard here."

Renn-Jaa said, "I'll do it. You search."

The bed wasn't much, basically a mattress on the floor, not joined by box springs or a frame. The sight made Sophia pull up a visual from Friday night, her dress being roughly pulled down and her panties being ripped off. Then the gladiator had his face between her legs, working her over with his tongue and mouth and the rubbing of his chin as he pushed her bra up and tweaked her nipples.

She shook it off.

The bathroom door was open.

Her lipstick was still on the mirror—"Thanks."

The sight made her pause.

Why hadn't he wiped it off yet?

Next to the bathroom was a walled room with a ceiling and a door. She tried the knob and found it locked.

A MacBook sat on a desk.

When Sophia lifted the top it asked for a password.

She closed it and turned her attention to the papers, lots of which were mail, with bills in one pile and non-bills in another.

Evan Starry.

That was the gladiator's name.

Evan Starry.

The bills were the normal stuff. Sophia opened the cell phone bill to see if the calls were itemized, which they weren't. Then she opened the Visa bill and ran through the charges. They were routine—gas, meals, cash advances, groceries, staples. She was almost folding it back up when something at the bottom caught her eye.

Concrete Flower Factory.

$500.

She memorized the name and reinserted the bill exactly like

she'd found it.

"What are you finding?"

"His name's Evan Starry."

"It doesn't exactly have that *Bond, James Bond,* ring to it, does it?"

"No, but I'll tell you one thing, he could kick the ass of any Bond that ever was. Any sign of him?"

"No. No Starry Night in motion."

"Starry Night?"

"Yeah, you know, the painting."

"What painting?"

"By Van Gogh. You never saw the painting Starry Night?"

"I don't know—"

"You had to have seen it," Renn-Jaa said. "You just don't know it by name."

"Whatever. Keep your eyes open," Sophia said. "If he finds us in here I'm going to say I came back for more and brought you along for a threesome."

Renn-Jaa smiled.

"If he's actually like you say he is maybe we should wait until he gets back and give that line a try."

"Not funny."

"Not meant to be. See if you can find a picture of him that he won't miss. Maybe Teffinger can run it through a database or something." A beat then, "Shit! He's coming!"

"Are you sure?"

"He's almost all the way up!"

38

Out of the shower Teffinger tucked a white cotton shirt into jeans, put on a blue tie with the knot trim but the action loose, and found some fairly clean black leather shoes for down below. His hair hung damp, towel dried but not blown. He roughed it up with his fingers then headed for work with a coffee mug at his side, steering with one hand once he got to the 6th Avenue freeway. The sun busted over the horizon, through his eyes and straight into his brain.

He hadn't read the notes.

He hadn't burned them either.

He needed coffee.

Checking his phone messages as he passed Sheridan Boulevard, he found one from yesterday that he didn't expect:

"Hey, Nick, it's me, Kelly Ravenfield. Long time, huh? I just wanted to let you know that I'm in New York and I think I saw Michael Northway on the street. I'm not positive it was him, there was some distance, but I'm about as positive as I can be. Anyway, I thought you should know." A beat then, "Okay, well, that's it, goodbye. Wait, one more thing. I'll be back in the office tomorrow, Wednesday, if you feel the need to give me a call for whatever reason."

Her voice was a song, a song wedged deep in his bones, a

song that he didn't realized he missed until just now.

Kelly.

Kelly.

Kelly.

He pulled up an image of jumping down into the cold rising waters of a mine, lifting her up and holding her tighter than tight. Another image quickly followed, down at B.Ts., with Kelly drunk at the bar, rubbing her ass into Teffinger's crotch and telling him how she was going to screw him silly later.

Kelly.

Kelly.

Kelly.

Thinking back, he couldn't remember why it ended. She was the one who broke it off, that was true, but did he do everything he could have to reverse it?

No.

He didn't.

He was in the middle of a horrible case and that was his excuse.

It was valid at the time.

Now, in hindsight, he wasn't as convinced.

Maybe she was testing him and he failed.

The image of Michael Northway wasn't pleasant. He was a hotshot lawyer, the head of Denver's largest law firm at the time, the firm Kelly was in, who got himself mixed up with a serial killer to the point of becoming a co-conspirator. When it came to the decision of Northway going down or Kelly going down, he chose Kelly. Luckily he didn't succeed. The killer met his match at Teffinger's hands on a dark stormy night up in the minefields above Central City but Northway escaped, never to be seen or heard from again.

Teffinger spent the next two weeks trying to pick up the man's scent.

The FBI helped.

Nothing materialized.

No one found even so much as a broken blade of grass where his footstep had been.

Teffinger's best guess was that the man had offshore accounts and fake passports. He was probably laying low in the underbelly of Bangkok or Rio, spending his time on sex and current affairs, maybe bar tending or doing something equally the opposite of lawyering.

Teffinger checked the rest of his messages hoping that the newscast last evening brought someone forward who knew something about the longhaired man who saved Sophia from Jackie Lake's killer.

He hardly listened to the words.

His thoughts were on Kelly.

For whatever reason.

That's what she said.

The meaning was clear.

Teffinger had never rekindled a relationship, not once in his life, not even back in high school or college. When things were done they were done. There was never a need to go back. Going forward was too easy. Something new was always just a step up the road. That was his problem according to Dr. Leigh Sandt, "Women come too easy to you, Teffinger. That's why you're still single."

That was true but deep down there was more.

He was addicted to falling in love.

There was nothing in the world like that initial free-fall into lust with a stranger.

It was shortsighted and shallow, he knew that and even admitted it to himself on rare occasions. That didn't mean he could control it, though.

Kelly had gone deeper into his bones than any woman.

Maybe it was time to end the addiction.

If he did, who would it be with?

Kelly was one of two possibilities.

The other was Sophia.

The 6th Avenue freeway doesn't go through Denver and swing out the other side. Instead it runs smack at the city on a suicide run and abruptly ends at a stoplight where it morphs into a street.

He looked up to find something he didn't expect.

He was right there at the end.

The cars ahead were stopped.

He slammed on the brakes with every ounce of strength in his body. The Tundra's antilocks grinded and the rubber fought the momentum, eventually bringing the vehicle to a jerky stop not more than two feet from the ass end of a shiny yellow Challenger.

An arm came out the driver's side window.

The middle finger on the hand of that arm extended.

Then the hand moved up and down.

Teffinger took his death grip off the wheel, waved to say he was sorry, then felt something on his crotch.

Coffee.

He dabbed at it with a dry hand and then pulled into the parking lot of a donut place. A Beach Boys' song came from the radio, "Don't Worry Baby." He was ten years old when he heard his first Beach Boys song and this was it. He still remembered the moment, in his room with the radio on, playing video games.

Life was simple back then.

It was pure.

It was the way life was supposed to be.

He swung through the side streets and back onto the freeway,

heading west. Twenty minutes later he was home. In the kitch-
en, the wind had blown the notes off the counter.

He gathered them up and took them to the sink.

There he ripped them in half, then quarters, then eighths.

Then, a few pieces at a time, he burned them to ashes with
a lighter.

He flicked on the disposal and washed the ashes down the
drain.

Outside the sun felt like an old friend.

He headed back for the freeway, trying to get a song.

Nothing good was there.

He punched off the radio and sang "Don't Worry Baby."

39

Yardley turned at the sound behind her and determined it was something small rustling through the bush, a field rat or a snake, something of that order. A crack in the glass had a solid sliver of light coming through it. She put her eye to it and got a narrow band of vision into the structure.

Deven was roped spread-eagle on a mattress, visible from the waist up.

She was naked.

Cave wasn't in view.

His voice came from somewhere near the foot of the bed, out of sight. "I was stupid. I actually believed that your little bitch friend Yardley was telling me the truth as to who hired her. She was lying though. Do you understand what that means?"

Suddenly his body appeared.

It was naked.

A beer was in his left hand.

He sat on the bed, tweaked Deven's nipple then poured beer on her face.

She twisted wildly.

"It means that I was actually going to let you go but now I'm not," he said. "Not in a million years. You're dead and so is your stupid little friend."

"She wouldn't set you up," Deven said.

Cave made a face of surprise.

"Oh no? Really? Then why did someone take a shot at me? No, not a shot, three shots; bam, bam, bam; one, two three. Do you want a hint? Because they knew I was coming. Do you know how they knew I was coming? Because a little birdie told them. Little birdies like that end up with broken wings. So do their friends."

Deven pulled at the ropes.

"That has nothing to do with you and me," she said. "Look, we have chemistry. I know you can feel it because I can. Let me join you. We'll be a team. I can get Yardley to tell me what's going on and who all's involved. I can help you bring all of them down."

Cave brought his mouth close to hers.

"Chemistry," he said.

She arched her face up to kiss him.

He pulled back, just out of reach.

"Don't lie," she said. "You know it's there. You can trust me."

"Really?"

"Yes, really," she said.

He stood up and looked down at her.

"I know when someone's lying to me."

"There are no lies here," she said. "Just give me a chance, you'll see. One chance. You won't be sorry. I promise. I promise you with everything I have and everything I am."

He swallowed what was left in the can, then crushed it in his fist.

"One chance, huh?"

Her face brightened.

"Yes."

He studied her.

"I'll tell you what," he said. "You say there's chemistry? I'll give you a chance to prove it."

He untied her ankles.

She pulled up to bend her arms as much as she could.

Cave pulled her back down.

"Stay," he said.

"Okay."

"Tell me to fuck you."

She didn't hesitate.

"Fuck me," she said.

"Say fuck me hard."

"Fuck me harder than I've ever been fucked in my life," she said.

He nibbled on her stomach.

It was taut and trembled under his touch.

She closed her eyes and wiggled her hips.

Yardley silently eased down off the log, picked the gun off the ground and made her way through the darkness to the front door. She put her hand on the knob and turned it ever so slowly.

It was locked.

Damn it.

What to do?

Two options came to mind. One, get back up on the log, bust the window out and shoot Cave. Take him by complete surprise. If she did that, she'd first have to wait until he was clear of Deven. Two, wait until he eventually came out of the structure, then jump out from around the corner and shoot him before he even knew she was there.

She'd never killed anyone before.

She was hungry.

She wore only short sleeves.

The cold night air worked with a growing wickedness on

her flesh.

By morning she'd be dangerously frayed.

She crept over to Cave's car and tried the driver's door to see if it was unlocked.

It was.

She let the door release only an inch then pushed it silently shut with her body before the interior lights came on. It was too dark to see if the keys were in the ignition. The more she wondered if they were, the more she needed to know.

She opened the door.

The interior lights came on.

The keys were in the ignition.

She pulled them out and stuck them in her pocket.

Then she had a better idea, replaced the keys and let the air out of the front tire.

40

B y the time their bodies reacted, the gladiator was so close that his footsteps were audible as they slammed up the steel steps. Getting through the door to the stairwell in heels before he got in would be impossible. They ducked into the bathroom, stepped into the tub and pulled the curtain.

Sophia's chest pounded.

Surprise!

That's what she'd say if he came in.

That trick was limited though. It would work for a minute or two but not in half an hour. She should use it now while the using was good.

She should.

She absolutely should.

Her brain was clear on the matter but her body balked.

A deep warning told her to hold off until she thought it all the way through. If he's the one who killed Jackie Lake, he knew she was a witness.

He'd kill her, right here, right now.

Renn-Jaa too.

He'd dump their bodies tonight where they'd never be found.

Stay still.

Just stay still.

Renn-Jaa put her mouth close to Sophia's ear. Sophia pulled back and shook her head.

No.

No.

No.

The woman's eyes darted, wide and twitchy.

The fear was palpable.

Sophia squeezed her hand.

They kept their bodies perfectly still.

The fridge opened and a can tab pulled. The gladiator took a long swallow of something, then the bulk of his weight moved in their direction.

He came in.

A zipper came down.

Sophia held her breath.

A long, strong piss followed, not more than three feet away.

Just as it ended a cell phone rang.

"Starry," the gladiator said. A beat then, "Damn it Sweeton, I told you never to call me on my cell. The stupid records stay forever." Silence. "I don't give a rat's ass if you're calling from a pay phone." A pause, listening, then, "Meet me at ten-thirty tonight, the same place as last time."

A zipper came up.

Ten seconds later the man was out of the loft, scampering down the fire escape.

41

Locke & Banner, P.C., was a hundred-plus law firm that had forsaken the typical high-rise financial district venue in lieu of an old warehouse conversion in the trendy section of Market Street just north of the 16th Street Mall. The litigation department was located on the third floor, which was also the top floor. Kelly Ravenfield's office was at the back, overlooking an alley and staring into the hundred-year-old bricks of another building immediately across that alley.

Teffinger didn't make an appointment and used his one blue eye and one green eye to talk the receptionist into letting him wander back without announcing him in advance.

Kelly was faced the other way working at a computer.

The office was decorated in shades of panic, replete with piles of files, yellow post-its galore, and a half-empty pot of coffee on a hotplate.

The woman's hair was blond and loose, cascading down the backside of a crisp white blouse. Down below was a pinstriped skirt, riding up thigh-high over nylons. Leather shoes with a two-inch heel were slipped off and sitting on the floor next to her feet.

Her left hand had no ring.

There were no pictures of men to be seen.

Teffinger's heart raced.

He cleared his throat.

When the woman turned, she was just as beautiful as ever, with those green eyes and her slightly crooked smile. Her face registered surprise, then something primal.

"Someone said you're still hot for me," Teffinger said. "I thought I'd stop by and see if that's true or not."

She came around and hugged him tight, stomach-to-stomach, then kissed him on the lips. With her arms around his waist, she leaned back and checked him out.

"How'd I ever let you get away from me," she said.

Teffinger cocked his head.

"It was a push, if I recall."

"Yeah well, in hindsight it looks like I should have zigged when I zagged," she said. "You're here about Michael Northway. You want some coffee?"

Teffinger shook his head.

"I quit coffee," he said.

The look on her face was what he expected.

"Honestly? You did?"

He smiled.

"No, of course I didn't and yes, I'll take some."

She punched him on the arm.

"You haven't changed."

"Yeah, old dog, no new tricks."

She poured a cup and handed it to him.

"There was nothing wrong with the old tricks if I remember correctly," she said. She took a sip of coffee and studied him over the rim. "Here's the deal on Northway. I was in New York yesterday taking a deposition. During the lunch break, I saw Northway across the street, this was on 42nd in Manhattan, a little before one. He looked the same as always with his surfer boy hair and cocky smile, except the power tie and tailored suit were gone. He was in jeans and a gray and white striped shirt with a collar, cotton, sort of sporty. He wore tennis shoes and had sunglasses hanging in the v-neck of the shirt. A woman was with him. She was younger, a lot younger, twenty-six or thereabouts, nicely dressed, very nicely dressed in fact, even by New York standards. She struck me as a lawyer."

"What color was her hair?"

"Blond."

"So she was sort of like you," Teffinger said.

Kelly nodded.

"Apparently old habits die hard," she said. "They disappeared around a corner. By the time I got across the street and on their tail, they were gone." A pause, "Here, let me show you exactly where they were." She pulled it up on Google Earth, first as an aerial view, then down to street level. "They were right there."

The street was jammed with office buildings.

"Take me around the corner," he said.

She did.

There was more of the same.

"Would you recognize the woman again if you saw her?"

Kelly shook her head.

"Doubtful," she said. "They were at a distance and I was a lot more interested in Northway than I was in her. What I said is about all I can remember of her. Nick, I'm not positive it was him. You need to understand that."

"You're pretty sure, though," he said.

She nodded.

"Right, pretty sure," she said. A beat then, "Have you talked to Sydney lately?"

Yes.

Every day.

"Did she say anything about me?"

The question confused him.

"No. Why would she?"

"We meet about once a month or so for lunch," she said. "Did you know that?"

No.

He didn't.

"What for?"

"You want the truth or lies?"

He shrugged.

"Whichever is easiest."

"That would be the lie," she said. "I'm going to go the hard way though and tell you the truth. We do it so I can keep up with what's going on with you. I made her promise to never tell you. It looks like she kept her word."

"Apparently," he said. "Remind me to talk to her about that."

The woman downed what was left in her coffee cup, then closed the door and locked it.

She shut off the lights.

She pulled the window covering.

Then she sat on the edge of the desk in front of Teffinger, leaned back on her arms and dangled her legs, saying nothing.

Teffinger put an index finger on each knee and moved them slowly outwards.

The woman's legs spread.

The nylons were held up with a black garter belt.

White cotton panties peeked out from between taut golden thighs.

"I have a confession to make," Kelly said. "You're the best lay I ever had."

"Is that what I am to you, a lay?"

She ran her fingers through his hair.

"I miss sitting in that old car of yours on those stormy nights."

He ran an index finger in a circle on her knee, then looked

into her eyes and said, "I ripped up every picture I had of you, ripped 'em up and burned them."

"You hated me."

He nodded.

"That's right."

"Do you still hate me?"

He considered it.

The answer surprised him.

"Yes," he said. "I didn't realize it until just now, but the answer is yes."

"Good."

"How is that good?"

"It's good because hate is another form of love." She pulled her skirt up. "Show me how much you hate me, Nick. Make me sorry I ever hurt you."

42

Yardley spent the night in the darkness around the corner of the building, curled up with her back against the structure, slipping in and out of consciousness. She must have fallen asleep because there was now a low-lying amber seeping into the sky. She stood up, took a few steps over and relieved herself on the ground. The more she thought about killing Cave the more it weighed on her. She'd try to wound him if possible then escape on foot. If he ever came after her down the road, she'd kill him without a second thought. He would have had his chance and blown it at that point.

The dawn got lighter.

The terrain took shape in the form of rolling prairie filled with scraggly pinions, yuccas, rabbit brush and grasses. To the west not more than twenty yards distant was a string of cottonwoods sucking up to a dried creek bed. Beyond that the foothills rose up.

Voices came from inside the structure.

Cave was up.

Yardley hugged the side of the building with the gun in hand waiting for the man to emerge. More than an hour passed, then he finally stepped out.

"Damned stupid tire!"

A stream of piss landed on the ground outside the door,

then the trunk of the car popped up and Cave rummaged around getting the spare and jack out. Yardley took a quick look and found Cave on the other side of the car out of sight, working the jack.

She was focused but not afraid.

She had a gun.

He didn't.

She crept around the corner and made her way to the door of the structure.

It was open.

She stepped in and found Deven naked on the bed, tied but in a different position. Instead of spread-eagle, her wrists were tied behind her back and one of her ankles was roped to the frame.

Her eyes were open.

She had enough wits about her to know not to talk.

Yardley looked around for a knife to cut the ropes, found nothing, then set the gun on the mattress and worked at the knots with her fingers and teeth.

Cave was outside swearing, broadcasting his position.

The knots were tight.

It took time.

Finally they came undone.

Silently, Deven put her shoes on; not her clothes though, there was no time for the clothes; those she picked up and carried.

They got to the door and waited until Cave got the spare on and knelt down to put the lug nuts on. Then they slipped outside and around the edge of the building.

Neither woman talked.

They made their way to the cottonwoods and followed them for a hundred yards where they ended.

Back at the structure a gun fired.

Yardley cursed herself for not being smart enough to grab Cave's weapon while she had the chance.

"Come on!"

They ran.

Deven was slow.

"Hurry," Yardley said. "We need to get over that ridge before he spots us."

"I'm trying!"

"Try harder!"

43

Back at the law firm Sophia kept her ass in the chair and cranked out billable hours until midafternoon, then did a web search for Concrete Flower Factory, the mysterious $500 credit card charge on Starry's bill. It turned out to be a dungeon in an industrial area on the north edge of the city, up I-25 near furniture row.

When she told Renn-Jaa, the woman's response was fast. "We need to get over there and find out what Starry's game is."

"Why?"

"I want to see the women he uses for one," she said. "I want to see if they look like you. I'd also like to know if he's into suffocation or strangulation or oxygen deprivation or whatever it is they call it. That and/or rape fantasies. Maybe that place is his release valve until he just can't stand it any more and has to do it for real."

Sophia cocked her head.

The woman made sense.

"Okay," she said.

"We'll go tonight," Renn-Jaa added.

A pause.

"Sure."

"Bring bribe money."

"How much?"

"I don't know. A thousand?"

"*A thousand?* Are you kidding?"

"I don't know. Just bring as much as you can and we'll try not to use it all. All I'm saying is that we need to have enough to get the job done. Do you have a thousand laying around?"

"I wouldn't call it laying around," she said. "I'll have to make a run to the bank."

"Fine. Get fifties or smaller."

"Okay."

Ten minutes later Grayson Condor walked into her office, closed the door and settled into one of the chairs in front of her desk.

"How you holding up?"

"Fine."

"Are you sure?"

Good question.

She smiled.

"Pretty sure."

"*Pretty sure,*" he said. "Well that's better than I would be. What do you think about having a bodyguard, at the firm's expense? I've made a few calls. There's an outfit called Personal Security Specialists. They're actually in our building on the tenth floor. They have a female on staff named Lea Skye, she's an ex-Marine with a long list of credentials. She looks like a lifeguard. She could sleep on your couch. You wouldn't have to feel weird about having a man in your place."

Sophia exhaled.

"Can I think about it?"

"Sure. Go down and talk to her. If you decide to go ahead, just let her know. The firm's already made arrangements."

She nodded.

"I'll talk to her."

"Good. If you need any time off—"

She shook her head.

"No, thanks, really; I appreciate it, but what I need more than anything right now is just to have my posterior firmly planted in this chair."

He understood.

Enough said.

Ten minutes later her phone rang and the voice of the California investigator, Aspen Gonzales, came through. "I have some news for you. It's not particularly pretty."

Sophia braced.

"Let me have it."

44

K elly was an animal, a dirty filthy little sex-starved animal who screwed Teffinger like a pack of wild ban-
shees, then slumped down on her sweaty back and
panted.

"Damn," she said.

Teffinger got his pants situated.

"You're going to have some 'splaining to do, Lucy. You were
pretty loud."

"I was?"

He nodded.

"Trust me."

"I don't care," she said.

By the look on her face she was telling the truth.

Teffinger was back on the street within minutes, passing wom-
en, able to sense the ones who were animals. A raven-haired
beauty approaching from the opposite direction held his gaze
longer than appropriate, almost as if daring him to seize the
moment.

"How you doing?" he said.

"Fine."

They passed.

"Hey," he heard over his shoulder.

He stopped and turned.

The woman approached. She wore an aqua tank that rode three inches above cutoff jeans. A flat little belly button peeked out. She pulled a tissue out of her purse and wiped lipstick off Teffinger's mouth, then shoved the tissue in his shirt pocket.

"There, all better," she said.

"Thanks."

She smiled for a heartbeat and then walked off.

When he arrived at the office, Sydney got in his face and said, "I watched the Tequila Rose surveillance tapes this morning. The guy that Sophia eventually left with, the gladiator, was checking her out long before she knew it."

Teffinger filled a disposable cup with coffee.

"I would have been too," he said.

"Not like that," she said. "More like in a creepy way."

"He was stalking her?"

"They didn't meet by accident," Sydney said. "He got in her space. Outside, he arrived fifteen minutes after her. It's possible he tailed her there."

Teffinger took a sip.

"Was he with anyone?"

"No, alone."

"Is any of his left ear missing?"

"Unknown," she said. "His hair's always over it." She grabbed a napkin and dabbed at the corner of Teffinger's ear, then held it up to show him.

It was lipstick.

"Kelly's or Sophia's?"

A pause.

"Kelly's."

"Jeez, Nick, that fast?"

He shrugged.

"I guess so."

"What about Sophia? She's out?"

"No."

"So she's in?"

"Nobody's anywhere. Things are just happening, that's all." He took a sip, filled her in on the information Kelly gave him about the Michael Northway sighting and said, "Coordinate with our counterparts in New York. See if you can sweet-talk them into rounding up surveillance tapes."

She frowned.

"On the list of a hundred things I need to do, where do you want me to put this one?"

"At the top. Oh, call Leigh Sandt and fill her in too. She's always complaining I don't keep her in the loop."

"You don't."

"Loops take time," he said.

"So does coffee."

"Yeah, but coffee trumps."

He raked his hair back with his fingers.

It immediately flopped back down.

"Time to do some gladiator work."

45

Yardley awoke in her bed Wednesday afternoon to the sound of someone knocking on her door. Deven was soundly asleep next to her. A strong Colorado sun muscled its way through the window coverings. She grabbed the gun, released the safety and walked barefoot across the loft, pausing and listening at the door before finally saying, "Who's there?"

"Madison Elmblade, the lawyer."

Madison Elmblade.

She was the bait Cave was supposed to take last night.

"Are you alone?"

"Yes."

Yardley opened the door far enough to where it got snagged by the chain, found things as the woman said and let her in.

"I've left you ten messages," she said. "Why haven't you called me back?"

"I'll explain," she said. "Just give me a minute."

She got the coffee pot going, splashed water on her face at the kitchen sink and dried it with a paper towel.

"Cave came for you last night," she said. "I was the one who fired the shots."

"That was you?"

Yes.

It was.

"Why?"

She explained.

The more she told the story, the more Elmblade paced. At the end the woman said, "So that's great that Deven's safe, but what do you think happens now?"

"Simple," Yardley said. "Cave will contact me sooner or later. I'm going to explain to him how I could have killed him ten different times but didn't do it. I'm going to tell him we're even. He needs to go his way and me and Deven are going ours."

The lawyer wasn't impressed.

"Do you really think that's going to work?"

"It has to, it's all I got."

"You got nothing," Elmblade said. "Less than nothing. What you got is Cave biding his time and figuring out a way to get both you and Deven tied up tighter than tight in his next little lair. You got nothing until he's dead. Then you have everything."

Yardley's chest tightened.

She already knew deep in her bones that what Elmblade was saying was a possibility. Hearing the words out loud gave them a bigger proportion.

She poured two cups of coffee, handed one to the woman and said, "So what do you propose?"

"We kill him."

She said the words and let them hang.

Yardley pictured it.

It wasn't pretty.

She frowned and shook her head.

"To be honest, I don't think I'm cut out for that," she said.

The woman wrinkled her brow.

"I need you to be the bait. We need to lure him somewhere

where I can do it and not have to worry about a thousand witnesses. Then we need to dispose of the body where it will never be found."

Yardley shook her head.

"There's no such place. Not in this day and age."

"Wrong, there are a million places and I know at least ten of them," Elmblade said. "That's not the issue. The issue is whether you'll be the bait. You are already, whether you admit it or not. The only question is whether you want me in the shadows waiting for him when he comes."

"Lovely picture," Yardley said. She flicked hair out of her eyes. "If I help you, Deven needs to stay out of it. I don't want her to play any part whatsoever. I don't want her involved even an inch."

"That's fine. You can stick her on a plane to Greenland for all I care."

46

When the California investigator said she had news and it wasn't particularly pretty, Sophia braced but not hard enough.

"Okay, the woman you asked about, London Winger, was an attorney here in Malibu," she said. "She was friends with the other woman, Chiara de Correggio."

"Okay."

"One day, both of the women mysteriously dropped off the face of the earth," she said. "Well, that's a slight misstatement. They didn't disappear on the same day. Chiara disappeared on a Tuesday and London disappeared the following day, Wednesday. Chiara just vanished; she didn't cash out a bank account or anything like that. London, on the other hand, did cash out a bank account. The following week, Chiara's body was found at the base of a cliff just south of Big Sur. She'd been dead for several days."

Sophia's heart raced.

"The police came up with a theory that the two women had a falling out. London killed Chiara, dumped her body and then went on the run before the walls closed in."

Sophia swallowed.

"How'd Chiara die?"

"I don't have that yet," she said. "The detective on the case is a man named John Maxwell. He's a no-nonsense alpha-type. He found out I was snooping around and actually called me. He wants to know what my interest is in all this."

"What'd you say?"

"I told him no interest at all, just curious." She exhaled. "Like I said before, I don't know what your interest is in all this and I don't want to know. I'll tell you this, though. If you're mixed up in any of this, I'd back down and do it fast."

Sophia considered it.

"Find out how Chiara died," she said.

"Are you sure?"

"Yes."

"Okay, but remember, it's against my advice."

"I understand."

She hung up and looked out the window.

She was a murderer.

She killed Chiara.

Why?

She had no memory, not a spark.

There was no question that she was London Winger. That was clear from the driver's license and photographs from her closet.

How did she end up in Denver?

How did she become Sophia Phair?

Her phone rang and Teffinger's voice came through. "According to Sydney, your gladiator friend from Friday night had you in his crosshairs the whole evening," he said. "When you bumped into him, it wasn't a real bump. It was something he staged."

"I know," she said. "I saw the same thing in the copy you sent me."

"When you left, you went to his place, not yours, right?"

"Right."

"Where was that? Do you remember?"

She did.

He wrote it down.

Then he said something. She heard the words and knew he was talking but a sudden dark thought wouldn't let her focus.

Maybe her past life as London Winger was somehow connected to what was happening here in Denver. Maybe Jackie Lake was dead because of something in Sophia's past.

"Hey, you there?"

"Yes."

"You left me."

"Sorry."

"Did you hear what I said?"

"No."

"I said, you should spend the night at my place tonight," he said.

"Okay."

"Good."

She exhaled and said, "Can I ask you something personal?"

"That sounds serious."

"No, not really, but I was just wondering if you ever killed anyone, you know, in the line of duty or whatever."

Silence.

"Yes."

"Will you tell me about it tonight?"

"I don't like to talk about it."

"Is that a no?"

"No, it's a yes with a qualifier."

When Teffinger signed off, Sophia dialed the California investigator and said, "Aspen, it's me, Sophia."

"Did you change you mind about pressing forward?"

"No," she said. "The opposite, actually. I have something

else I want you to run down. Find out if London Winger or Chiara de Correggio had any connection to a man named Evan Starry. That might not be his real name. He's about thirty, six-four and built like a gladiator."

"Sounds yummy."

Sophia smiled.

"We definitely need to meet at some point," she said. "We like the same foods."

47

Midafternoon Teffinger got a call from a very, very, very pissed female who said, "Check your emails you bastard." The line went dead. He knew the voice but couldn't place it. Sydney came over and said, "Problems?"

He raked his hair back with his fingers.

"Always."

He logged on to his email account, which pulled up unceremoniously on a large flat-panel monitor. At the very top was an email from September Tadge, the attorney, with a short, sweet message: "How dare you put my life in danger?"

Teffinger swallowed.

Behind the words was a link.

He clicked it to find that it took him to a video. He watched himself from an outside camera, sneaking into the back window of September's law office, then from other cameras inside, rifling through lower level rooms before heading upstairs. There a camera picked him up pulling an expandable file out of a cabinet, copying the contents and replacing it.

His face was clear.

There was no question it was him.

When it ended, Teffinger looked around the room to see if anyone had been eavesdropping. If they were they didn't let on.

Sydney watched it without saying a word.

She gave Teffinger a sideways glance and walked away when he looked at her.

"Sydney."

She kept going, not looking back, walking briskly out the door.

"Hold on."

She didn't.

She sped up.

The elevator door opened just as she got to it and the chief came out. She sidestepped him, ducked in and pressed the close button repeatedly.

The doors shut just as Teffinger got to them.

He nodded at the chief, who was now stopped, and bounded down the stairwell. He didn't catch Sydney until she was out of the building and half a block up Bannock. He grabbed her elbow and jerked her to a stop.

"Let me explain," he said.

"Get your hands off me."

"It's not like it seems," he said.

She looked defiantly into his eyes.

"How dare you get dirty?"

"Look—"

She pushed him on the chest, hard enough that he had to step back.

"There are no *looks*," she said. "Why is nobody ever who I think they are?"

"Sydney—"

She walked away.

When Teffinger followed she turned and pointed a finger at him.

"Don't," she said. "Just don't."

He stopped.

She walked away.

He watched until he couldn't stand it, then turned the opposite way and took one step after another.

He had no idea where he was going.

It wasn't back to homicide.

The sun beat down.

He wiped sweat off his forehead and sped up.

"Come on, bake me to death. Just drop me on the sidewalk right here, right now."

Then he punched a stop sign.

The streets of Denver slipped by, unfocused, blurred by adrenalin and anger; anger at what he did, anger at getting caught, anger at putting September at risk, anger at jeopardizing the case, anger at putting Sydney in a difficult position.

An hour passed.

That's how long it took, a full hour of walking at breakneck speed, before his brain began to focus again.

He called September from a pay phone.

"We need to talk," he said.

"No, no talking," she said. "There's only one thing you need to know. I've entrusted a copy of the tape to a friend of mine. If I end up dead, he's going to turn it over to the police. You'll pay for what you did. That will be my present to you from the grave."

"Look, there's no way he could ever find out."

"You don't know that."

The line went dead.

48

Yardley drove Deven to DIA Wednesday evening and gave her an envelope stuffed with money. "Remember, call me and let me know you got safe to wherever you decide to go but don't tell me where it is."

"This is wrong," Deven said.

"No, this is right. What's wrong is if I have to worry about you instead of focusing on business."

"We should be doing the business together."

Yardley gave her a kiss on the check.

"Next time."

"We've always been in things together before," Deven said.

"Well, this time is different."

"If that's true then come with me," Deven said. "We'll both just disappear."

"And look over our shoulders for the rest of our lives? No thanks. Everything will be settled by this time tomorrow. Indulge me until then."

Yardley gave her a hug, hopped in the car and waved goodbye as she drove off.

There.

Done.

Now it was time to meet with Madison and set the bait.

49

The black lens of twilight settled over Denver, dropping the temperature, washing away the stress of the sun and preparing for the sins of the night. Sophia and Renn-Jaa drove north on I-25 in shorts and Ts, en route to the Concrete Flower Factory, with the radio turned to hip-hop.

They didn't talk much.

Sophia couldn't clear her mind of the fact that she killed a woman—a friend, no less—in her not-too-distant prior life as London Winger. She didn't know why but did know there was no acceptable excuse. No matter what led to it, she should have been able to find a resolution short of what happened. The fact that she let herself kill someone spoke to her underlying genetic composition. That flawed foundation would not have changed simply because her memory was faulty.

It was with her right now.

It was drilled into her bones.

She couldn't survive prison.

A cage would kill her.

She not only knew that now, but undoubtedly knew it back then. That was the jolt that morphed her from London Winger into Sophia Phair.

John Maxwell.

That was the detective after her, John Maxwell, a "no-nonsense" man.

Sophia could feel his reach.

She could feel his breath on the back of her neck.

"Are you okay?"

The words came from Renn-Jaa, over the radio.

"Yeah."

"You sure? We can call this off if you want, or I can do it myself. You can wait in the car."

"I'm fine."

A mile clicked off, then another and another. In five minutes they would be at their exit. From there it was only a mile or two to their destination.

Sophia shut her eyes.

The vehicle glided effortlessly.

Suddenly an image flashed in her brain. It was night, deep, deep night, pitch-black. She was driving through a heavy fog down a road she knew well. To the left, cliffs dropped off into the pacific. She kept an eye on the rearview mirror, looking for headlights. There were none.

Her heart pounded.

A turnoff appeared up ahead on the left.

She crossed the centerline and swung into it.

Dust kicked up.

She opened the door.

The dome light kicked on and lit up the interior. Her hands, now visible, were stained with blood, blood that she'd wiped off earlier but not completely. On the seat next to her was a towel.

She unrolled it.

Inside was a bloody knife.

She grabbed it by the handle, stepped outside and walked to the edge of the cliff one careful step at a time. The pounding of the ocean against the cragged rocks below cut through the darkness.

She cocked her arm back and threw the knife with all her might.

Then she looked around for headlights.

There were none, not in either direction.

She got back in the car and took off. A mile down the road she swung to the side and threw the towel over another cliff.

That was the easy part.

The hard part was yet to come.

She drove for another two miles. A guardrail appeared on the left side of the road, a guardrail that marked a dangerous curve at the top of a steep cliff, a guardrail that she knew well. There was no shoulder on either side. She pulled into the oncoming lane and brought the vehicle to a stop not more than a foot from the rail.

She could see in both directions.

There were no headlights coming either way.

She got out, ran around to the back and opened the trunk. An unpleasant odor escaped. She looked around one more time, then pulled a woman's body out.

It landed on the ground with a thud.

She dragged it to the guardrail, then got on the other side and pulled it over.

Her heart pounded.

Her lungs fought for air.

She dragged it as close as she dared to the edge of the cliff, then got on the other side and pushed it with her foot until it dropped over.

Then she got the hell out of there.

50

Teffinger dragged his exhausted feet back to homicide, hoping against hope that Sydney had returned, which she hadn't. He set about trying to get background information on the guy who didn't exist, the gladiator. Five o'clock came and went. Detectives and staff drifted off to their non-work lives, their real lives. The last one, Richardson, got up at 6:15, stretched and said, "You're in charge."

"Thanks."

"I'll expect a written report in the morning."

Teffinger smiled.

"It'll be on your desk."

He leaned back and closed his eyes just to rest them for a second. Just before he lost consciousness his cell phone rang. It turned out to be Condor, the managing partner of Sophia's law firm. When Teffinger recognized the voice, he expected the call to be about Jackie Lake or Sophia.

He was wrong.

"This isn't a call I ever wanted to make," Condor said.

Teffinger leaned forward and rubbed his eyes.

"What's going on?"

"I'm calling on behalf of a client of mine," Condor said. "Her name is September Tadge."

"The lawyer?"

"Right." A beat then, "I've seen the videotapes."

The words hung.

Teffinger swallowed. "Go on."

"To be honest, I'm sort of torn," Condor said. "On the one hand, I admire the hell out of the fact that you're doing whatever it takes to find out who killed Jackie. If I was in your shoes, I could only hope that I'd have the same intestinal fortitude. It takes guts to get dirty. What you're doing in effect is putting the case before your own well-being. So don't think I don't appreciate what's going on."

Teffinger waited.

"But," he said.

"But, that said, I also have a duty to my client," he said. "My duty to her is to follow through with whatever it is that I agree to do. In this case, she wanted my promise that if anything happened to her, I would turn the videotape over to your chief and another copy over to the D.A.'s office." A beat then, "I told her I would do that."

"I understand."

"Okay, then."

"One thing," Teffinger said. "Just so you know, I had second thoughts about what I did after I did it. I never looked at the files. I burned them. They're history."

Condor exhaled.

"That's admirable," he said. "Unfortunately, this is one of those genies that you can't put back in the bottle. I really hope that nothing ever happens to September and we can both go about our business in peace."

"Let's hope so."

"By the way, this file is being kept under lock and key," he said. "September hasn't told anyone else and neither have I."

"I appreciate that."

Silence.

"One more thing," Condor said. "If there's anything the

firm can do to help you find Jackie's killer, just let me know."

"You can tell me his name."

"Van Gogh."

"I mean his real one."

"I don't know it. Neither does Sophia. She already told you that."

Teffinger called Sydney for the tenth time and got dumped into her voicemail for the tenth time. This time he left a message.

"Call me," he said. "You can hate me, you can be disappointed in me, you can think anything you want. I won't bother you about it. I can't let the case suffer though. I need you back and I need you now."

He hung up.

Five minutes passed. Sydney didn't call.

She would have picked up the message by now.

The fluorescent light directly over his desk hummed with all the subtlety of a jackhammer, no worse than it had for the last two weeks but suddenly intolerable. He took his shoes off, got up on his desk and muscled it out.

Then he swapped it for one in the chief's office.

There.

Better.

He walked over to Sydney's computer and pulled up her emails. Two were from detective Adam Coulter of the New York homicide unit, with attached videotapes from two security cameras, one from a bank and one from a hotel.

They weren't long but they were long enough.

There was no question that the man on the street, the one Kelly Ravenfield thought was Michael Northway, was indeed Michael Northway.

Teffinger paused a frame and then enlarged it.

The man was smiling, happy, smirking even, with his surfer-boy hair and his big white grin.

"Got you," Teffinger said. "Even if I get fired, I'm going to come out there and get you."

51

Yardley called Cave shortly after dark and said, "We need to call a truce. When I shot at the house, I wasn't shooting at you. All I was doing was trying to get you to abort and head off with me in the trunk. All I was trying to do was get Deven back to safety."

"You're certainly the clever one, I'll hand you that."

"Look," she said, "we both know that I could have shot you ten different times out there in the sticks. I didn't. For that, you owe me."

"You should have killed me while you had the chance."

"Maybe but the fact remains that I didn't," she said. "Here's my proposition. We call it even. You go your way and me and Deven go our way."

Silence.

"The one who hired you to send me to Miami is that lawyer, Madison Elmblade, right?"

"Right. I didn't know anything about it being a setup. I thought it was just business as usual. If I had any inkling it was anything other than a hundred percent legit, I would have tipped you off."

"For the moment, let's assume that's true just for the sake of argument."

"It is true."

"If it is then prove it by helping me get her," he said. "Do that and then we'll be even."

A beat.

"Look, we're already even on account of the fact that I didn't kill you," she said. "If it wasn't for that, we wouldn't even be having this conversation."

Cave exhaled.

"Let me make it clear," he said. "My way or no way."

"Damn it."

"Decide."

"What exactly do you want me to do?"

"I'll give it some thought," he said. "Meet me in one hour at the Rikki. Come alone and don't do anything stupid."

"Okay."

The line went dead.

Yardley powered off and looked at Madison, who had been listening to the exchange, pacing.

"He wants to meet me in an hour at the Rikki," she said.

Madison tapped two cigarettes out of a pack, handed one to Yardley and lit them both up with a gold lighter. She flicked the lid closed harder than necessary.

"It's a trap," she said. "He's trying to flush you out."

"So what do we do?"

"Simple. We oblige him."

52

The Concrete Flower Factory turned out to be a large, creepy building buried between an industrial complex and railroad tracks. A spiraling dark parking lot out front was packed sardine-tight with everything from shiny new euros to rusty old pickups. Renn-Jaa found a spot at the end of the line and killed the engine.

"Popular place."

"Yeah, I'm surprised."

The entry was an unceremonious red door with the name stenciled in black paint. Immediately inside was a riveting blond dressed in black accents—black stilettos, a short black skirt, black cuffs on her wrists and ankles and a black collar around her neck.

She fixated on Sophia, kissed her on the lips and then did the same to Renn-Jaa.

"Yummy," she said. "Are you here for a session or the Gathering?"

Sophia shifted feet.

"A friend of ours comes here," she said. "His name is Evan Starry. He uses someone and recommended her, but I can't remember her name."

The blond wrinkled her nose.

"Evan Starry," she said. "That doesn't ring a bell."

"He's about six four and built like a gladiator."

Her face lit up.

"I know who you mean," she said. "He mostly uses Secret. Hold on."

She checked a notebook and said, "She's in a session; she'll be free in about forty-five minutes. The Gathering's a fifty dollar donation, but since you're getting a session, you can wait in there for free if you want."

Renn-Jaa looked at Sophia and shrugged.

"Sure."

"I'll come and find you when Secret's free."

"Sounds good."

The Gathering was down a long hallway to the left, which emptied into a large space that must have housed manufacturing of some sort back in the day.

Smoke and perfume and sex permeated the air.

Rap dropped from ceiling speakers.

Bodies were everywhere.

Not just men, either, plenty of women too.

Most of the guys were normally dressed, some up, some down, but not too much that would raise an eyebrow on the street.

The women were the opposite.

They were flaunting skin and tattoos and panties and hair and attitude.

Drinks were being served from makeshift bars.

At first it looked like an ordinary rave.

When they got a few steps inside, however, they saw a rack with a woman stretched out tighter than tight, naked except for a black thong. Her mouth was open and another woman was licking her tongue.

Not far down was a second setup.

A woman was hogtied on a table with her face in the crotch

of a second woman.

Sophia and Renn-Jaa bought glasses of white wine, five dollars each, and made their way around the room.

There were ten or twelve stages all told.

Most had at least two or three women in line, waiting their turn.

Someone came up behind Sophia and wrapped their hands around her stomach. Lips nibbled the back of her neck. She turned to find the blond from the front door.

"I'm on break," she said. "I'm up next on the rack. I want you to be the one to dominate me."

"Me?"

The woman nodded.

"Yeah, what do you think?"

"What am I supposed to do to you?"

"Whatever you want," she said. "You can tease me or tickle me or make me come or put clothespins all over my body or whip me or whatever you want."

Sophia pictured it.

"You don't have to get naked or anything," the woman added. "You can if you want but you don't have to."

"What would you like the most, if I agreed?"

"The most? Stretch me out tight and make me come."

Silence.

Then Sophia shook her head.

"I'll do that if you want, but it would need to be in private."

The woman looked at Renn-Jaa.

"How about you? Are you up for it?"

"No."

"Are you sure?"

"No."

"No meaning no, or no meaning you're not sure?"

"No meaning I'm not sure. To be honest, I'm half tempted."

"Then say yes."

Renn-Jaa exhaled, deciding.

The woman grabbed her hand and pulled her towards the rack. Over her shoulder she said to Sophia, "You can join her if you want. Do a tag team on me; pain and pleasure at the same time, or whatever you want."

Sophia wandered around the room then made her way over to the rack. Renn-Jaa and the blonde had their arms around each other's waist, waiting for the device to free up.

Sophia put her face next to the blonde's ear.

"I'll make you a deal," she said. "This is confidential so don't repeat it."

"Okay."

"I might be getting into a relationship with the guy I told you about, Evan Starry."

"The gladiator."

"Right, the gladiator," she said. "That's why I came down here tonight, to find out what he does down here. Are you privy to that information?"

"Yes."

"Well, if you fill me in, I'll join in on that tag team."

"Stick your tongue out."

Sophia obeyed.

The woman sucked it, wet and deep.

Then she said, "You have a deal."

53

The glare of the sun gave way to shadows, which gave way to long shadows, which gave way to all shadows. Full night was next, not more than 45 minutes away. Sophia left a message for Teffinger; she was safe with Renn-Jaa and would call him later.

Today had been the worst.

Teffinger still hadn't identified the longhaired man who saved Sophia and could identify Jackie Lake's killer.

He had zero information on the gladiator.

His little trick at September's office was about to drag him down into an eternal black abyss.

As far as Michael Northway went, the videotapes were golden but that's all there was. Teffinger's counterparts in New York couldn't get Northway's image on the news since the case didn't involve a child or a missing person in imminent danger. Also, they didn't have time to try to identify the woman who had been walking with Northway. The FBI profiler, Leigh Sandt, was more of the same, sympathetic and willing but overworked and unavailable.

His phone rang.

"Are you at home?"

The voice belonged to Kelly.

"Yeah, why?"

"Do you have a woman with you?"

"No."

"I'm coming over."

The line died.

When she showed up, Teffinger was showered and in fresh jeans with a white cotton shirt rolled at the cuffs. Towel-dried hair, damp but not dripping, hung over his face. A cold blue can was in his left hand, half empty from two long swallows.

Kelly looked good.

No, not good, way beyond.

She wore Daisy Dukes and a minimal cerulean tank, with white ankle socks and Sketchers down below. Her hair was loose and ruffled.

Teffinger handed her a glass of white wine over ice, then ran an index finger around her bellybutton.

"Hi," he said.

"Hi back."

Behind Teffinger's house, Green Mountain dropped into his yard, almost to the back door. Up that incline at the top of the property was a redwood deck that looked over the roof and onto the billion city lights that twinkled to the east. That's where they ended up.

The talk was light.

The temperature was nice.

Teffinger filled her in on the Michael Northway tapes, the fact that it was definitely him that Kelly saw, and that no one was available to run down the lead.

"Go yourself," Kelly said.

"Can't," he said. "I'm working that Jackie Lake case."

Kelly knew that.

It was all over the news not to mention the talk of the legal community.

"Send Sydney."

Sydney.

Sydney.

Sydney.

She still hadn't returned Teffinger's calls.

He took a swallow of beer and said, "I want you to be my attorney for a minute. If you agree, then you have to keep what I say confidential, right?"

"Yeah but there's a downside."

"What's that?"

"Attorneys aren't supposed to sleep with their clients."

He knew he should smile.

Instead he got serious and told her how he broke into September Tadge's law office and copied the file on a suspect, Van Gogh, who had committed several murders in the past identical to Jackie Lake. Teffinger ended up getting caught on office security tape, which was now in the hands of Grayson Condor who was acting as September's attorney. "He's keeping the tapes under lock and key so they stay private, but if anything happens to September, *i.e.* Van Gogh pops out of a shadow and kills her, then Condor's under instructions to turn the tapes over to the D.A.'s office, plus my chief."

"God, Nick, this is serious."

He swallowed what was left in the can and then crumpled it in his fist.

"I know."

"You could lose your job."

"I know."

"Not could, would," Kelly said. "They'd have to protect the system. They wouldn't have a realistic option to do otherwise, no matter what your track record's been."

Teffinger exhaled.

"I'm telling you because I don't know where this thing between you and me is going," he said. "You need to know that I might not have a job or an income down the road."

"That doesn't matter," she said.

"I wish it was that simple."

"I know of September Tadge but don't know her personally," Kelly said. "She does criminal defense so our worlds don't really intersect. I could talk to her though. Maybe I can get her to back off; maybe even destroy the tapes."

"You think?"

She patted his knee.

"Even so, though, we still have the problem of Grayson Condor," she said. "That firm's extremely political. Having dirt on the person in charge of Denver's homicide unit could have a value in some way at some point down the line. I wouldn't put it past him to keep a copy of the tape even if September tells him not to."

"Do you really think he'd do that?"

"Yes."

Teffinger exhaled.

"Is there any way around it?"

Kelly took a sip of wine.

"Maybe," she said. "It only shows a break-in if September says so. If September were to say, for example, that she hired you to enter like that as a test run to be sure her security system was working the way it should, then it wouldn't be dirt at all."

Teffinger frowned.

"Right now she won't even talk to me," he said. "Having her lie on my behalf is something I can't even imagine. Plus, what about Condor? He could contradict her story and say she hired him because I'd broken in."

Kelly shook her head.

"No he couldn't, not if she didn't give him permission. Anyway, we're getting way too far down the road," she said. "I'll talk to September tomorrow, as your attorney." A beat then, "There's one thing nagging at me. She obviously has some type of connection to Condor to choose him as her attorney. In fact, he's sort of a weird choice because he's almost in a conflict position. I mean, here he is working against you while you're the guy trying to find out who killed an associate in his firm. If I was September, I would have picked someone outside the firm to represent me. She must have chosen Condor because they have some past relationship together."

Teffinger shrugged.

It made sense.

"In that case, if she asks him to return the tape and not make a copy, maybe he will," he said.

"Maybe."

"You don't sound convinced."

"Here's what I'm getting at," she said. "She knew that her mystery client was the prime suspect in Jackie Lake's murder. I have to imagine that if she already had some kind of relationship with Condor, she would have mentioned it to him. If that's true, why didn't Condor tell you?"

"I don't know. Confidentiality requirements?"

Teffinger stood up.

"Want to take a ride?"

"Where?"

"There's a guy I'm curious about who may be Van Gogh," he said. "I want to swing by his place."

"What's his name?"

"Evan Starry," he said. "He was stalking Sophia Phair on Friday night. He's built like a gladiator."

She studied him.

"Who's Sophia Phair?"

"She was at the scene when Jackie Lake got murdered," he said. "This is confidential by the way. She may have been the intended victim, not Jackie Lake." He exhaled and added, "She's also the woman who wrote on my mirror."

She wrinkled her face.

"What mirror?"

"In the master bathroom."

"She wrote something on the mirror in your bathroom?"

He nodded.

"When? Today?"

"No, six months ago."

"She wrote something on your bathroom mirror six months ago and it's still there?"

Yes.

It was.

"What'd she do, scratch it in?"

"No, it's written in lipstick."

"Lipstick?"

Right.

Lipstick.

"Show me."

54

The Rikki—where Cave told Yardley to meet him—had a checkered past, starting life as a biker bar, then morphing into a disco, then a drug-driven hard rock club and now a theme club, with hump day being British Invasion night—Peter & Gordon, Beau Brummels, Kinks, Stones, Who, and of course those four guys from Liverpool. The crowd stretched from 21 to 35. Tie-dyed shirts, headbands, peace signs and bikini tops were the attire of choice.

It was located east of the South Platte, backing up to the BNSF line.

The side and back parking lots were full.

Latecomers lined the service road, both sides, for a good hundred yards in each direction. That's where Yardley found a slot, fifty yards up on the opposite side of the street, next to the culvert.

There were no streetlights.

The only light came from the neon signs of club or the cut of headlights.

Yardley killed the engine.

Madison stuffed a gun in her purse.

"Don't leave the club," she said.

"I won't."

"Even if he sticks a barrel or a knife in your ribs, don't

leave the club. He won't kill you inside no matter how much he might pretend to."

Yardley nodded.

"Where are you going to be?"

"Somewhere across the street where I can see the exit," she said. "Do you know if the club has any security cameras?"

"I don't have a clue."

"Look around when you get near," Madison said. "See if there's anything mounted on the side of the building shining on the entrance or the parking lots. If there is, call me when you get inside. If I don't hear from you I'll assume the negative."

"Okay."

Yardley got out, walked up the road to the club and paid ten dollars at the door.

Inside, "Paint it Black" pounded through the air.

Yardley made her way to the bar, squeezed in and ordered a rum and coke.

The place was jammed to the walls with bodies.

She looked around for Cave.

His James Dean face didn't appear.

She was ten minutes early.

Knowing Cave, he'd show up at exactly the appointed minute.

Ten minutes passed.

Yardley stayed put.

Cave would find her.

She ordered another rum and coke. Time passed; Cave's face wasn't appearing. Thirty minutes later, Cave would have had plenty of time to scout every corner of the club.

Where was he?

Yardley called Madison and said, "There's no sign of Cave. Did you see him come in?"

"No."

"So what do we do?"

"Let's give him a little more time."

Ten minutes passed.

Then twenty.

Yardley's phone rang. She expected it to be Madison telling her to call it off. She was half right; it was Madison. The message wasn't what she expected though.

"There's a bunch of cop cars down the road, on the other end from where we parked. Something's going on down there. Any sign of Cave yet?"

"No."

"We'll give him another ten minutes then call it quits," Madison said. "I'm going to stroll down the road and see what's going on."

"Don't let anyone see your face."

"I won't."

Five minutes later Yardley's phone rang and Madison's voice came through.

"There's a dead woman on the ground," she said. "That's what all the commotion is about."

"What happened?"

"I don't know; I kept my distance. It could be a hit-and-run or a drug overdose or something like that. The important thing from our perspective is that there's going to be flashing lights there for hours," she said. "I doubt Cave will show with anything like that going on. Give me five minutes to get back up the road, then come out. I'll meet you across the street and escort you back to the car."

"Okay. I wonder why Cave didn't show?"

"Maybe he did and he's out here in the shadows somewhere waiting for you to leave," Madison said. "We need to be careful. Do you want me to come in and get the car keys from you? I can pick you up in front with the car if you want."

"No, we can walk it. Even Cave wouldn't make a move with so many cops around."

55

From the Concrete Flower Factory, Sophia and Renn-Jaa headed for the gladiator's loft with plans to tail him to the mysterious ten-thirty "Sweeton" meeting. They made a pass at 9:53 to find his space dark.

"Damn it, he's already left."

"Maybe he'll bounce back. You want to hang for a while or call it a night?"

"Let's hang. It can't hurt."

They found a parking space with a view and waited with the radio on rap, not saying much. Sophia took the opportunity to call Teffinger, got pushed into his voicemail and left a message, "It's me, I'm with Renn-Jaa, no problems, everything's fine. Can I spend the night at your house? Let me know. Call me."

"Me too," Renn-Jaa said.

Sophia slapped her thigh.

A solitary figure walked down the sidewalk in their direction, nothing but a dark silhouette at this distance. The motion was erratic.

"Someone's had too much to drink."

"Been there."

Sophia focused on the figure but used most of her concentration on the mysterious pieces of her past. She killed Chiara out in California. There was no question about it. The more she pictured dumping the body off the cliff, the clearer it became. She could feel the weight of the body as she pushed it with her foot. She could hear the scraping of the body on the ground. She could smell the decay.

She killed Jackie Lake, too; she knew that, not just because of the flashbacks, but because it was vibrating way down in her bones.

There were others too, other murders.

She could feel them out there in the night, standing there and watching her like dark shapes, waiting for her to look in their direction.

As the figure got nearer, it took shape as a woman, a young black woman, drunk or drugged to the point of hardly being able to walk. She was singing. The words were sloppy and incoherent.

Suddenly figures appeared behind her.

There were three of them.

They were bigger.

"Hey, baby, where you going?"

The voice was deep.

It belonged to a man.

In no time they were up to her, then had her in a circle.

The men were black.

They moved with agility.

Words got exchanged but they were too muddled to make out.

"This isn't good," Sophia said.

"No."

Then with lighting speed, the men dragged the woman into a parking lot. They were holding her down, ripping her clothes off, slapping her face. Words came from her mouth, trying to be screams but coming out muffled and inarticulate.

"They're raping her."

Sophia reached for her phone.

Suddenly another figure raced at the scene, screaming some kind of war cry.

The men got up.

They spread out.

A blade flashed.

The charging figure stopped just short.

"Go," he said.

Sophia recognized the voice and the posture.

It was the gladiator, Evan Starry.

The men stepped closer.

One of them said, "Fuck you asshole!"

Then they sprang.

It took time but the gladiator dropped two of them to the ground.

The third escaped.

One of the men on the ground started to move, contorted, broken. The woman brought a rock down on his head. He dropped to the ground and didn't move again.

The gladiator snatched up the woman's clothes and grabbed her hand.

"Come on!"

They got the hell out of there.

56

Kelly didn't have much to say about the lipstick on Teffinger's mirror other than, "So you've had it up there all this time and never wiped it off?"

True.

"Do you have a picture of her?"

No.

He didn't.

In the Tundra heading east on 6ᵗʰ Avenue en route to the gladiator's loft, Kelly kept her face pointed out the windshield and said in a voice almost too quiet to be heard, "Do you love her?" Her face was serious. She clearly didn't want the wrong answer but was braced for it. She turned long enough to catch Teffinger's eyes, then looked away.

"I don't know."

"What about me?"

He exhaled.

"Same answer."

"Well that's interesting."

"Interesting isn't the word I'd use. You were both in my past, you both left, now you're both back—ironically, almost at the exact same second," he said. "Assuming you're back, which might be incorrect."

"It's not incorrect, as far as I can tell so far."

"Well that's good to hear."

"Is it?"

"Actually, yes."

Kelly put her hand on his knee.

"I'm going to be honest with you Nick," she said. "Every minute you spend deciding isn't going to be easy for me. That said, whichever way you go, I want you to be absolutely sure it's the right way."

"I'll be honest right back," he said. "I'm not enjoying this. I know it sounds like every guy's dream but it isn't mine."

"Does she know about me?"

Teffinger shook his head.

"There was no *you* until noon," he said. "I haven't even seen her since then."

"Are you going to tell her?"

"Of course."

Right after they passed Wadsworth, Teffinger's phone rang. It was Barb from dispatch, the proud owner of new breast implants and a few new gentlemen callers. "Got some job security for you," she said.

"Who's on call?"

"Sydney."

"Call her and put her on it," he said. "If she doesn't confirm that she's on it, tell her she's fired and then call me back."

The woman chuckled.

"I heard about that little spat you two are having," she said. "What's that all about?"

"Do you really want to know?"

Yes.

She did.

"Do you promise you won't tell anyone?"

"Absolutely."

"Okay, here it is," Teffinger said. "There was one cup of

coffee left in the pot this morning. Sydney took it just as I was walking over to get it."

The woman smiled.

"May she rot in hell."

"She will," he said. "What's the location of the body?"

"It's at the Rikki."

Teffinger knew the place.

He'd gotten more than his fair share of sin there back in the day.

"I'm en route," he said. "Call Sydney like I said, but don't tell her I'm going."

To Kelly, "This is the gladiator's lucky night. I got a body at the Rikki. Do you want me to drop you off or do you want to hang around."

"I'll hang around," she said.

The scene was roped off when Teffinger got there, not as large as he would have liked, but not bad. Kelly said, "If I'm not here in the truck when you get back, I'm inside the club having a drink."

Fine.

No problem.

He headed over.

The body belonged to an attractive young woman. Her face was alive, even in death. Teffinger pulled up an image of her driving a little too fast with the windows down, singing to a song that was playing a little too loud.

She wore jeans and a blouse.

Her hands were tied behind her back.

The knot of a rope was in her mouth with the ends of the rope stretched tightly to the back and tied, in the nature of a poor-man's gag.

A screwdriver was pounded into her brain through the ear, buried all the way up to the handle.

Blood was on her blouse and on the ground, meaning she was killed here and not just dumped. A purse was on the ground next to her.

Teffinger touched nothing.

He let the crime unit document the scene.

Sydney showed up ten minutes later.

She walked over to him, all business and said, "Nice."

Teffinger nodded. Right. Nice.

"I want you to take the lead in processing the scene," he said.

She gave him a mean look.

"Tell me something. Am I supposed to turn you in like the book says or am I supposed to become an accomplice by not turning you in?"

Teffinger frowned.

He'd put her in a bad position.

There was no denying it.

Then he said, "The easy thing to do would just be to turn me in. That way you stay clean." A beat then, "That said, I think the whole thing might end up resolved without anyone needing to know anything. Kelly came up with a plan."

"Kelly?"

Right.

Kelly.

"Pure little sweet innocent Kelly?"

"Yes."

"I can't believe you dragged her into this."

Time passed.

Eventually the purse got bagged and the contents processed. An envelope of cash was inside, a lot of cash. So was the victim's driver's license.

She was someone named Deven Devenshire.

DAY FOUR

July 21
Thursday

57

Thursday morning Yardley opened the bookstore for business and hid two guns in strategic locations. Fifteen minutes later Madison called and said, "Did you hear about the dead woman at the Rikki last night?"

No.

She didn't.

"It was Deven," she said. "We need to meet and decide what to do." A beat, "Hello? Are you there?"

She was.

Her chest was tight.

The room was unfocused.

"Are you sure it was Deven?"

"Yes, it's all over the news. Obviously Cave killed her. Where are you right now?"

The bookstore.

She was at the bookstore.

"Get out of there right now," Madison said. "Get in your car and drive until you're a hundred percent positive Cave's not on your ass. Then call me and we'll arrange to meet somewhere." Silence. "Are you getting this?"

"Yes."

"Pull yourself together and do it. Do it now."

Yardley obeyed.

She was in the car.

She was driving.

She was checking the rearview mirror.

Why didn't Deven get on the plane like she was supposed to? That's all she had to do, just get on the stupid plane. How hard was that?

Damn it.

Damn it.

Damn it to hell.

She must have decided to stay around and watch Yardley's back. She knew Yardley would never agree to it so she did it in secret.

Cave was a dead man.

Dead.

Dead.

Dead.

Yardley should have shot him when she had the chance.

She wound all over Denver then back into the center, parking by the library and walking over to Civic Center. She sat down in the shade and leaned against a pillar at the amphitheater, then called Madison and told her where she was.

"I'll be there in fifteen minutes."

"I'll be waiting."

Ten minutes later her phone rang.

She expected it to be Madison asking for more specific directions, but the voice belonged to Cave.

"Deven is your fault," he said.

"You're a dead man."

"All you had to do was follow through with what you said you would do," he said. "If you did that, I was going to let her go. That's the honest-to-God truth."

"Bullshit."

"You shouldn't have brought your little friend with you last night," he said. "I saw her over there in the shadows. I drove right by her. She never even looked at me. She was staring at the club. You should have played straight with me. Instead you decided to get fancy. That's why Deven's dead right now. Her blood is on your hands. I hope it feels good."

The line went dead.

Five minutes later Madison showed up.

Yardley filled her in.

They agreed that going to the police wasn't an option. Too many people would drop, including both of them. At the end Yardley said, "I'll fill in Marabella and see what she wants us to do."

"She better want us to kill Cave," Yardley said, "because that's what's going to happen."

58

Thursday morning Sophia set about summarizing a deposition because it was the most brainless thing she could do. Her world was unraveling, she could feel it. She was spiraling out of control and there wasn't a thing she could do to stop it.

The incident of last night received some print in the paper but not much. Two black men were beaten to death. Police were investigating.

Renn-Jaa came in, closed the door and said, "Do you still think we did the right thing, not telling the police what we saw?"

Yes.

She did.

The men had it coming.

The drunken woman was a victim and the gladiator, at least at that particular moment in his life, was a hero. It wouldn't do any good to drag them into it, not to mention that Sophia and Renn-Jaa wouldn't have a good reason for being in the vicinity. There was one more consideration, too. One of the men got away. If Sophia and Renn-Jaa came forward as witnesses, the guy might think they saw him—which they did, but not his face. He might decide he didn't need any witnesses running around.

"So what do we do after work?" Renn-Jaa said.

"I don't know. Let's wait and see."

An hour later Sophia's phone rang and the voice of the California investigator, Aspen Gonzales, came through. "Okay, I have a little more information for you. The murdered woman, Chiara, died from a slit throat."

Sophia's blood raced.

That's the exact memory sprang into her brain yesterday.

"With what?"

"A knife."

"What kind?"

"I don't know; they never found it," Aspen said. "Something big and sharp I'm guessing. The reason it took a while for the body to show up is because it got thrown off a cliff. It ended up snagged in an outcropping ten or twenty feet above the tide line. A fisherman spotted it five or six days later."

Sophia swallowed.

"Where was the cliff?"

"Up near Big Sur," Aspen said. "Reportedly there was a seriously dense fog in that area the night Chiara got murdered. The theory is that someone drove to the cliff, pulled the body out of a trunk and threw it over."

"Was there a turnoff or something?"

"I don't know."

"Is there any way to find out?"

"Why?"

"I'm just curious."

"Hold on."

Silence.

A minute passed then, "Okay, I have the GPS coordinates of where the body was found. I'm pulling them up on Google Earth." A beat then, "No, no turnoff. In fact it's sort of a weird spot to dump a body. The road bends right there. There's a guardrail on the cliff side and rocks on the other. There isn't even a shoulder on either side."

"Can you give me those GPS coordinates?"

"Sure."

After Sophia hung up, she closed her door and pulled up the scene on Google Earth.

It was the exact scene from her memory.

From that location, she scrolled south down the road. It took time, but she eventually came to the place where she threw the knife off the cliff.

She paced back and forth by the window.

Her palms were wet.

Her breath was short and quick.

She called Teffinger.

He answered, groggy.

"Did I wake you up?"

Yes.

She did, but no problem.

"Sorry about last night," he said. "I had two homicides. First a woman out at a club called the Rikki, then two black men downtown, actually not too far from where your gladiator friend lives. I didn't get home until four."

"When can I see you?"

"Whenever you want."

"How about right now?"

"I just got up."

"I'll come to your house."

"What about work?"

"Work can wait. I'm on my way. Be there, okay?"

"Okay."

59

Teffinger found Sophia in the kitchen firing up the coffee pot when he got out of the shower. She wore Saturday-night legs encased in nylons, a hip-hugging white skirt and loose raven hair. His hands went around from behind and squeezed her breasts.

She turned just enough to give him a quick peck on the lips.

"I'm sorry I'm in your face this morning," she said. "I hope you don't mind too much."

No.

He didn't.

"What's going on?"

She turned and put her arms around his neck.

He wore jeans but no shirt or socks or belt.

"I've had a couple of flashbacks," she said.

"From Jackie Lake's?"

"No, from a year or so ago."

Teffinger moved his hand down and fondled her ass.

"Good."

"They weren't pretty," she said.

"What do you mean?"

"I may have done something," she said. "Something bad."

"Like what?"

She laid her head on his chest.

"I can't talk about it," she said. "I just wanted to warn you that I'm not the person I might seem to be."

Teffinger wasn't impressed.

"None of us are," he said. "We're all someone else."

"No, this is worse."

"I'm not worried about it."

Teffinger poured two cups of coffee, handed one to Sophia and said, "There's a woman I know named Kelly Ravenfield. She's a lawyer. Do you know her?"

"No."

"Well, me and her had a thing at one point," he said. "Yesterday our paths sort of crossed."

Sophia's face tensed.

"This thing, did you love her?"

He nodded. "Yes."

"Are you still in love with her?"

He shrugged. "I don't know. She's the one who ended it, not me. To be honest, I don't know if I can ever really feel secure with her again, deep down. What I do know is that my feelings for you haven't changed. I mean, except for that one night, we've only known each other a few days. But there's something there. Am I wrong?"

"No. So what happens now?"

"That's up to you," he said. "I'm just being as honest as I can."

"Does she know about me?"

He nodded.

"Yes."

"What'd you tell her about me?"

"I told her I might be in love with you."

She laid her head on his chest.

"I want to meet her," she said.

60

Yardley wandered the city lost in the fact that she was responsible in large part for Deven's death. She'd underestimated Cave.

That wouldn't happen again, not in a thousand years.

Madison called and said, "I talked to Marabella. She's bringing in someone fresh to take care of Cave. It's scheduled for tonight. In the meantime, you and me are to drop out of sight, separately not together. Either me or Marabella will call you when it's okay to surface."

"I understand."

"It will all work out."

"We'll see."

"By midnight it will all be over."

"I hope so."

"Trust me, it will."

Five minutes later she was crossing Sherman when her phone rang and Cave's voice came through. "Here's the deal," he said. "Your little friend Madison Elmblade is going to die. There's nothing in the world either you or her can do to stop that. She was going to kill me. That's first blood and first blood is last blood."

"Screw you."

She hung up.

Ten seconds later the phone rang.

"You better listen because this is your only chance," Cave said. "Elmblade's going to die but that doesn't mean you are. Tell me who's at the top. Do that and we're even."

"I don't know who's at the top."

"That's bullshit and we both know it," Cave said. "Tell me who's at the top and don't just feed me some stupid name, either. This time you're going to need proof. Do that and you can keep your pathetic little life. Don't do that and I swear that sooner or later I'm going to get you alone and your world will get very, very ugly. You have until six o'clock tonight to call me." A beat then, "And by the way, I already know that someone new will be brought in to kill me. It's not going to work. Even if it did, I'll be leaving something behind for the police to find. If I go down you'll all be coming with me. Six o'clock, not a minute later."

The line went dead.

Yardley did a one-eighty and headed back to her car over by the library, then drove back to the bookshop and opened for business.

"Come on Cave. Come on and get me."

Ten minutes later the door opened and a man walked in.

The power of his presence filled the space.

He raked his hair back.

It immediately flopped back down.

"My name's Nick Teffinger," he said. "I'm with Denver homicide."

"You're here about Deven Devonshire," she said.

He nodded.

"It's my understanding that she worked here."

Yardley started to answer but the words didn't come out. Instead she was focused on the man's eyes.

They were two different colors.

One was blue and one was green.

"I've seen you before," she said. "You were on the cover of a magazine; GQ, I think."

"You have a good memory."

61

From Teffinger's place, Sophia drove to Jackie Lake's house, parked a block down the street, snuck around the back and broke a window to get in. In the bedroom, she kneeled on the mattress in the position she would have been straddling Jackie if she was the one who killed her.

Her memory didn't jog.

She shut her eyes and focused.

Nothing happened.

She pounded the mattress.

Come on!

Come on!

Come on!

She squeezed her eyes as tight as they would go and pictured Jackie beneath her, panicked, desperate to stay alive. She pictured herself slicing the woman's ear off and strangling her over and over.

No memory sparked.

No vision entered her brain other than the one she forced there. It had been there before, though, clear as sin. She needed to get it back and extend it. She needed the next ten seconds to roll through her head.

It didn't happen.

Then she had a thought, namely, do it the other way. Become Jackie, looking up.

She rolled onto her back, put her arms up as if tied to the headboard, and pictured herself as Jackie, staring into the face of the person killing her.

Nothing happened.

She bounced her head up and down.

Nothing happened.

No vision appeared.

Then, bam!

A chill ran up her spine.

She was going to die and she knew it. She looked at the person straddling her.

It was her.

She was the one there.

"No!"

She screamed, rolled violently and fell to the floor.

She got the hell out of there and headed for the office, in desperate need of a sane environment. She hadn't been there more than two minutes when Renn-Jaa came in and closed the door.

"Where were you? You had me worried sick."

"Teffinger's."

"During working hours?"

Sophia exhaled.

"One of his old girlfriends came back into his life yesterday," she said. "She's a lawyer. Her name's Kelly Ravenfield."

"Kelly?"

"Do you know her?"

"Yes."

"Is she pretty?"

"Not as pretty as you."

"You don't sound so sure."

"Google her," she said. "You should be able to find a picture."

Sophia did it.

The woman was with Locke & Banner, P.C. The firm's biography page showed a stunning blond with a solid pedigree, including a clerkship with a federal judge back in Cleveland.

"I can see Teffinger's point," she said. "I'd probably do her myself."

"Maybe you'll get the chance."

62

Teffinger talked to the bookstore owner, Yardley White, for half an hour and learned that she had irresistibly hypnotic eyes. He also learned that the victim, Deven Devonshire, was a dependable worker, good with customers, honest, and had no known problems with men, finances, drugs or anything else. She wasn't in any kind of trouble, had no enemies and flossed after every meal.

"Thanks," he said.

He gave her his card and left.

She was withholding something from him, that's what his gut kept saying as he drove back to homicide. When he got there, Sydney was at her desk.

Teffinger headed for the coffee machine, poured two cups and carried one over.

"There, we're even," he said.

She smiled.

"You can't stay mad at me," he said. "It's physically impossible. People have tried. It's never worked."

She shook her head.

"The sad thing is, there's probably some truth to that."

He took a sip and studied her over the rim.

"I want you to go to New York and run down our lead on Michael Northway."

"We had three homicides last night. Three as in one, two, and then another one, three."

"I know, I'll handle them," he said.

"Northway's a cold case," she said. "Whatever leads are there will still be there in two weeks."

"Maybe, maybe not. Let me put it this way—*Please.*"

She cocked her head.

"You have Kelly Ravenfield on the brain," she said. "That's why you want to catch Northway, to score points with Kelly. Personally I like Sophia better."

"Good to know," he said. "When I invite you to a threesome, it will be with Sophia."

"I'll make a deal with you," Sydney said. "We'll do the threesome tonight and I'll leave for New York in the morning."

Teffinger smiled.

"I'm going to call your bluff one of these days if you're not careful." He took a sip and said, "Northway's a cold case but the lead is fresh. If I let it slip away I'll never forgive myself. So let me say it one more time—please?"

She exhaled.

"God I hate you."

He nodded.

"Thanks," he said. "Come back with something. I want that little insect behind bars before he eats his next steak."

She studied him.

"Kelly dumped you," she said. "If she did it once she'll do it again. Stick with Sophia."

"We'll see."

His phone rang and Kelly's voice came through.

"Bad news," she said. "I stopped over at September's office and had a chat with her. She wasn't receptive to my ideas. Sorry."

Teffinger's chest tightened.

It wasn't until that second that he realized how much he'd been hoping to get that little problem behind him. The specter of getting fired gnawed at his foundation once again.

"Okay," he said. "Thanks for trying."

"I might have a Plan B though," she said. "Why don't we meet for lunch and I'll outline it for you."

Fine.

Wong's.

Noon.

63

Yardley called Marabella to report Cave's demand for the name at the top no later than six. She also allowed herself a moment to evaluate whether she should make an anonymous tip to the police that Cave killed Deven. That, even on brief reflection, was a bad idea. Cave needed to silently disappear and then his apartment and office needed to be sanitized.

The detective, Teffinger, could be a problem.

Yardley had all the right answers to the man's questions but could feel the needle on his bullshit detector twitching. The most telling giveaway was that he didn't flirt with her, not an iota, even when she invited him.

Six o'clock.

Not a click more.

That's how long she had before Cave put on his freak suit.

She checked her watch.

Six o'clock would arrive in five hours and thirteen minutes.

What to do?

Her phone rang, not the store's landline, the cell. The incoming number was long distance, one her phone didn't recognize.

She answered.

A timid woman's voice said, "Hello, my name is Kimberly

Lee. I'm calling about an important matter and hope I can have a few minutes of your time."

"Sure."

"I had a brother named Rydell Rain. Is his name familiar to you?"

"Vaguely. I'm having trouble placing it though to tell you the truth."

"He disappeared a couple of months ago," she said. "The police haven't gotten very far with figuring it out."

"So why are you calling me?"

"The reason I'm calling you is that I was going through his old cell phone records in the past just to see if I spotted anything unusual, your number was one of the ones that came up."

"How long ago?"

"Let me see … more than a year ago; the fall of last year, October to be precise."

"October … I remember him now," she said. "He was looking to buy a book. It was going to be a gift for someone."

"A book?"

"I sell rare books," Yardley said. "I have a store in Denver."

"So he called you about a book?"

"Yes," she said. "I'm trying to think of which one it was … I don't know, it's evading me. Anyway, I remembered we had some negotiations and finally reached an agreement. He sent me money and I sent him the book. I probably have records if it's important to you."

Silence.

"You know, if you don't mind—"

Two minutes later she was back on the phone. "I have the receipt," she said. "He purchased a signed, first edition printing of Ayn Rand's *Atlas Shrugged*. Do you have a fax number?"

Yes.

She did.

"It's on its way," she said.

The talk continued until the fax arrived.

Then it ended.

After Yardley hung up she called Marabella and said, "We might have a problem."

64

Sophia called Teffinger midafternoon and said, "Before you said you'd give me the dates and locations of the women who were killed the same way as Jackie Lake, so I could compare them to my calendar as proof that I wasn't involved."

He wasn't amused.

"You're not the killer. Let it go."

"I want you to do what you said."

"Sophia—"

"Please."

A beat then, "Fine. Check your emails in half an hour."

"Thank you."

"You're welcome."

She almost hung up. "Are you still there?"

"Yes."

"Is my lipstick still on your mirror?"

"Yes. How'd you know?"

"I didn't. I was just hoping."

The email from Teffinger arrived twenty minutes later.

Her breath tightened.

All the Jackie Lake-type murders took place before she was Sophia Phair.

They were back in time when she was London Winger.

She had no memory of doing them or not doing them.

Everything was blank.

Renn-Jaa glanced in as she walked down the hallway, then swung in and closed the door.

"Are you okay?"

She forced her mouth to say, "Yes."

"Are we still up for the gladiator tonight?"

The gladiator.

According to the kinky little blond from the Concrete Flower Factory, the gladiator liked to bind women with rope, inextricably and beyond escape, with multiple wraps and fancy knots, taking up to an hour or longer just to get her fully tied. He brought his own rope, red, precut into assorted lengths. Once he got the woman fully bound he'd tease her, bringing her close to orgasm, then back off and start all over again.

It wasn't exactly the same as what happened to Jackie Lake.

It wasn't exactly dissimilar either.

There were overlaps.

"Hey, are you there?"

Yes.

She was.

"So are we still up for the gladiator tonight or not?"

"Yes."

65

Kelly had a corner booth at Wong's with two plates of almond chicken when Teffinger got there. She kissed him on the mouth, told him again about the disaster at September's this morning and said, "Here's Plan B. She has dirt on you so what we need to do is level the playing field and get some on her. Then we make a swap, silence for silence."

"What makes you think she has dirt?"

Kelly smiled.

"She's a human being, right?"

Teffinger chewed what was in his mouth and swallowed it down.

"Let me rephrase it," he said. "What makes you think we can find it?"

"There's no we involved," she said. "What I'll do is hire a private investigator. I'm going to do it anonymously and not even tell him who I am. I'll tell him I'm an attorney and have him agree to be bound by confidentiality. Whatever he finds out will be deemed attorney work product, meaning it will be privileged. I'll have the retainer delivered in cash upfront. We'll let him figure out what the dirt is and where it's hidden."

Teffinger cocked his head.

"What happened to the shy, straight-minded woman I first met?"

"She grew up." She dabbed at her lips with a napkin. "So do you want me to move forward or not?" Teffinger hesitated long enough that Kelly added, "If you end up fired it won't just be a blow to you. It will be just as big a blow to the city."

"I doubt that."

"You've put away a dozen guys that a normal detective wouldn't have even looked at," she said.

He shrugged.

Maybe.

"I sent Sydney to New York this morning," he said.

"Good."

"She's still mad at me but not as much."

"Do you think she'll find anything?"

He nodded.

"She's a long ways down the road from where she was when I first met her." A beat then, "Just like someone else I know."

"Whatever," she said. "Tell me I can move forward on Plan B."

He considered it.

"If we do it, the investigator needs to stay clean," he said. "He can't be doing anything illegal. He can't be breaking in or tapping her phone or anything like that."

"He'll be an independent contractor," she said. "He'll be responsible for the means he uses. The important thing from our standpoint is that I don't expressly or implicitly suggest that he break the law. That keeps us out of it."

Teffinger speared a piece of chicken.

"Do you have someone in mind?"

She nodded.

"There's a guy named Sanders Cave down on Market Street," she said. "Back in Northway's firm, some of the law-yers used him. I don't know him personally but the talk is that he gets the job done and knows how to keep his mouth shut."

Teffinger took a sip of tea.

"I'll totally keep your name out of it," Kelly added.

"What about payment?"

"I'll cover the retainer," she said. "You can pay me back in sex."

Teffinger raked his hair back.

His phone rang and a man's voice came through.

"My name is Rex. I'm the owner of the Rikki. You got a minute?"

He did.

What followed was good.

Very good.

He hung up and looked at his watch.

"Got to run," he said.

"What about Plan B?"

He shook his head.

"It's a good concept," he said. "I'm half tempted to go through with it just so you can front the retainer and I can pay you back in sex. The more I think about it though, I don't want any dirt on September. She came forward to help me in good faith. I'm the one who screwed up, not her. She needs to be left in peace."

66

Midafternoon Teffinger walked into Yardley's bookstore and said, "Do you have a computer with a DVD drive? There's something I want to show you."

Yardley wasn't in the mood.

Teffinger was trouble.

"What is it?"

"Well, the owner of the Rikki is a guy named Rex," he said. "Last night when I was processing the scene, he wasn't there. I talked to the manager on duty and several of the bartenders and everyone said the same thing, namely that there were no surveillance cameras anywhere on the premises. Well, today I got a call from Rex. It seems that one of the cash registers has been coming up short so, unknown to anyone, he personally installed a security camera above it last week, hidden up in the ceiling. The camera is mostly trained on the register but it picks up some of the peripheral area. Guess whose face showed up in that area for over a hour?"

Yardley swallowed.

"Mine," she said.

Teffinger nodded.

"Now, earlier today when I talked to you, you said you were home last night."

She stepped over to the window and looked out.

Her head was light.

"How much trouble am I in?"

Teffinger shrugged.

"I'm not sure yet," he said. "Assuming the timer was set correctly, you were in the club until after Deven got killed. So you didn't kill her."

"That's right, I didn't."

The man pulled a book off a shelf and thumbed through it.

"I'm not much of a reader," he said.

"Too bad."

"I'd like to, I just don't have the time."

"You need to make the time."

"Maybe someday." His face hardened. "I'm going to give you one free lie. You've used it up. I won't take kindly to a second one. That said, why don't you tell me what happened last night?"

Her mind raced.

There was no place she could begin that wouldn't eventually lead to lies.

"I can't," she said.

The man closed the book and slipped it back on the shelf.

"This is why I can never read," he said. "People are always making me do things the hard way." A beat then, "You're a pretty woman. Were you and Deven lovers?"

Yardley walked to the door and opened it.

"It's time for you to leave," she said.

67

Sophia pushed through the revolving doors at the base of the building and stepped out into the sizzling downtown heat. She headed over to 16th Street and settled into a brisk walk, letting the temperature bake her brain. When she stopped at a street vendor for a hot dog, someone behind her came to a parallel halt.

It was a man in jeans, a black T, a red baseball cap and dark oversized sunglasses.

He kneeled down to tie a shoe.

She left, eating the dog en route and trying to not drop catsup down the front, when she came to an art gallery with an angled window.

She peered in, ostensibly looking at something that caught her eye, but using the glass as a rearview mirror.

The man was twenty steps behind, stopped again, not staring directly at her but occasionally twisting the sunglasses slightly in her direction.

She stepped inside the gallery and called Teffinger.

He didn't answer.

She called Renn-Jaa.

"I'm on the 16th Street mall," she said. "Someone's following me."

"Call Teffinger."

"I did," she said. "He's not answering. What I need you to do is get in line behind him and wait for me to lose him. Then follow him."

"I'm already heading down the hallway. Describe him."

She did.

"Stay where you are and give me five minutes to get in position. I'll call you when I am."

"Done."

A nicely-dressed woman came out from behind a desk in the back to see if Sophia needed assistance, which she didn't.

She was just browsing.

The artwork wasn't bad, mostly oil landscapes and cityscapes, some realistic and some looser, not as good as the stuff in Santa Fe or Taos but still not bad.

Minutes later her phone rang.

"I'm in position," Renn-Jaa said. "I have him in my sights."

"Be careful."

"I will."

Sophia walked out and took an immediate right without pointing her face even peripherally at the red cap.

She walked a block then a second.

There she crossed the street and moved into Market Square, ducking into an alley as soon as she got out of line of sight.

She hid behind a dumpster.

The red baseball cap walked past.

Sophia couldn't see his face.

He was too small to be the gladiator.

Shortly thereafter Renn-Jaa walked past.

Her face was intense.

68

Teffinger could feel Yardley White's eyes digging into his back as he walked away from the bookstore. He was a block from the Tundra when his phone rang and Sophia's voice came through.

"I'm on the mall and someone is following me," she said.

Teffinger's blood drummed.

"Where is he now?"

"I shook him two minutes ago," she said. "Renn-Jaa's following him. They're in Market Square."

Market Square was six or seven blocks up.

"Describe him."

She did.

Jeans.

Black T.

Red baseball cap.

Sunglasses.

"Get out of there."

He hung up, called the dispatcher and said, "I have a possible sighting of the man who killed Jackie Lake. He's somewhere downtown around Market Square. I want every cop within a hundred miles down there right now. This is top priority, it trumps everything. Are you getting this?"

Yes.

She was.

"Give me his description."

He did.

She repeated it.

"Right, he said. "No sirens. Do you understand? I don't want to scare the little prick into a hole. If anyone comes in with a siren blaring I'm going to personally rip his face off."

Traffic was thick enough that he decided he could get there quicker on foot and headed off at a fast run. Every square inch of asphalt and concrete and brick and glass that had been soaking up the heat all day now flung little fireballs at him. It gripped him hard but he didn't have time to bend to it.

He kept going.

Seconds were everything.

Someone needed to spot the guy before he caught wind of what was going on and ducked in a door. The city was a rat's maze. A good rat could get out without even trying.

He slowed enough to pull out his phone and hit redial.

When Sophia answered he said, "Call Renn-Jaa and find out where the guy is. Then call me back."

"Will do."

A minute later his phone rang.

"The guy spotted her. He cut around a corner over on Market and disappeared."

"Market. Okay."

He relayed the information to dispatch then got back into a full run.

He was almost to 16th when he noticed a man turn the corner at a brisk pace on the opposite side of the street. He didn't have a red baseball cap or sunglasses but those could have been ditched. The rest matched, namely jeans and black T.

He ran faster, fifty yards off, trying to decide whether to

waste time on the guy or continue on to Market.

When he got to the corner, the guy was gone.

Teffinger continued on towards Market then did a one-eight thirty steps later and doubled back.

69

Too many walls were crashing in on Yardley. Cave would kill her starting at six tonight, Deven was dead, and now Teffinger caught her in a lie about being home when Deven was murdered. She had cash in the safe, plus the offshore accounts. There were three fake passports and a variety of driver's licenses with her photo on them. She'd prepared for flight, never thinking the need would actually materialize this early in the game but being overly cautious nonetheless.

Maybe it was time.

If she did it, it would still be prudent to sanitize everything; download the computers onto flash drives and then destroy the hard drives; shred all the papers; etcetera etcetera etcetera.

Part of her wanted to do it.

Leave.

Leave now.

Leave while the leaving was good.

Another part of her wanted to ride it out.

Cave might actually end up dead by midnight just like Marabella said.

Teffinger might sniff around but the bottom line is that Yardley had nothing to do with Deven's murder. The only threat Teffinger posed was if he worked his way too deep into Yardley's life and found out things he shouldn't.

What to do?

If she stuck it out, that would prove her loyalty beyond question. The assignments would get bigger and the money would follow.

She liked Denver.

It was sunny.

She had friends.

She knew the haunts.

In a strange turn of affairs, she might even take up with Teffinger. There had been a moment between them. Most men couldn't keep up with her long term. Teffinger could, he was built for distance. He had the strength for it. He had enough dimensions to him to keep her interested. She'd seen him on the cover of GQ two or three years ago. She remembered his eyes, one blue, one green, both so full of sex that it made her think nasty little thoughts.

Her phone rang and the voice of a man came through, a voice she didn't recognize.

"Yardley?"

"Yes."

"I'm a friend of someone who has invited me to come to Denver to resolve a problem," he said. "Are you familiar with what I'm talking about?"

She was.

"Good," he said. "I'm already here in town. The problem has gone underground. I'm going to need your help to bring the problem back out into the open."

Bait.

That's what he was talking about, bait.

Her mind flashed to Deven, alone and tied in Cave's trunk, then being dragged out into the night and stabbed through the ear with a screwdriver.

"Sure," she said.

"Yes?"

"Yes, whatever you want."

"Good," he said. "Keep your cell phone with you at all times. I'll be in touch shortly."

70

Sophia took refuge at homicide while Teffinger coordinated a small army from his desk via cell phone and emails. She kept his cup full, answered questions when he had them and fought back the urge to grab him by the tie and pull him into the coat closet.

The killer escaped.

In fact, not a single person including Sophia and Renn-Jaa got a good look at him. Teffinger's main ambition since the point of failure was to find a security camera that captured the guy's face. The army was out looking for those cameras and collecting tapes when they found them.

So far only one camera had a tape of interest.

That was from a second story location looking down.

The suspect's cap hid his face.

However, it also showed a tattoo sticking out the bottom of his sleeve on the left arm. The ink depicted the tip of a scorpion's tail, with 90 percent of the tattoo hidden.

Sophia had never seen that tattoo before.

The tapes were inspected not just for men in a red hat but for anyone and everyone wearing jeans and a black T, the thinking being that the lid and sunglasses could have been ditched.

Several persons of interest emerged.

On closer inspection, however, the Ts while black didn't

match the suspect's, which was plain. Two had AC/DC in white letters, others had writings or images.

At 9:15 Teffinger called everything off.

Everyone was out of the room by 9:39.

Only Teffinger and Sophia were left.

Outside, night had settled over Denver.

Sophia flipped the lights off.

The room fell into darkness.

She closed the door and wedged it shut with a folding chair.

She unbuttoned her blouse as she walked towards Teffinger.

"Is this going to be your first time doing it in here?"

She expected him to balk, to tell her how he couldn't, to flap his lips about how the cleaning lady could show up at any minute or how one of the other detectives might have forgotten something.

Instead he came at her.

His hands went to her ass and he pulled her up.

Her legs spread and her thighs gripped his waist.

Teffinger walked her over to the wall and backed her into it.

He kissed her hard.

He dropped her feet to the carpet then grabbed her wrists and pulled her arms up over her head. He pinned them with one hand and ripped her panties off with the other. Then he took her with all the force of his body, slamming her into the wall so hard that the windows shook.

71

With so many reporters hovering around to get a sound-byte out of Teffinger's lips, he decided it was best to not create a second story by carting Sophia home with him, so he put her in a taxi to Renn-Jaa's and listened to the oldies station as he headed west on 6th Avenue.

The music was good.

Neil Diamond, "Solitary Man."

The Four Tops, "Bernadette."

The Righteous Brothers, "You've Lost That Lovin' Feeling."

Johnny Rivers, "Secret Agent Man."

As he passed Kipling he checked his voice messages to find he had one from Sydney. "Hey, cowboy, I made it here to New York safe and sound if anyone cares. I've been flashing the photo of Northway and his female companion around at restaurants in the vicinity. So far no one recognizes Northway. A waitress recognized the woman but has no idea who she is. Later."

The message ended.

Teffinger looked at his watch.

It was almost 11:00, meaning 1:00 New York time.

Sydney would be asleep.

He dialed anyway because if he didn't he'd forget what he

was thinking by the morning.

She answered.

Her voice was scratchy and unfocused.

"The waitress who recognized the woman, did she work at a nice restaurant?"

"Teffinger it's one o'clock here. You're waking me up."

"I know, I'm sorry," he said. "The restaurant though, was it an expensive one?"

"They're all expensive," she said. "Do you want to know what I paid for supper?"

"You know what I mean."

Yes.

She did.

"It was a nice enough place."

"Was the woman decked out?"

"The waitress?"

"No, the other one."

"I didn't ask," she said.

"Tomorrow find out," Teffinger said. "If she was decked out and the restaurant was on the expensive side, I'm guessing she's a lawyer, particularly if she was with other people dressed like lawyers—ask the waitress about that tomorrow. If all those pieces fit then start concentrating on law firms but here's the important part, don't let her know anyone's looking for her. I don't want her tipping off Northway. In fact, the more I think about it, Northway might even be in the same firm."

"Practicing law?"

"Maybe."

"That's not possible," she said. "His license was revoked."

"He still has the skills," Teffinger said. "A license is a piece of paper. Just don't let them see you coming, that's the point I'm making."

"Fine, I'll wear my invisible suit. Anything else?"

"Yes," he said. "Did the—?"

"Teffinger, that was a rhetorical question."

"I know," he said. "I'm giving you the rhetorical answer. Did the waitress actually wait on the woman? Is that why she remembers her?"

"Yes."

"How long ago?"

"Several months ago, six, seven, eight, something like that. She wasn't real clear with dates."

"Okay, contact the manager, use your best charms and see if he'll give you the credit card runs for that time period."

"Okay, good night."

"Aren't you going to ask if there's anything else?"

"I already made that mistake once," she said. "Where are you, in your truck?"

Yes.

He was.

"What's that song?"

"Jan and Dean, Little Deuce Coupe."

"It sounds like a cartoon. When I get back remind me to show you where the real stations are."

72

Thursday evening Yardley took the elevator from her loft down to the parking garage, fired up her silver 3-series BMW and merged into the Denver twilight. From the trendy buzzing streets of LoDo she wove over to Santa Fe and headed south. Six o'clock had come and gone. She hadn't called Cave with the name of the person at the top.

He hadn't called to give her one final chance.

As she headed out of the guts of the city the lights got less bright, the traffic lights got farther apart and the taillights thinned.

Cave was behind her somewhere.

She could feel his breath on her neck.

The miles clicked off.

The city gave way to less city.

The buildings got shorter and fewer.

The streetlights disappeared.

The speed limit increased.

Still, even this far south, traffic existed.

She kept going.

Headlights were behind her, not right on her ass, but definitely there. A large green sign indicated to exit here for the Chatfield Reservoir. In a couple of miles the road would cut left into I-25.

She was in no-man's land.

She kept her eyes peeled on the road and both hands tight on the wheel.

Then she saw what she was looking for, namely a 2x4 with nails sticking out, near the centerline.

She pointed her left front tire at it and held her breath.

The wheel hit it.

The tire exploded.

The vehicle jerked to the left.

She got it under control, pulled over to the shoulder, stopped and put the hazard lights on.

If everything went as planned, Cave was behind her somewhere. He'd see her at the side of the road and pull over to take his kill. That's when the man from out of town would take him down.

She got out and opened the trunk, ostensibly looking for the spare.

The night was coffin quiet, broken only by a faint chatter of crickets and a slight twist of wind. A low blanket of clouds hid whatever stars and moon might be above.

"Are you out there?"

No response.

She kept her cool.

Of course he was there.

He was the one who placed the two-by-four.

Headlights came up the road, only one pair now with no more behind, a couple of hundred yards away.

A chill ran up her spine.

When she was being instructed earlier this evening as to what to do, it seemed simple. Now the night played with her. Cave might simply slow down, shoot her through the passenger window, and keep going.

Bam.

One shot.

Game over.

The car approached.

It slowed as it got closer.

She shouted into the darkness, "This could be him. Are you ready?"

No one responded.

The silence forced a terrible thought upon her.

What if the man who called her earlier wasn't the person Marabella brought in to do the work? What if he was actually a friend of Cave's?

What if this whole thing was a setup?

What if Cave was the one who placed the two-by-four?

73

Sophia and Renn-Jaa stared up at the gladiator's loft from the same parking space as last night. This time the lights were on. Also this time no drunken woman staggered down the sidewalk. Sophia had her window open with her arm dangled out. A cigarette hung from her fingers. She took a puff and then pulled it back outside.

"What do you think?"

"I think I saw a shadow shift," Renn-Jaa said. "I'm about 90 percent sure he's home."

Sophia checked the time.

It was 11:12 on a Thursday night.

"He's in for the night," she said. "We're wasting our time."

"Ten more minutes."

Sophia took another puff, flicked the butt to the sidewalk and closed her eyes.

Teffinger.

Teffinger.

Teffinger.

No one had ever taken her the way he did.

Not even the gladiator.

A scene sprang into her head, as if she was sitting in a dark theater and the screen suddenly sprang to life, flickering at first with a jagged surrealism and then becoming vividly focused.

She was in a desperate fight.

Chiara had a fistful of her hair.

She was trying with all her might to rip it out of Sophia's head.

Sophia twisted and dropped to the carpet.

Chiara fell with her but kept her grip.

Sophia punched her in the face, again and again, getting only glancing blows, unable to strike a direct hit.

Chiara kneed her in the gut.

Vomit shot into her mouth.

Then hands came to her throat.

They tightened with deadly intent.

She twisted, desperate, but the woman was on top of her. There was too much weight to shift off. She flailed her arms and got a hand on a wine bottle. She brought it upside the woman's head with a terrible thud.

The woman fell to the side.

She groaned for a heartbeat then went limp.

She wasn't dead.

Her chest moved.

Breath came in and out of her mouth.

Sophia watched her for a moment while dark thoughts filled her brain. Then she walked into the kitchen and looked for a knife.

"Are you okay?"

The words came from Renn-Jaa.

The image vanished.

The screen went black.

"Yes."

"Look," the woman said, pointing.

Sophia followed the woman's finger to the gladiator's loft. The lights were going out.

"Either he's going to bed or stepping out," Renn-Jaa said.

Two minutes later the gladiator emerged at ground level, walked half a block to a car and took off.

"We're up," Renn-Jaa said.

74

When Teffinger got home the house was an oven. He opened the windows, charged up the ceiling fans and sat on the front steps with a cold one.

The night was black.

A light breeze rustled the leaves.

Dry lightning flashed to the east somewhere over Denver.

Bugs sucked up to a streetlight. A bat swooped in with jagged flight and snatched one out of the air. Survival; it was everywhere, all the time.

Teffinger had always envisioned himself with kids one day.

Kelly would be a good mother.

Sophia was a lot wilder than Kelly but that didn't necessarily mean she'd be selfish. It wouldn't hurt a kid to have a little wildness in his blood. That would increase the chances of not being snatched out of the air by a bat.

His street dead-ended at a turnaround as far up into Green Mountain as civilization went. His house was third from the end on the left side. Coyotes, deer, fox and rabbits were rampant; rattlesnakes, too. In fact Teffinger almost stepped on a four-footer on the back patio last month.

He was caught between Kelly and Sophia, dead center, smack in the middle, a helpless piece of metal between two equally powerful magnets.

He'd made no promises to either but still he felt like he was cheating on both of them. He needed to make a choice but neither of them was letting go. If he had the time to concentrate on nothing else, things would probably get pretty clear pretty fast.

He didn't have that time though.

That was the problem, that was *always* the problem, not just with this but with everything.

He pulled a quarter out of his pocket.

"Heads Kelly, tails Sophia."

He tossed it up and missed the catch.

It bounced on the concrete and rolled into the grass.

"I'll take that as an omen."

He swallowed what was left of the beer, crushed the can in his hand and headed inside. In the kitchen something sticking out from behind the toaster caught his eye.

It was a piece of paper.

It was one of the pages he copied from September's file on Van Gogh.

"What'd you do, blow back here when I wasn't looking?"

He debated, wondering if he should read it or not.

Then he decided that even though he was getting the blame, the moral concepts were the same now than they were before. He burned it and washed the ashes down the sink.

75

The solitary headlights approached with a whining of tires and the blare of a radio. Yardley stood on the shoulder side of her car, not knowing if Cave was coming down the road or sneaking up behind her or somewhere else altogether.

The headlights slowed as they came alongside.

It became clearer that the vehicle was a convertible.

Voices shouted louder than the radio.

As it got alongside, the voices took shape as belonging to teenagers, a bunch of them. Two were standing up, waving their arms, and one of them shouted, "Bottle bomb!"

Bottles flew at Yardley's car.

Glass shattered.

Pow!

Pow!

Pow!

Then the vehicle sped up and the taillights receded up the road.

Suddenly Yardley heard a noise behind her.

She turned.

A shadow was there.

She ran up the road.

"Get back here!"

She ran harder.

Footsteps closed in.

The gap shortened.

Then a fist punched the back of her head. Her feet gave out and her body went down, landing with a terrible blow to her chest before she could get her arms in front.

The oxygen slapped out of her lungs.

Colors spun in her head.

Then everything went black.

She retained consciousness at some point thereafter in a confined space with her hands tied behind her back and a rope gagged around her mouth.

She was in the trunk of a car.

She had one thought and one thought only, namely that this was the exact position Deven had been in before she was yanked out and stabbed with a screwdriver.

Cave had tricked her.

She'd underestimated him.

Now she'd die for being stupid.

First, Cave would have his fun with her.

He'd take his time.

He'd be creative.

He'd enjoy himself.

DAY FIVE

July 22
Friday

76

During the break-in last night, the gladiator didn't jump out of a corner with killer hands, or charge up the fire escape with a knife in his hand, or mysteriously drop out of the ceiling with a war cry. Every noise and flicker of light in the universe seemed like one of those but in the end none were.

Things were much the same as before.

One exception was that Sophia and Renn-Jaa found a full drawer of neatly coiled lengths of red rope, with labels ranging from four to twenty feet.

The other exception was the laptop.

This time when they flipped it open, instead of getting a password screen the display sprang to life. They found a number of flash drives in a drawer, grabbed one and copied the document files.

In the process, Sophia knocked over a small green banker's lamp, which shattered on the wood planking.

They left it where it was and got the hell out of there.

That was last night.

Now it was morning.

Sophia got two hours of seatwork under her belt then pushed the gladiator's flash drive in her laptop and took a look. One of the folders was labeled "Rope." In it were hundreds of photos of naked women tied in intricate bondage.

She scanned a few of them and closed the folder.

Then she saw a folder that grabbed her by the throat, a folder labeled "Sophia Phair."

She clicked it open to find a number of JPEG images of herself spanning back two weeks, long before Friday night when they ostensibly first met. Many were snapped downtown in the financial district or on the mall; she was dressed in attorney attire, often with Renn-Jaa going to lunch, plus a couple with Condor as they walked to the courthouse the week before last. She had a leather briefcase in her left hand.

There were three with her walking with Jackie Lake.

Those weren't the creepy ones though.

The disturbing ones were at her loft, taken from LoDo below as she stood on her balcony. There would have been some of her in bed if the guy could have gotten an angle.

With the door closed, she showed the images to Renn-Jaa who said, "We have to get these to Teffinger right away."

Sophia frowned.

She knew that.

They'd broken in.

In a perfect world, Teffinger would never know about that. Unfortunately the world was getting less and less perfect.

"This is actually good," Renn-Jaa said. "As long as we have to confess to Teffinger what we've been up to, we can tell him about the three guys who attacked the black woman."

Sophia ran her fingers through her hair.

"We can get disbarred," she said. "Both of us. Breaking into to someone's place—twice no less—then stealing information from a computer, that's pretty serious conduct for an attorney no matter what the motivation."

Renn-Jaa contemplated it.

She didn't argue.

"I don't care about me," Sophia said. "My life's pretty much screwed up at this point and I don't see myself recovering. You're a different story though."

"What do you mean? Your life's screwed up—"

Sophia stood up and looked out the window.

"We need to be smart," she said. "We need to get all this information to Teffinger without implicating ourselves."

"How?"

"We'll hire an attorney," she said. "What we say will be privileged. She can then transmit everything to Teffinger without specifically mentioning our names."

Renn-Jaa tilted her head.

"Her?"

"Right."

"Do you already have someone in mind?"

Sophia nodded.

"Kelly Ravenfield," she said. "She has Teffinger's ear."

Renn-Jaa shook her head.

"She's trying to get Teffinger," she said. "I can see her letting it slip that you and me are her clients. She can get a leg up that way."

Sophia shook her head.

"If she purposely betrays our trust, Teffinger wouldn't look very favorably on it. She'd just be shooting herself in the foot. Besides, Teffinger already graduated from third grade, meaning he's going to put two and two together anyway." She looked at her watch. "Let's see if we can get Kelly to meet us for lunch. He'll know we broke in. My concern is that we never formally admit it."

Renn-Jaa smiled.

"This has nothing to do with anything," she said. "You just want an excuse to meet Kelly."

77

Teffinger's night of so-called sleep dripped with dreams of scorpions. He didn't realize why until he woke up and remembered the arm tattoo of the man who stalked Sophia yesterday. He got the coffee pot charged up and let it do its thing while he took a three mile pre-dawn jog through the silent streets of Green Mountain, then headed to work with a bowl of cereal in his lap and a thermos of the good stuff laying on the passenger seat.

En route he called Sophia to be sure she survived the night.

The call woke her.

She was fine.

"You were quite the little ride last night," she said.

"I could say the same."

He was the first one to work as usual. When he opened the door and flicked on the fluorescents, something happened he didn't expect. The light above his desk hummed like a flock of angry mosquitoes. He walked down to the chief's office and turned on the lights. No humming came from above.

He smiled.

How'd the man figure it out?

He was half tempted to switch them back but decided he didn't have time right now, later, but not now. Instead he got the coffee dripping and searched the net for scorpion tattoos in hopes of finding an identical match to the suspect in question.

Nothing popped up.

He pulled up a listing of tattoo shops in Denver and found that most of them opened at ten, meaning it was too early to start calling.

He printed off a copy of the suspect's tattoo and tacked it on the wall behind his desk. While he was at it he printed off a copy of Michael Northway walking through the streets of New York and stuck that up too.

His phone rang and Sydney's voice came through from New York.

"You were right," she said. "The woman with Northway was a lawyer. Her name's Michelle Twist. She's a partner in a big firm here in Manhattan by the name of Block, Winters & LaJunge. Northway isn't a member of the firm. I went through all the bio photos and he's not there."

"Good work."

"Thanks, but here's the big question. Now what?"

Teffinger chewed on the options.

"Here's what we'll do," he said. "I'm going to email you photos of D'endra Vaughn, both alive and dead. Stake out the base of the law firm's building and see if you can catch the lawyer—"

"—Michelle Twist—"

"—Right, her, see if you can catch her coming out. Get her alone. If she comes out with someone else, back off. The key is to get her alone, the sooner the better but tonight at her house or apartment if that's what it takes. When you get her alone, show her the photos and explain the background. At that point, hopefully she'll give you the name Northway's using and where to find him, even if he's a client. Tell her your conversation with her never existed. No one will know what she tells you. All you want is the information."

"What if she doesn't cooperate?"

"That will depend on whether she says that Northway's a client or not," he said. "If he's a client and she refuses to give him up, quite frankly I don't know what we're going to do. But if he's not a client, if he's just a friend or lover or something like that, then make it clear that we'll be forced to determine whether she's harboring a fugitive. Remind her that's a felony."

"Sounds good."

"Hopefully we don't get to that point," he said. "Give her every opportunity to talk off the record."

Silence.

"You still there?" she said.

He was.

"Northway has a way with women," she said. "She'll tip him off and he'll disappear again. Maybe we should just lay low and stay in the shadows. Do we have enough to tap her phone?"

Teffinger raked his hair back.

It flopped back down.

"Doubtful," he said. "Show her the photos. Hopefully they'll convince her to do the right thing."

"That's your plan? To hope she does the right thing?"

"Yes."

"Has it ever worked before?"

"No but there's always a first time."

78

Yardley woke on a raggedy mattress in a strange room with her left wrist in a metal cuff chained to the bed frame. The first rays of light were just beginning to creep into the sky. An old blanket covered the window, nailed to the plaster. No sounds came from anywhere, not from inside or outside. She was in a cabin or farmhouse away from civilization.

She didn't call out.

She quietly tried to work the cuff off her wrist.

It was too tight.

The chain was secured with padlocks at both ends. The bed frame was thick, heavy metal. She was a hundred percent stuck. There was no way out.

Cave had her.

She was still dressed in the same clothes as last night. She hadn't been roughed up or raped.

Pee.

That's what she needed to do, not in ten seconds, now.

Next to the bed was a bucket half filled with water.

Was that her bathroom?

Apparently so.

Next to it was a roll of toilet paper.

Next to the toilet paper was a jug of drinking water and a

box of crackers.

She listened intently for signs of Cave, got none, then used the bucket as quickly as she could, before he could interrupt her.

She called out.

"Cave."

No one answered.

No sounds came.

"Cave, are you here?"

Silence.

She dragged the bed to the window and pulled the blanket to the side. Outside was prairie topography. A dilapidated barn occupied a position fifty yards to the left. The boards were loose and many had fallen off. Whatever red paint once existed was now peeled and flaked. The base was choked with weeds. No discernible path or road led to it.

She pulled the blanket off and tried to open the window.

It wouldn't budge.

To many layers of paint kept it locked.

She wrapped the blanket around her hand and punched the glass out, then chipped away at the jagged ends. A cool morning breeze entered the room.

Not a single sound filtered in from the outside world.

She pulled the bed farther to the window, getting the end of the chain directly under it. Then she climbed out and dropped to the ground. Three feet, that's how far she could extend from the side of the house. That didn't get her to where she could see around either corner. The only visible universe was more prairie.

She called out.

No one answered.

Wherever she was, it was remote.

Cave could make her scream as loud as he wanted. The end

of her voice wouldn't come within a mile of a human ear.

Suddenly she heard a car, very distant but heading her way.

Cave was coming back.

She tugged wildly at the chain.

The shackle cut into her wrist.

The skin broke.

Blood dripped out.

She pulled harder.

79

By most talk the Blue Ricochet Eatery & Pub on Walnut was more worthy of the pub part of its namesake than the other part. The lights were dim, the waitresses wore little schoolgirl outfits and the male patrons didn't complain. Sophia wandered in there on a drunken bar-hopping night three months ago and ended up leaving with the drummer of a band she'd never heard of. It wasn't until the next day that she learned the band had played at Red Rocks earlier in the evening.

She opened the front door and stepped inside at 12:05.

The interior was a cave but she knew the layout and headed for the restroom, which was almost as dark as the rest of the place. The lock for the door was broken so she held it shut with her foot as she did what she came to do.

That was better.

She was a human again.

She checked her face in the mirror and fluffed her hair.

This was it.

It was time to meet the enemy.

With adjusted eyes she spotted Renn-Jaa in a dim corner booth sitting across from a blond.

As she walked over things got bad.

She hoped the blond wouldn't be as attractive as her law

firm bio photo.

In fact it was the opposite.

She slid in next to her, gave her a peck on the cheek and said, "We finally meet. I'm Sophia Phair."

Kelly studied her.

"Kelly Ravenfield," she said. "I was hoping you'd be ugly."

"Back at you."

"Black hair, blond hair," Kelly said. "Teffinger has a real yin-yang thing going on, doesn't he?"

"So it seems." Sophia spotted a penny sitting on the edge of the table and picked it up. "You want to flip for him?"

Kelly smiled.

"I can see what he sees in you," she said. "So what's this mysterious meeting about? Why am I here? Are you going to drag me out into the alley to settle things with a good old fashioned cat fight?"

"Nothing that dramatic."

They ordered salads, got informed by a ponytailed waitress with a full-sleeve tattoo that they "might want to avoid the produce today," and changed to soup.

"That comes from a can, right?" Renn-Jaa said. "It's not mixed up in a 55-gallon drum in the back or anything, is it?"

No.

It wasn't.

"Okay then, the soup."

Sophia explained why they were here; namely, she got picked up by a gladiator at the Tequila Rose on Friday night, the club's videotapes showed he had been stalking her, so she and Renn-Jaa had broken into his loft to see if they could find anything.

"That was a risky move," Kelly said.

"Stupid is more like it," Sophia said. "Anyway, we downloaded his laptop onto a flash drive last night. It turns out he's taken a hundred or more pictures of me all over town, dating back to at least two weeks prior to Friday night."

Kelly put a serious expression on her face.

"That's Van Gogh's MO."

"Precisely," Sophia said. "I need to get the flash drive to Teffinger without being implicated in any type of criminal activity. Me and Renn-Jaa are hiring you as our attorney."

"There needs to be a reason," Kelly said.

Sophia nodded.

"We know that," she said. "The reason is this. We're going to give the flash drive to you and it comes with a request for a legal opinion which is, *Was it okay to break into the gladiator's loft and download the information contained on that flash drive, or did we commit an illegal act?*"

Kelly smiled.

"I think I could probably answer that for you, given enough time to do the research."

"I thought you could," Sophia said. "Now, if it turns out that Teffinger somehow ends up with the flash drive off the record, then that's what happens. Our hope is that after he knows what he can find, he'll think of a way to get a legitimate search warrant and then inadvertently stumble on the laptop. Don't mention our names to Teffinger though."

"He'll know."

"We don't care if he figures it out," she said. "What we care about is the fact that legally we have a confidential communication taking place here, by which I mean it's fully within the attorney-client privilege, by which I mean no one loses their license."

Kelly nodded.

"Devious," she said. "Beauty and brains. I think I may be in trouble."

"You'll take the case?"

"Of course. Did you bring the flash drive with you?"

"Yes; and a retainer. Is ten dollars enough?"

"That sounds fair."

Sophia looked around for her purse.

It wasn't on the table.

It wasn't on the seat next to her.

Then she remembered.

She set it on the back of the toilet when she was in there ten minutes ago.

She headed for the restroom with a terrible feeling in her gut. When she got there the feeling exploded into something much worse.

The purse wasn't there.

It was gone.

So was the flash drive inside it.

80

The Ink Box was sandwiched between a gay video arcade and a medical-marijuana joint in a seedy stretch of Broadway on the south edge of the city. Teffinger parked on a side street, made double sure the doors were locked and headed over.

Inside with her feet propped up on a desk was an attractive woman in her early twenties, heavily pierced and inked, with raven punk hair, wearing a short white tank and low-riding jeans, reading a magazine.

"You're Angel," Teffinger said.

She nodded and said, "You're not what I expected."

"No?"

"No."

"What'd you expect?"

"I don't know but not you," she said.

Residual pot hung in the air. Some kind of alternative music spilled out of a black Bose radio on the desk. "I have that same exact radio in my bedroom, except mine's white," Teffinger said.

"Small world."

"Mine doesn't get that station though."

"Next time you come bring it with you and I'll fix it for you."

"That'd be nice."

She ran her eyes up and down his frame.

"You're what we call a clean canvas," she said. "We should dirty you up before you leave."

"You think?"

She nodded.

"Can I show you something?"

"Sure."

She stood up, pulled the tank over her head with a sexy slither, and tossed it on the desk. Perky attributes emerged, as good as Teffinger had ever seen. The woman shook them.

"See this right here?"

She pointed to a tattoo on her left breast.

It was a scorpion.

The tail looked exactly like the tail on the man who was stalking Sophia yesterday.

She took Teffinger's hand and put it on her breast. "Go ahead and touch it," she said. "It doesn't bite."

He squeezed.

"Nice."

She sat on the desk and dangled her feet.

"I dance down at B.T.s," she said. "A guy came in one night, saw this bad boy right here and asked me where I got it. He wanted one just like it on his arm. Two days later he showed up and I inked it on him."

"Did you find the records on him yet?"

She shook her head.

"I'm still looking," she said. "This was two years ago. We don't do paper anymore, everything's on the computer. We back up onto flash drives but to be honest we're not very good at labeling them." She pulled the top drawer of the desk out and pointed to eight or ten sticks. "I've gone through three of them so far with no luck. You want me to keep going?"

Yes.

He did.

"I'm going to lock the front door," she said. "Otherwise there will be a hundred potheads from next door barging in here looking for a lap dance."

"You give lap dances here?"

"Yeah but don't spread it around," she said. "Twenty dollars. I'm going to give you a free one after we find the information you want."

It took twenty minutes, twenty topless minutes, but the time was worth it.

The scorpion guy's name was Jack Plant.

His address was over near Washington Park.

Teffinger folded a printout of the invoice and shoved it in his back pocket.

Angel put her arms around his neck and rubbed her chest against him.

"Time for that lap dance, cowboy."

"I'd like to but—"

She grabbed his hand and pulled him towards a door that led into a back room.

He stopped, pulled out his wallet and gave her two fifties. "That's for the work you missed while you were taking care of me. I'll get that lap dance from you down at B.T.s some night."

"You go there?"

"Yes."

"I work Friday and Saturday nights."

"I'll hunt you down."

"I'll bet you will."

81

Yardley screamed for help as the drone of the approaching car got louder. No voices responded, no faces magically appeared, nothing sane happened. Her initial thought was to stay outside and make Cave kill her there, in hopes that someone was off on a distant ridge with a pair of binoculars. Then she pictured Cave dragging her in through the window over the jagged glass and tearing her flesh to shreds. She climbed in, left the bed where it was and cowered under it.

The front door opened.

Footsteps approached.

The bedroom door opened.

"Stand up."

The words took her by surprise because they didn't belong to Cave. They belonged to someone else. She stood up to find a large man, six three or more. He looked like an Indian with a mean face and long braided hair.

He cast his eyes on the broken window and said, "You've been a busy girl."

She suddenly realized where she knew the voice from.

He was the one she talked to on the phone, the man who was brought in to take care of Cave.

"Why am I chained up?"

"For your own good," he said. "I was hoping that our little trap last night would draw Cave in and that I could kill him and that would be the end of everything. When he didn't show, I had to go to plan B, which is to keep you secluded until I get him."

"I don't get it."

"It's simple," he said. "Marabella wants to be absolutely sure Cave doesn't get his hands on you and find a way to make you talk."

"I don't need to be chained for that."

He exhaled.

"It's important that you stay here and that I'm absolutely sure you're here at all times," he said. "I can't have you be a distraction."

"I won't be," she said. "I'll stay here but at least give me the run of the house."

He studied her.

"I'll unchain you while I'm here," he said. "It's going back on though when I leave."

Yardley said, "Fine."

She'd worry about it later.

All she wanted right now was the steel off her wrist.

He turned out to be an Apache named Ghost Wolf who whipped up pancakes and coffee on a propane stove, which they ate on the front steps. The world in front of the house was as abandoned and empty as behind. A rutted, weed-invested drive snaked off into the distance, a feeble umbilical cord to civilization.

"What is this place?"

"It's Apache."

"We're on a reservation?"

"No, it's Apache-owned but not part of a reservation," he said. "Three thousand acres. We're on the eastern plains, fifty miles east of Denver."

"What's it used for?"

"Lots of things," he said. "In this case, Cave's body will end up buried out there."

Yardley took a sip of coffee.

"How many other Caves are already here?"

He grunted.

"By my hand, eleven," he said. "By others, more."

"So you've been at this awhile."

"Three years."

"That's all?"

He nodded.

"That's when someone I knew got stumbled on one night by a shit-faced pack of cowboys who thought she'd be a good little ride," he said. "Afterwards, they figured she'd be a good witness too, so they took care of that little problem."

"They killed her?"

He nodded.

"Strangled her to death. Five of them are out there in the field now. One is yet to come."

"Was she your wife?"

"No, someone else's wife," he said. "My lover."

"What'd the husband do?"

"That broke-dick dog? Nothing. He got drunk and forgot about it."

He pulled a pack of smokes out of his back pocket, tapped one out and held it out to see if Yardley was interested, which she was. He lit them up from a book of matches and blew smoke.

"So where's Cave?"

"I don't know," Yardley said. "I do know one thing though. You're not going to get him without me. Let me help you."

"I'll think about it."

"There's nothing to think about." She took a long drag and

stood up. "We're wasting time. Let's get going."

82

Losing the flash drive to a bathroom opportunist was a blow but not a fatal one. The importance of the JPEGs wasn't the images themselves so much as the fact they spanned back more than two weeks. That information could still be communicated from Kelly to Teffinger irrespective of the lack of proof. It wasn't until Sophia was walking back to the law firm that she realized the more important aspect of the loss, namely that she never checked the other files to see if they related to any of the Van Gogh victims.

Not doing that had been stupid.

So was not making a copy of the drive.

She cancelled her credit cards and got back into bill-able-hour mode. Midafternoon her phone rang and the voice of the California investigator, Aspen Gonzales, came through.

"Two things," the woman said. "One, I got a hold of the autopsy report on Chiara. Check your emails, I sent it to you."

Sophia swallowed.

She remembered slitting the woman's throat following a brutal fight. The report would either confirm or refute that memory.

"How'd she die?"

"She had lots of contusions on the face and neck indicative of a fight," Aspen said. "That wasn't the cause of her death though. She died from having her throat slit."

Sophia's head felt light.

Her memory was accurate.

"Thanks."

She went to hang up but stopped when a muffled voice continued talking.

"Hello? Hello? Are you still there?"

"Yes," Sophia said.

"I thought I lost you for a second," Aspen said. "The second thing is this; that detective I told you about, John Maxwell, has been following me all over town. I can't throw a stone without hitting his face."

"Why?"

"It's his way of putting pressure on me," she said. "We're on extremely thin ice at this point. My advice is to shut this case down and shut it down fast. I wouldn't put it past this guy to tap my phone."

"You said he was a straight shooter."

"He is," she said. "He'd get a warrant. But that doesn't mean that people won't go out of their way to help him. Hell, he could connect us just by getting my phone records. Tell me to shut it down."

Sophia hesitated.

"No, don't."

Silence.

"Look—"

"Keep pressing ahead," Sophia said. "Please."

A beat then, "If Maxwell connects us he may very well pay a surprise visit to you in Denver."

"I understand."

Sophia went to the restroom and studied her eyes in the mirror. They were the eyes of a killer. Now that she was looking for it, it was easy to see.

Back at her desk she opened the autopsy report.

As Aspen said, Chiara had been in a violent fight.

There was also an important fact that Aspen hadn't mentioned, namely that Chiara had suffered a severe blow to the side of her head.

Sophia pictured herself desperately searching for anything to use as a weapon and then suddenly finding the wine bottle in her hand.

She needed to know the cause of the fight.

All she could hope is that she wasn't the one who initiated it.

Even that, though, was a point of interest at best.

Chiara was unconscious when Sophia went into the kitchen looking for a knife. Even if Sophia had been in a mode of self-defense up until that point, the act of slitting the woman's throat as she laid there helplessly was anything but.

That was an act of murder.

A knock came at the door. Sophia looked up expecting to see Renn-Jaa.

Instead it was Marabella Amberbrook, one of the uppity-ups from the forty-second floor and a member of the firm's board.

The woman smiled and said, "Got a minute?"

83

Clay Pitcher, district attorney, was a barrel-chested man with permanently stained cigar teeth and a closet full of tan blazers. On a good day he looked like a used car salesman. This wasn't a good day. Fourteen months away from retirement, he was putting in his eight, Monday to Friday, and talking more about opening a boat rental in the Bahamas than about his cases. Still, he had a damn fine pedigree and could be a top-notch lawyer if the right facts got him riled up enough.

These weren't the right facts.

He told the chief and Teffinger they didn't have enough evidence to support a search warrant for Jack Plank, the possible Van Gogh. "We can convince a judge that Plank's the guy who was following Sophia around yesterday, based on the tattoo," he said. "We can also convince him or her that it's certainly suspicious and that the reason he was following her around is because she witnessed him killing Jackie Lake and now he wants to get her all dead and silent."

Teffinger nodded.

"Right."

Clay scrunched his face.

"The problem is that although it's suspicious, that's all it is," he said. "He never talked to the woman, he never got closer than thirty steps, he didn't threaten her in any way and as far as we know he didn't break into her house and kill her cat."

"She doesn't have a cat," Teffinger said.

"I'm speaking metaphorically," Clay said. "Suspicion doesn't get you a warrant. Probable cause does. And that's what we don't have here boys and girls, probable cause."

Teffinger raked his hair back.

"Clay, quit screwing around and go get me a warrant," he said.

They both looked at Chief Tanker.

He was behind the oversized wooden desk leaned back in a worn leather chair with his fingers laced behind his head. The flag was to his left. Behind him on the wall were photos, mostly of him with persons of relevance—businessmen, athletes, politicians—not just posing for a stupid snapshot but biking or fishing or kicking it up.

He slipped forward in his chair, creased every wrinkle in his 50-year-old face and looked at Teffinger.

"Clay's here to give advice," he said. "Now, I'll admit that 95 percent of the advice he gives is wrong in hindsight. But all we have at this point is foresight."

Teffinger shuffled in his chair.

He was beaten.

He could argue but it wouldn't get him anywhere.

He looked at the ceiling.

"Nice lights up there," he said. "Mine buzz to hell and back."

Tanker smiled.

"That's too bad."

On the way back to the Tundra, Teffinger got a call from Kelly to the effect she wanted to meet ASAP, for business reasons, not to screw—although screwing would be fine tonight.

"Business?"

Right.

"It relates to the gladiator," she said.

84

Yardley couldn't convince Ghost Wolf to let her ride along with him today but did have enough persuasion in her sexy little body to at least keep him from chaining her up while he was gone.

"Be sure you keep your ass right here."

She nodded.

"I will."

He looked at her sideways.

"Don't make me regret this."

She patted his hand.

"Don't worry."

She waited a full fifteen minutes after he left to be sure he wasn't doubling back for some reason, then put her shoes on and headed up the so-called road, following the ruts and broken weeds. The guy was too creepy to be around. More importantly, her captivity here might not actually be in the name of her own safety. She might be here because Marabella had determined things had gotten too messy. Right now someone might be sanitizing her store and loft. Once that was done and no complications twisted to the surface, Yardley would be officially expendable.

Admittedly the likelihood of that scenario was small.

Still, it wasn't non-existent.

It was particularly disturbing that Ghost Wolf so easily mentioned he'd killed eleven people and buried them on the property. That wasn't exactly the kind of information a professional would broadcast if there was any possibility of it being repeated. Maybe he told her because he thought they were kindred spirits, each in as deep as the other. On the other hand, maybe he pictured her dead in 24 hours.

She needed to get to the bookstore and see if it was being sanitized.

The sky was blue and cloudless.

The sun was in her eyes and on her chest.

She was only ten minutes into it and already sweating.

The air was still and quiet.

The daily breeze wouldn't kick up until eleven or so.

She kept her eyes on the horizon. If a car approached she'd get down low, make her way into the brush and lay flat.

What she was doing was risky.

She knew that.

Marabella had a legitimate concern that Yardley not fall into the hands of Cave. With Yardley back in the world and defiant as to Ghost Wolf's efforts to keep her safe, Marabella might decide she had no option but to eliminate the problem once and for all.

Who would she send to do the job?

Ghost Wolf?

Probably.

He was already in town and knew the situation.

Bringing in someone new would only make a complicated situation even more complicated.

Ghost Wolf would be the one.

He'd probably enjoy it too, after she'd tricked him.

Not a sound pierced the air.

Her mind wandered.

An old Shakira song, "Hips Don't Lie," got stuck in her head and wouldn't come out.

Then she had to relieve herself.

She stopped, wiggled out of her shorts and panties, held them in her left hand and squatted down.

It felt good.

When she stood up, a figure was charging up the road towards her at full speed.

It was Ghost Wolf.

85

When Marabella shut the door for privacy, a cold chill ran up Sophia's spine and straight into her brain. The woman took a seat in front of the desk, crossed her legs and said, "I'm going to get right to the point. There's talk at the water cooler to the effect that the blow you took to the head might have been more severe than you've let on."

Sophia forced a confused expression onto her face.

"What do you mean?"

"What I mean is, you've been having blank looks when people talk to you about things in the past."

Sophia shrugged.

"Maybe a little."

"Do you remember anything yet about what happened at Jackie Lake's house?"

No.

She didn't.

Not a wisp.

"What about other things? Are you having memory issues with respect to other things as well?"

"Maybe a little."

Marabella nodded.

"Let me ask you this," she said. "Do you remember the

circumstances under which you joined the firm?"

No.

She didn't.

"Circumstances?"

"Right, circumstances," she said. "Do you remember the discussions you and I had when you first came to the firm?"

"No."

"Do you remember a woman named Yardley White?"

"No."

"No?"

"No. Who is she?"

Marabella didn't answer.

Instead she studied Sophia. She picked a pencil off the desk and twisted it in her fingers as if contemplating the next words. Then she said, "Do you remember what you did out in California?"

The words ricocheted in Sophia's skull.

California?

How did Marabella know about California?

Play dumb.

Play dumb.

Play dumb.

"No," she said. "What did I do out in California?"

"You honestly don't remember?"

"No."

The woman wrinkled her forehead.

"This is going to be painful but you better know it since you're spending so much time hanging around that detective Teffinger," she said. "You killed a woman. Her name was Chiara de Correggio. She was a friend of yours."

Sophia swallowed.

"How'd I do it?"

"You slit her throat."

"How do you know about it?"

"You told me. You killed her and dumped her body over a cliff. You had a different name back then. It was London Winger."

Marabella exhaled.

"I'm going to ask you something and I want you to tell me the honest to God truth," she said. "Did you kill Jackie Lake? Did you do to her what you did to that woman out in California?"

Sophia's instinct was to rise and run.

Instead she turned her chair until her face was hidden and squeezed her eyes shut.

Water came out and rolled down her cheeks.

Marabella said nothing.

The silence was thick.

Seconds passed, many seconds, slow seconds, one after another after another.

Then Sophia slowly swiveled the chair back. She tried to look into Marabella's eyes but couldn't. "I'm pretty sure I killed Jackie Lake," she said.

"Why?"

"I don't know."

Marabella reached over and held Sophia's hand.

"I thought it was you. Don't worry, I'm not going to tell anybody."

86

Kelly was at the curb outside her office when Teffinger swung over. Traffic was thick and he was blocking it so he didn't notice much about her other than she looked professional. When she slid in, the cab filled with perfume. The rustling of her nylons worked at his senses.

"Where are we going?" she asked.

"To rattle a tree."

"What's that mean?"

"It means we got the identity of the man who was following Sophia yesterday," he said. "His name is Jack Plank. I'm almost positive he's Van Gogh and the one who killed Jackie Lake. Clay says we don't have enough evidence for a search warrant so I'm going to rattle the guy's tree."

"Clay's too conservative."

Teffinger worked his way around a blue hair in a faded Volvo going ten under.

"That's true but he's probably right on this one," he said. "So tell me about the gladiator."

Kelly adjusted her body in the seat.

Her skirt rode up.

"This is off the record," she said. "The gladiator has a laptop in his loft. On that laptop are a lot of JPEG images of Sophia Phair. They're clicks of her walking around downtown and up on the balcony of her loft. Here's the important part, they go back at least two weeks prior to Friday, when he supposedly met her for the first time. He was stalking her for at least two weeks, exactly like what September Tadge told you about Van Gogh."

"How do you know all this?"

"I can't tell you," she said. "That part's confidential. It's true though. What you need to do is figure out a way to get a legitimate search warrant based on something else, pretending you have no idea about the computer, then accidentally stumble on it."

Teffinger wrinkled his brow.

"Did you break into his place?"

"No."

"Did you hire someone to break into his place?"

"No."

"Have you actually seen the JPEGs?"

"No, they were described to me."

"By who?"

"That's confidential."

He got silent.

Two blocks later he looked over and said, "Sophia broke in, didn't she?"

"I can't tell you any more than I already have."

He raked his hair back.

It immediately flopped down.

A squatty fat guy in a Hummer cut him off.

Then his phone rang.

Sydney was on the other end from New York. She sounded like she just stepped off a roller coaster before it came to a complete stop.

"Big news," she said.

"How big?"

"Bigger than what's in you pants," she said. "Two inches."

Teffinger laughed.

"I met with the lawyer and showed her the pictures of D'endra," she said. "That made an impact. It was there on her face. She wouldn't admit one way or the other if Northway was a client of hers but that's the impression I got. She listened patiently but in the end she said she couldn't help me. She said her hands were tied."

"Damn it—"

"Wait, I'm not finished," Sydney said. "We met for a light lunch, that's where I talked to her, in this little rinky-dinky place halfway down an alley. Anyway, throughout the whole meal, she had her cell phone sitting on the table. At the end, when she said she couldn't help me, she got up to leave. I said, *Hey, you forgot your phone.* She looked at me and said, *No, it's in my purse.* It wasn't, of course, it was sitting right there on the table. It took me a second to figure it out, but then it hit me that she was losing her phone on purpose. It's not a violation of an attorney-client communication to simply lose a physical object."

"Clever. So what's in the phone, anything?"

"There's no *Northway* listed. I've gone through all the text messages and none seem to relate to him. So what we have are all the incoming and outgoing numbers. My suspicion is that one of them belongs to Northway."

"Run with it."

Teffinger hung up and filled Kelly in on the parts she wouldn't have picked up. She had a right to know given that Northway almost killed her last year, not to mention that she was the one who spotted him on the street.

"Back to Sophia," he said. "Now I'm confused. We have this guy Jack Plank with the scorpion tattoo following her all over downtown yesterday. We also have the gladiator stalking her for at least two weeks. Which one am I supposed to concentrate on?"

She shrugged.

"Both. Maybe they're working together."

87

Yardley ran but was no match for the warrior feet of Ghost Wolf. He was closing dangerously fast and would be on her in seconds. She was off the road in the prairie sprinting south, hoping beyond hope that the man would twist a foot or step on a cactus or slam down face first into a boulder.

That didn't happen.

The gap closed.

A fist grabbed her by the hair and yanked her head back with a force that snapped her feet out from under her and sent her slamming to the ground on her back.

The wind slapped out of her lungs.

She couldn't breathe.

Ghost Wolf towered over her, a menacing silhouette blocking the sun. He shifted a large knife from his left hand to his right.

Yardley raised her arms to protect her face.

"Don't!"

He kicked her.

"All you had to do was stay in the house. That's all you had to do, one simple little thing."

"You were going to kill me."

"Shut up."

"I have money," she said. "I can pay you. We'll go get it right now. It's at my bookstore. It's more than a hundred thousand."

"Sorry, baby."

"But—"

He kneeled down, grabbed her hair and pulled her face to his.

"You don't like me," he said. "You didn't like me from the first minute you saw me."

"That's not true."

"You think I'm ugly."

"No I don't."

He grabbed her blouse and ripped it open with a violent motion that sent buttons flying. Then he grabbed her bra and tore it off. Holding her down with one hand, he wedged a knee between her legs, then the other

"One last ride before you die," he said. "That's my gift to you."

He was undoing his belt.

Yardley flailed her hands wildly, searching for a rock or stick or anything.

There was nothing.

Nothing.

Nothing.

Nothing.

The man grabbed her face and squeezed.

"You're going to like this," he said.

His eyes were crazy.

Slobber dripped from his mouth.

She reached for the knife.

She was fast.

He was faster.

He held it at length, taunting her.

"Is this what you want?"

He tossed it to the side, far, twenty or thirty feet.

Then he pinned her arms above her head with one hand and reached between her legs with the other.

She struggled to get her wrists free.

They wouldn't budge.

The man's strength was absolute.

88

arabella's question—*Do you remember a woman named Yardley White?*—pounded inside Sophia's brain with the strength of a hundred maniac drums. Somehow that woman, whoever she was, had something to do with Sophia's past.

Luckily the woman lived in Denver.

According to the Internet, she owned a bookstore on Wazee that specialized in collectible and valuable books. The scope of the business was international; the store's website was offered in five different language selections.

The name of the store, Extraordinary Books, was vaguely familiar.

She'd heard it before.

Either that, or maybe she wandered in one day.

No.

Wait.

She'd seen the name in the paper, recently too, about a third of the way down the page.

She headed to the firm's library on the middle floor and flipped through the stacks. It took twenty minutes but she eventually found what she was looking for. As soon as she saw it, she remembered. It was an article about a woman named Deven Devenshire who was murdered outside a club called

Rikki. The victim worked at Extraordinary Books.

The article felt like a black nail being pounded into Sophia's soul.

She'd killed a woman in California in her past.

Yardley White was mysteriously a part of that past.

An associate of Yardley White's just got murdered.

Sophia dialed the number of the store.

No one answered.

She grabbed her purse and headed for the elevator.

89

The scorpion tattoo guy, Jack Plank, lived in a small brick bungalow on Marion, two blocks east of Colfax, awash in a sea of the same. None of the houses had driveways or garages meaning that curbside parking was at a premium. Teffinger swept by the house after putting Kelly in a cab back to the firm. The windows were open and the front curtain was twisting whimsically as if being pushed by a fan. The screen door was closed but the wooden one behind it was open.

Teffinger found a space big enough for the Tundra two blocks away and doubled back on foot.

An alley ran behind the houses.

The suspect's 7-year-old Mustang was parked in that alley. The driver's window was down. Teffinger felt the grill; it was warm, not from the sun, from driving.

Jack Plank was home.

Teffinger rolled up his sleeves, swung around to the front, walked up the cracked concrete to the door and knocked.

A man answered.

Gone were the jeans and black T of yesterday. Now he was well dressed in a gray summer suit with the jacket on as if Teffinger caught him just before he was about to leave.

He had a rough, manly face.

"Sophia Phair," Teffinger said.

"What about her?"

"You were stalking her yesterday."

The man tilted his head.

"Now I recognize you," he said. "You're that detective all over the news." He opened the door, "Come on in."

Inside the place was simple but neat.

"I wasn't stalking her I was guarding her," he said. "I'm with Personal Security Specialists, we do bodyguard work among other things. We were hired by Grayson Condor to keep an eye on Sophia and make sure nothing happens to her."

"Does she know about it?"

"No."

"Condor offered it to her early on but she wasn't interested," he said. "Yesterday his nervousness caught up to him and he hired us on the sly. We're in the same building as him, down on the tenth floor. Our mission is not to be intrusive to the point of infringing on the woman's privacy but keep her close enough to protect her if anyone makes a move."

Teffinger called the law firm.

Condor confirmed the story.

Teffinger shook Plank's hand.

"Sorry about the mix-up." He was halfway out the door when he turned and said, "How come you aren't following her today?"

"We rotate," he said. "Lea has her today."

"Lea?"

Right.

Lea.

"A female?"

Plant smiled.

"Trust me, you wouldn't want to mess with her."

"What does she look like?"

"A lifeguard."

"Okay."

"Blond."

"Okay."

"Tanned."

"Okay."

Teffinger pulled up an image.

Plank said, "I don't know if this is worth anything but I saw a guy yesterday. There was nothing suspicious about him and I only saw him once but for some reason he rubbed me the wrong way. I told Lea to keep an eye out for him today just in case."

Teffinger raked his hair back.

"What'd he look like?"

"Huge," Plank said. "Six-four or thereabouts and built like a warrior."

"A warrior?"

"Right, ripped."

"Like a gladiator?"

"Right. Warrior, gladiator, same thing."

"Did he have long hair?"

Plank wrinkled his brow.

"Yeah, halfway down his back. Do you know him?"

90

Ghost Wolf had his body on Yardley's, his bare stomach flat on hers, his tongue licking her face, his pants around his knees and his hips maneuvering for penetration, when he suddenly froze. The hate in his eyes gave way to something different. He was consumed with something directly behind Yardley's head.

Then a rattle shattered the silence.

It was a snake.

It was so close that the earth behind Yardley's head vibrated.

For several seconds Ghost Wolf didn't move.

Then he slowly lowered his face so it was pointing directly at Yardley's chest and began to slither backwards down her body one inch at a time.

The rattles grew more agitated.

Yardley braced for a bite to her cheek or neck.

Her face suddenly felt cooler and she lifted her eyes to find the head of a massive rattlesnake bobbing directly above her, in and out of the sun, casting shadows across her eyes.

The reptile wasn't looking at her.

It was fixated on Ghost Wolf.

Yardley closed her eyes.

She didn't want the snake to snap at them.

Ghost Wolf had his face all the way down to Yardley's navel. He was almost free. Then with a quick jerk he drew back and stood up.

The snake lunged.

The distance was too great.

The forward momentum of the snap brought the reptile onto Yardley's chest.

It was heavy.

It was thick.

It was hot.

The rattle shook with a fierce warning directly above her face, striking her nose and ricocheting off her forehead.

She didn't breathe.

She didn't move.

Suddenly the snake lunged a second time.

Ghost Wolf screamed.

His massive body tumbled hard and bounced on the ground.

The snake was off Yardley.

She opened her eyes and twisted her head but couldn't see it.

Ghost Wolf was twitching on the ground with his hands between his legs. When he pulled them back, his cock was an awful purplish color and grotesquely swollen.

Blood dripped from it.

It took thirty minutes for Ghost Wolf to die.

Yardley watched every minute of it.

When the man finally stopped twitching and showed no reaction to being nudged, Yardley stuck a hand into his pants pocket in hopes she'd find a set of car keys.

The wait was worth it.

They were there.

A lighter was in there too.

Cigarettes were in his back pocket.

In the other back pocket was a wallet. The man's driver's

license showed he was Ghost Wolf Ki-Jaka from New Mexico. In the fold was $2,300 cash. Yardley stuck the bills in her pocket, wiped the leather as clean as she could of prints and dropped it on the ground.

Half a mile up the road she found the car, locked with the windows down a couple of inches.

She fired up the engine, lit a cigarette, made her way to an abandoned country road she'd never seen before and headed west.

The air conditioning was heaven.

The smoke in her lungs was an oasis.

As the miles clicked by her thoughts turned to Marabella. It wasn't clear if the woman had given Ghost Wolf orders to protect Yardley from Cave or to pretend that was his goal. She needed to get home and find out if her loft or store was being scrubbed of loose ends.

It took an hour and twelve minutes to get back to the city limits, less than she thought. She swung down C-470 to the west end of the light rail, dumped the car on a side street off the 6th Avenue frontage road, and took the tram east into downtown.

Her blouse was tied but not perfect.

Anyone who focused on it could tell it had been ripped off.

She kept as covered as she could, ostensibly reading a newspaper, and made her way to the loft without drawing any direct questions as to whether she was okay or what happened to her.

There she walked through the lobby, took the elevator down to the parking garage and got the spare key she kept hidden on top of the sprinkler pipe over in the corner.

Then she headed up to her loft.

Everything inside was normal.

No one had entered.

It hadn't been sanitized, meaning Ghost Wolf hadn't had instructions to kill herl

She took a long hot shower, slipped into panties and laid down on the couch.

Her eyes closed.

Everything was fine.

Everything was good.

She didn't fall asleep, almost but not quite. Twenty minutes later she got dressed and headed for the bookstore on foot.

She needed to know if it had been sanitized.

She needed to be positive that Marabella was a friend and not a foe.

91

Cutting through downtown on the shady side of the street, Sophia turned directly into the path of a skateboarder carrying a box. They both went down, the box flew and the skateboard skidded upside down to a stop.

It happened fast.

Sophia didn't know if it was her fault.

The person next to her on the ground was a teenager, high school age, a girl, with a ponytail pulled through the back of a Rockies hat. Sophia helped her to her feet. The girl's knee was bleeding.

"Sorry. Are you okay?"

The girl wiped the blood off.

"I'm fine," she said. "You?"

Sophia checked.

Her nylon had a run and the side of her skirt was dirty.

Stuff was all over the sidewalk.

Sophia helped gather it up. There were paperbacks, CDs, folded up posters, pens, a calculator, a clock radio, makeup, perfume and lotions.

The girl's name was Netta.

They shook.

Sophia grabbed the last thing down, a DVD, and glanced at the cover. There was something striking about it. The title was

"Rebel Without a Cause." Netta must have seen something in Sophia's face because she said, "Have you ever seen that movie?"

No.

She hadn't.

"Take it."

"No, I couldn't."

"For helping me pick everything up—"

She shrugged.

"Thanks."

The movie went into her purse.

They hugged.

Then they parted.

Half a block later Teffinger called and said, "Where are you?"

She told him.

She was outside knocking skateboarders to the ground.

"Outside?"

Right.

"I'd rather you stayed at the firm," he said. "It turns out that the gladiator may have been following you yesterday. Look around and see if there's a female blond lifeguard-type tailing you."

She turned.

It was true.

There she was, back fifty steps, paying attention to something in a store window.

"Who is she?"

"Her name's Lea," he said. "She's today's equivalent of the scorpion guy from yesterday who turned out to be a non-event. Both of them were hired by Condor to guard you."

"To guard me?"

Right.

That.

"Condor didn't tell me anything about that."

"He thought you wouldn't approve."

"Well, he was right." A beat then, "I need to see you. When?"

"I don't know. Tonight?"

"Deal."

"You were a bad girl," he said. "You broke into the gladiator's place."

"You talked to Kelly?"

He did.

"So what's next?"

"I'm not sure yet."

Politely, Sophia called Condor and expressed appreciation for his concern but respectfully asked that he call off the troops.

He argued but didn't win.

Sophia walked down the sidewalk as if to nonchalantly pass the bodyguard, then stopped at the last second and held her hand out.

"You're Lea," she said. The shock on the woman's face was palpable. "Nice to meet you, I'm Sophia."

Right.

The woman knew.

"You've been called off," Sophia said. "Call your office and confirm if you want. Have a nice day."

She turned and headed for Wazee.

It was time to see what she could find out about the mystery woman from her past, Yardley White.

92

Teffinger climbed a rusty fire escape up seven floors, questioned the sanity of what he was doing, then took a peek inside an industrial, single-paned window. He wasn't prepared for what he saw. The space was just that, space, broken by no walls or interior obstructions other than a few support columns. A young Asian woman was bound to one of those vertical shafts with multiple wraps of red rope. She was standing with her back strapped to it. Her feet were separated with a stretcher bar and her arms were pulled up tight, putting her in the form of an inverted Y. The rope was as snug as it could be without digging into her flesh. A red ball gag was in her mouth.

She wore no clothes.

The gladiator was kneeling at her left foot with his back to Teffinger, working yet another wrap of rope into place.

He wore jeans but no shirt or shoes.

Head-banger riffs jagged through the air.

Teffinger rapped on the glass.

The man's head turned, not all the way, just enough to concentrate on whether he had actually heard something.

Teffinger rapped again.

The gladiator turned, saw him and stood up.

His body was ripped.

He was tall, too, at least one and maybe even two inches taller than Teffinger. He flicked his head and the motion ricocheted through a thick mane of black hair.

Seconds later the door opened and Teffinger was face-to-face with the man.

"What the hell do you want?"

"I'm—"

The man cut him off.

"I know who the hell you are," he said. "That wasn't the question. The question is, what the hell do you want?"

"I came here to give you a friendly piece of advice," Teffinger said.

"Like what?"

"Like leave Sophia Phair alone, because if anything happens to her I'm going to personally rip your head off and piss in the hole."

"Is that a threat?"

"That's absolutely a threat."

The gladiator narrowed his eyes.

Then with a lightning motion he punched Teffinger in the gut, grabbed him by the face and pinned his head against the door.

"Here's a little piece of advice for you," he said. "Don't fuck with the wrong person."

He threw Teffinger down.

"Now go and piss back to where you came from you little broke-dick dog."

Teffinger grabbed the railing for support and forced his body up into a vertical position.

He brushed his jeans off.

The knee was ripped.

"You've been warned," he said.

Then he was gone.

93

Yardley swung by the bookstore on the opposite side of the street, detected nothing unusual and entered from the back. Everything was as it should be. The computer hadn't been taken or copied, everything in the vault was intact, all the books were on the shelf and her gun was still in the top drawer.

The place hadn't been sanitized.

Someone tried to turn the front door knob, found it locked and knocked.

Yardley peered out the window and saw the last person on earth she expected, Sophia Phair. She unlocked the door, grabbed the woman's arm and pulled her in.

"This is a breach of protocol," she said.

The woman was confused.

"I don't understand."

Yardley slapped the woman's face.

"You've put us both at risk," she said. "How dare you?"

It took time, but Yardley eventually learned what was going on. The woman had a memory loss and was trying to reconstruct her past. She didn't remember anything about Yardley, not word one. She only became aware of her earlier today when Marabella mentioned her name.

Yardley studied her, deciding.

Then she headed into the kitchen, pulled two cold diet Cokes from the fridge and sat the woman down.

"I'm going to assume Marabella won't mind me talking to you," she said. "You were fully a part of everything I'm going to tell you."

"Thanks. I'm scared to death," Sophia said. "Did I kill someone out in California?"

Yardley nodded.

"Chiara de Correggio," she said. "You honestly don't remember doing it?"

No.

She didn't.

"I could forget a lot of things," Yardley said. "But I don't think I could ever forget anything like that."

"Well I did."

"Lucky you."

"I feel like I'm waking up from a beautiful dream to find that the real me is a nightmare," Sophia said.

"Nightmare may be a little strong," Yardley said. "You definitely have a past though and it's not particularly pretty."

The woman grabbed her hand.

"Tell me," she said. "Tell me who I am. Tell me what I did—no, I already know that—tell me why I did it. That's what I can't figure out. I don't know what happened. I remember killing Chiara but it only comes in flashes of images. I don't know why I did it. Was it justified? Did I somehow get provoked? Was it self-defense?"

Yardley felt the corner of her mouth go up ever so slightly.

"Justified? You're kidding, right? You slit the woman's throat wide open while she was unconscious."

"How do you know?"

"Are you serious?"

Yes.

She was.

"You told me," Yardley said. "You dumped the body over a cliff that same night. It was foggy out."

The woman receded.

She remembered.

Yardley could see it in her eyes.

She could smell it on her skin.

Everything.

That's what Sophia wanted to know, every stinking detail.

Yardley got a glass of ice, poured Coke in and topped it off with a splash of rum.

"You too?"

Yes.

Definitely.

Yardley took a deep drink and organized her thoughts. "First of all, you have to promise not to go all goody goody schoolgirl on me and run to the police with what I tell you."

"I won't."

"I don't mean maybe," she said. "I need a one hundred percent guarantee."

"You have it."

Yardley chewed on it, still not sure.

Then she clinked glasses with Sophia, they downed them and mixed two more.

"Marabella—the upity-up lawyer in your law firm—runs an organization," Yardley said. "Basically it's a game of lawyer swap. I do all the nuts and bolts work. What we do is find a lawyer who's been disbarred or is on the run from something, usually someone who's out to kill them for one reason or another, and we match them with another lawyer who's sick and tired of the whole legal rat race and wants to get out."

"I don't get it."

"Let me clarify," Yardley said. "The outgoing lawyer applies for admission in another state through reciprocity. The new lawyer shows up, pretending to be the old lawyer. We arrange placement of the new lawyer with a firm, with someone on the inside who knows what's going on and gets a cut of the action."

"What's in it for the old lawyer?"

"Money."

"How much?"

"It varies," Yardley says. "To a large part it's determined by their goals. Sometimes all they want to do is open up a spa, which they can float for a couple of hundred grand. Sometimes they need a million or more."

"Where does the money come from?"

"The incoming lawyer," Yardley said. "We only approach people with deep pockets." A beat then, "There's one exception to that formula. You're one of the people who fall into that exception."

Sophia swallowed.

"How so?"

Yardley took a long swallow. "It isn't pretty," she said. "There are cases where the incoming lawyer doesn't have the funds."

"That was my situation."

She nodded.

"After you killed Chiara, you cleared out your bank accounts but that wasn't anywhere near enough to get into a scheme like this," she said. "Marabella fronted the money for you. Sophia Phair was a real lawyer. She got her money, disappeared with a new name and papers that I put together for her, and that was that."

"So where does that put me? Am I supposed to pay Marabella back?"

"You really don't remember?"

"No."

"Okay, it goes like this," Yardley said. "You and Marabella came to an agreement. She'd front the money for you and get you into the program. In return, she'd call on you one day to do a job for her."

"What kind of job?"

Yardley shrugged.

"That would be up to her when the time came," she said. "It was made very clear to you that it might very well be something extremely risky and probably illegal."

"I agreed to that?"

Yardley nodded.

"There was full disclosure and your eyes were wide open," she said. "You had every opportunity to turn it down. Back then your name was London Winger."

Sophia drank what was left in her glass, more than half, in one long swallow.

"So what you're saying is that I sold my soul to the devil."

Yardley tilted her head.

"Something like that." She leaned forward. "Let me give you a piece of advice. Someday when Marabella asks you to do whatever it is that she asks you to do, do it without question. Don't screw with her. Don't double-cross her." Yardley saw the wheels spinning in the woman's head and added, "You can't just run away from this. You can't just hop on a plane and disappear."

"Why not?"

"Because Marabella always has collateral to call on," she said.

"What kind of collateral?"

"Your family, your friends, whatever it is that's dear to you at that point in time," she said. "And when it starts it doesn't stop. It doesn't stop until you come back. What happens at that point, you don't want to even know." She patted the woman's hand. "There's no reason to dwell on it. Just do what she says when the time comes."

Sophia exhaled.

"What if I killed myself?"

"The collateral still gets collected. It's a message to others."

"So I'm trapped."

"That's the wrong way to think about it," Yardley said. "Marabella liberated you. Your past is behind you. You're not rotting away in a jail cell. Instead, you're out here in Denver practicing law and living the good life. All you have to do is hold up your end of the bargain."

The woman stood up to leave.

"Think it through," Yardley said. "You'll get used to it."

Sophia took two steps and turned.

"One question," she said. "How did you find me? I mean, I was on the run from the law, right?"

"Right."

"So how'd you find me when the law couldn't?"

"Normally I do all the finding," Yardley said. "That's the hardest part of my job, finding good incoming candidates. You were an exception. Marabella found you. She never told me how. I don't know if you two bumped into each other walking down the street or met at a bar or whatever. It was a fait accompli by the time I got pulled in."

The woman headed for the door.

"Thanks for all the honesty," she said. "I won't say a word to anyone."

"That'd be smart."

94

Back at the law firm, Sophia went to Marabella's office, closed the door and said, "I went to see Yardley White. She filled me in."

"And?"

"And I may be a lot of things but I don't screw people who help me," she said. "I just wanted you to know."

Marabella hugged her.

Sophia hugged her back.

"I don't understand how you found me. Yardley didn't know either."

"I didn't find you," Marabella said. "I stumbled into you."

"And I told you I killed someone?"

The woman nodded.

"Why would I do that? Why would I say something like that to a complete stranger?"

Marabella smiled.

"You don't remember?"

No.

She didn't.

"When we met, you had the barrel of a gun in your mouth," she said.

"I was going to kill myself?"

She nodded.

"You were ten seconds away from it. You had nothing to lose by telling me anything."

"You talked me out of it?"

"I did."

"You saved my life then."

The woman shrugged.

"You would have done the same."

"Did I ever say thanks?"

"Five hundred times."

Sophia hugged her again and said, "Let's make it five oh one."

"Okay but no more."

Back at her office there wasn't much left of the billable day but she deposited her ass in a chair and forced herself to salvage as much of it as she could.

Teffinger called her cell.

"I stopped by to say hello to your little gladiator friend. We didn't chat long. He was busy stringing a little Asian girl up with red rope."

Sophia flashed back to the Concrete Flower Factory.

"Yeah, he's into that."

"You knew?"

"Well, sort of. What'd you two talk about?"

"The weather mostly," Teffinger said. "Mainly I wanted to see if he had a piece missing from his left ear."

"Did he?"

"No. Both ears were normal," he said. "If you see him anywhere, I don't care if he's a mile away, you let me know immediately. Deal?"

Sure.

Deal.

"Are we still on for tonight?" she asked.

"Absolutely."

When she stuck her phone back in the purse, something scraped the back of her hand. She investigated to find it was that movie, Rebel Without a Cause.

She studied the cover.

The man on the front was gorgeous. The rebellious angst on his face was real.

He was James Dean.

Sophia remembered the name as soon as she saw it on the cover.

James Dean.

He died young, if she was thinking of the right guy.

She set him on the desk and got back to work.

Ten minutes later when her eyes inadvertently fell back on the man, an image jumped into her brain.

She was at Jackie Lake's house.

James Dean was at the woman's dead body.

He was flexing his fingers open and closed and open and closed, as if he had just done something hard with his hands and was working the pressure out.

He looked at Sophia, shocked to find someone else there, then charged.

She ran.

She toppled a blue lamp in front of him as she bolted through the living room. It slowed him just enough that Sophia made it to the front door.

Then she was outside.

She ran.

He was closing the gap.

She could hear his breathing.

He dove.

A hand caught her foot.

She slammed forward.

Her head struck something hard.

Then everything went black.

The memory vanished.

She was covered in sweat.

She called Teffinger.

"Jackie Lake's house," she said. "Was there a blue lamp in the living room?"

"Yes."

"Was it knocked down?"

"Yes."

"Was it smashed?"

"Yes, what's going on?"

"I think I just had a partial memory flash," she said.

"Good."

"I saw the killer's face," she said.

"Was it the gladiator?"

"No," she said. "Here's the weird part. It was James Dean."

Teffinger laughed.

"James Dean the movie star?"

Yes.

Him.

"Damn, you had me all excited there for a minute."

"It was so real—"

95

Teffinger called Sydney and said, "When you were going through the FBI's Van Gogh files, did red rope show up anywhere?"

"Are you in your truck?"

"Yes."

"What's that song playing on the radio?"

"I don't know."

"Put the phone by it."

"Sydney—"

"Just for a minute."

He did.

"That's an old Beyonce song called Crazy in Love," she said. "Pat yourself on the back. You finally got something good. How'd that happen?"

"It didn't," he said. "I was flipping the dial and that's where it was when you answered. Red rope, yes or no."

"No."

"Are you sure?"

"No," she said. "Oh, and I'm fine by the way, thanks for asking. I've been running down those numbers from the lawyer's cell phone. I've been able to eliminate a lot of them. There's one that has my interest. It came from a pay phone in San Francisco."

"San Francisco."

"Right. As in California," Sydney said.

"Why does that ring a bell?"

"That's where Jackie Lake was coming back from the night she got killed."

Right.

"Did the call come before or after she got killed?"

"Before," she said. "Three days before, actually."

"Was she in town yet?"

"No. She was still in Denver at that time."

Teffinger raked his hair back.

It flopped back down over his forehead.

"Do you have any other numbers of interest?"

"Yeah, more than I need," she said.

"Concentrate on those." A beat then, "Drop by the lawyer's house tonight. Tell her we appreciate the gesture regarding the phone but we don't have time to decipher codes. See if she'll just tell you point-blank where we can find the little asshole."

"I'll try."

He hung up and listened to the song for a few heartbeats. It wasn't bad but it wasn't the Beatles. He punched to the oldies station, got Martha & the Vandellas, Dancing in the Street, and left it there.

Back at the office he pulled the Jackie Lake file and confirmed that the lamp broken in the living room was blue. He dialed Sophia and asked, "The blue lamp has me curious. You'd been in Jackie's house before, right?"

Right.

She had.

"Maybe that's why it's in your memory," he said, "because you saw it there before."

"I'd been in her house before but I really don't remember seeing that lamp." A pause then, "Hold on. That's not true. It was in her bedroom. That's where I saw it, it was in her bedroom."

"Okay."

On his desk was a half-cup of cold coffee. He poured it in the tree-sized snake plant over by the window, got a fresh cup and went through Jackie Lake's old photos.

Several were in the bedroom.

One showed the blue lamp in there.

So, maybe Sophia's memory was accurate after all.

If the blue lamp part of it was correct, maybe the James Dean part was too, only instead of it being the real James Dean, maybe it was his ghost—someone who looked like him.

James Dean.

Did your ghost kill Jackie Lake?

He called Sydney.

"Another question," he said.

"Wait, first answer me this," she said. "After we hung up, did you let Beyonce finish her song or did you cut her off?"

He smiled.

"I'll tell you what, when you come back I'll let you program my whole radio. I won't change it for a week."

"You're messing with me."

"No, I'm serious," he said. "Now answer a question for me. When you were going through those FBI files, did the name James Dean ever come up?"

"James Dean?"

"Right, the actor."

"He's dead."

"I know but—"

"Dead people don't kill live people, Teffinger," she said. "That's Homicide 101."

96

From the terrace of her loft Friday evening, Yardley called Cave and said, "The people I report to want a truce. You get a million dollars in cash and leave town. Everyone goes their separate ways. No hard feelings. If that's acceptable, they'll have it together by tomorrow. No tricks, no double-crosses, no lies. This would be a final deal."

Silence.

Then, "I have an account in the Cayman's," he said. "You can wire it there."

No.

No electronic footprints.

"You get cash. You can wire it yourself if you want." A beat then, "Yes or no?"

"I'll think about it."

The line went dead.

Yardley knew that Cave knew it was a lie, but she also knew he was a greedy little bitch.

He'd want to believe it was true.

He'd keep himself off balance, at least for tonight, going over and over that 1 percent possibility that maybe it was legit.

That would give her time to figure out how to kill him.

She poured a glass of wine and stuck Billie Holiday in the player, getting a sultry lamenting of love gone wrong. The terrace was in the shade. The temperature was perfect. Down below, trendy little LoDo was starting to warm up its night moves.

Lights were turning on.

The shorts and Ts of the day were giving way to more formal attire.

She reclined in a lounge chair, safe.

Safe from Cave.

Safe from Ghost Wolf.

Safe from Teffinger.

Save from having to think.

Safe.

Safe.

Safe.

Safe from everything.

The wine dropped down easily and went straight to her blood.

It felt nice.

It freed her.

It lifted her.

It made her human.

She poured another glass, carried it to the railing and looked at the world below. The sun was gone. Sin, seduction and shadows were around the corner.

She loved the night.

Night was when all the stress went away. Night was when people became clearer versions of themselves. Night was when the men got hornier, the women got looser, the dangerous people woke up and the lights and music melted everything together.

She needed it, not from a distance, she needed it all around her, all over her, she needed it right there where she could touch it.

She jumped in the shower, towel-dried her hair until it was damp but not dripping, and dressed in heels, a short black skirt and a sexy black blouse that she tied in a knot below her breasts so her belly showed.

Then she headed out.

She needed to get laid.

She needed it badly.

She needed it now.

Nothing else mattered.

Nothing.

97

S ophia paced back and forth in front of the windows at homicide while Teffinger finished up one more thing at his desk. They were the only ones in the room. Outside the sun was setting

Several photos were tacked to a board behind him.

One of them was Jackie Lake.

Another was a man.

For some reason he looked vaguely familiar.

"Who's that?" she asked.

Teffinger turned.

"Michael Northway," he said.

"Who's he?"

"A schmuck."

She smiled.

"He looks familiar," she said. "I've seen him around some-where."

"Where?"

"I don't know."

"He used to be a hotshot lawyer here in town," he said. "You probably crossed paths with him at some point."

She nodded.

That was probably it.

"Where is he now?"

"New York." He powered his computer off and stood up. "Are you ready for your surprise?"

Yes.

She was.

"It involves something kinky, I hope."

He slapped her ass.

"You'll have to wait and see."

The Daniels & Fisher Tower sat in the heart of Denver on the mall. The 17th floor, just below the 2-story clock facade, had a wraparound observation deck. From there, inside the structure, a ladder led to the top of the building above the clock, which was an open bell cap protected by a narrow deck. That's where Teffinger took Sophia.

Below, Denver spiraled out in all directions.

The Pepsi Center, the Auraria campus and Elitch Gardens looked like toy replicas. The 6th Avenue freeway was a ribbon of headlights coming in and taillights going out.

Immediately below, the mall buzzed with Friday night life.

Teffinger wiggled out of a backpack, got a bottle of white wine out, poured two glasses and handed one to Sophia.

She clinked his with hers and took a swallow.

It dropped into her stomach and sent a warm chill into her brain.

"You're on the 20th floor right now," Teffinger said. "Not many people make it up here. Even the 17th floor deck is only opened up to the public once or twice a year."

"Why are you so special?"

"We had a homicide here two years ago right where we're standing," he said. "I got to know the maintenance guys. One of them was storing his pot up here in a weatherproof case. I never told anyone. He was appreciative."

"You'd be a good lawyer," she said. "You know how to horse trade."

"Yeah but I can't lie good enough."

"That's true. You'd need to work on that. I could teach you."

He smiled.

Then he put a serious expression on his face.

"I did some follow-up on your James Dean flash," he said. "I got to thinking that maybe you were seeing someone who looks like James Dean. I mentioned it to Kelly Ravenfield who turned me on to something."

"What?"

"There's a private investigator in town by the name of Sanders Cave," Teffinger said. "Kelly's old law firm used to hire him for projects. He has a remarkable resemblance to James Dean."

Sophia's heart raced.

"Do you have a picture of him?"

Yes.

He did.

He pulled an image up of the man's driver's license on his cell phone and tilted it so Sophia could see.

"Is this the guy you saw?"

She couldn't believe it.

"It could be."

"What's that mean? Maybe yes, maybe no?"

"I'd say 90 percent yes," she said.

"Ninety percent," Teffinger said. "Could you pick him out of a lineup?"

"No."

"No? I don't get it."

"I can't say he was the person I saw at Jackie's," she said. "He's the person I saw in my flash. I can't say that the flash was a memory, though. It was more like I was watching a movie. Maybe the movie came from a memory but I don't have an actual memory. The more I think about it, the whole thing may have materialized in my head because I'd been looking at the cover of 'Rebel Without a Cause.' I have to be honest, Nick. If

Abraham Lincoln's face had been on the cover, it might have been him that I saw in my flash."

Teffinger stared at the lights.

"Can you get a search warrant for his house?"

"Not based on what you've told me," he said. "What you're saying is that you saw him more in something like a dream than a memory."

She nodded.

"Sorry. I wish I could say otherwise."

Teffinger pulled her to him.

"I'll tell you a secret," he said. "Right now at this second I don't care about anything except one thing."

98

Teffinger swung past the gladiator's place, found the lights on and decided to hang out for a while and see if the man made a move. The chances were remote but remote was still more than zero. He parked a half block down the street, killed the engine and left the radio on.

The Zombies sang Tell Her No.

Teffinger could still smell Sophia in his clothes and taste her in his mouth. She might be a lawyer but she was built for sex and not afraid to prove it.

A shadow moved in the gladiator's window.

Frankly, Teffinger wasn't sure he was staking out the right man.

Cave was still a contender in his mind.

The gladiator, however, had more concrete evidence against him. He'd been staking out Sophia for at least two weeks. Admittedly there could be a non-lethal explanation. Maybe the gladiator saw her somewhere, got infatuated and decided to do a little recon before making a move. Guys have done stranger things. Still, the gladiator didn't really need recon, not if the only goal was to impress a woman. He carried all the persuasion he needed right there in his smile and his muscles. He was more the kind of guy who could just look at a woman and suck her in.

Teffinger needed access to the man's laptop.

He needed to find out if the guy had photo files on any of the other Van Gogh victims. What would really be nice is if Teffinger could find a bottle of ears. He had to resist the urge to break in. If the evidence was there and he tainted it through an illegal entry, that would be irreversible.

A light went out.

Then another.

Two minutes later the man walked out of the building to a car and pulled into the night.

Teffinger turned the radio off and followed.

"Head to Sophia's house," he said. "I dare you."

If the gladiator was going for Sophia, he was doing it by way of a fifty mile detour, heading east on 6th Avenue all the way to Golden, then cutting to the left and winding up Lookout Mountain.

The road snaked up with an endless string of hairpin switch-backs, winding ever higher. The lights of Denver twinkled to the east, stretching farther and farther out as the road climbed.

Teffinger stayed back as far as he dared and, in fact, didn't even have a visual of the gladiator most of the time.

He came around a switchback.

The gladiator was parked in a turnoff, standing in front of his headlights.

As Teffinger came around, the man waved him in.

The smart thing to do would be to keep going.

He pulled in, killed the engine and stepped out.

"Nice view, huh?"

"Yeah, real pretty," Teffinger said.

"I killed a man here once," the gladiator said. "I was seventeen. He was twenty-three. His girl liked me better than she liked him. He didn't take too kindly to that and wanted to settle things man-to-man. I said sure but he'd have to throw the first punch. You know why?"

Teffinger said nothing.

"Self-defense," the gladiator said. "Once that first punch is thrown, a man has a right to defend himself."

He took his shirt off, slowly, one button at a time and then neatly placed it on the hood.

His chest was steel.

His arms were pythons.

"How about it Teffinger? Do you feel like taking that first punch?"

Teffinger took a step towards the man and squared off.

"Why don't we both take it?" he said. "On the count of three. I'll even let you do the counting."

The gladiator hardened his face.

He raised his fists.

"Good enough," he said.

Teffinger put his fists up and said, "This is for that little Asian girl."

One ...

Two ...

Three!

99

Yardley ended up in a throbbing club filled with nasty thoughts, hot bodies and a driving beat. She got three rum and cokes in her gut on top of the wine and wedged into the center of the dance floor. The music took control. She surrendered to it, her arms up, her hips grinding, her lips parted, her eyes unfocused.

A body ground into her from behind.

A hand reached around and cupped her stomach.

She didn't turn around.

She went with the beat.

She went with the moment.

The hand moved up and went to her breast. Yardley pushed the hand in tighter. A nibble came at the back of her neck.

She turned and found herself face-to-face with a stunning woman.

A stranger.

A perfect stranger.

A perfect stranger with lagoon eyes, soft blond hair and pink lips.

They kissed.

The woman's mouth was soft.

Her tongue was wet.

Her perfume was sex.

She put her mouth to Yardley's ear and said, "I've been looking for you."

Yardley pulled up an image.

They were in bed.

She was on her back.

The woman was above her, naked from the waist down, straddling Yardley's face, rocking her hips, grabbing a fistful of Yardley's hair with hard tight fingers and pulling her face up tighter into her pussy.

She squeezed the woman's hand.

"I live close," she said.

"Let's go."

DAY
SIX

July 23
Saturday

100

Teffinger regained consciousness to find he was outside in the dirt, in the middle of a black night, with a seriously damaged face and a body that may or may not be broken. He got to his knees and used the Tundra for support to get upright. The lights of Denver came in and out of focus to the east. He was still up on Lookout Mountain.

The gladiator had beaten the shit out of him.

It was one-sided from the get.

In fact, Teffinger couldn't even remember if he got one solid punch to the man's face.

The guy could have killed him.

The next time he would.

This was a warning.

He got into the truck and sat there until the dizziness in his head dissipated, then made it home alive. The bathroom mirror wasn't kind. It showed a seriously swollen lip, a half-shut eye, ragged cuts, and a large number of nasty bruises on his arms, neck and torso. Under his hair was a lump the size of an egg. As far as he could tell, no bones were broken. He got in the shower, cleaned up as good as he could, left all the wounds uncovered and fell into bed.

When he woke up it was 10:16.

He got the coffee going and ate cereal from the left side of his mouth. Chewing was tough. There was a deep cut on the inside of his mouth where his cheek had been punched into his teeth.

Traffic on the drive in was thicker than usual.

Just as he passed Federal, his phone rang and Sydney came through.

"Bad news," she said.

"Why? What happened?"

A beat then, "You sound weird."

"My lip's swollen."

"From kissing?"

He grunted.

"Yeah, kissing fists. Give me the bad news first."

"First? There's only bad news, Teffinger. There's no bad news followed by good news. There's only bad news."

"Okay, give me that first then."

She smiled.

"I haven't been able to get to the lawyer yet. She didn't go home last night. I don't know where she went. Worse though, I think we've been tricked," she said, "and when I say we, I mean me."

"How so?"

"That cell phone that she left on the table? I think it was a decoy," she said. "I've run down every number in it. As far as I can tell, not one of them was to or from Northway. In hindsight, what I think happened is that the lawyer left it on the table pretending to help us but actually to obstruct us. My suspicion is that she called Northway as soon as she left the table. He's probably in Bangkok by now." A pause then, "The sad thing is there probably isn't anything we can do about it. She never specifically said we'd find anything in there."

"Maybe you missed something."

She sighed.

"I've already double-checked," she said. "Do you want me

to triple-check?"

He considered it.

His brain hurt, right behind his eye.

It felt like someone was inside his skull trying to break out with a hammer.

"No," he said. "Try to make contact with the lawyer again. Tell her we need his location and need it now. If we get it, it never came from her. Nothing about her ever goes into a file. If we don't get it though and it turns out that she tipped him off, tell her we're going to treat that as being an accessory after the fact."

"Okay, but you still sound weird."

When he got to the office things got worse. It turned out that the chief wanted to see him. Tanker closed the door, wrinkled every crease in his 50-year-old face and said, "This is a conversation I hoped to never have."

With that, he showed Teffinger a DVD.

It was the one of Teffinger breaking into September Tadge's law office, copying confidential and privileged files and sneaking out.

Teffinger went to speak but Tanker cut him off with a wave of the hand.

"Don't say anything," he said. "September Tadge's lawyer, who turns out to be none other than Grayson Condor, dropped this off this morning on behalf of his client. He says you not only stole files from Ms. Tadge but you're also bedding Sophia Phair, who's a prime witness in the case, and maybe even a suspect."

Teffinger's mouth opened.

Tanker frowned.

"Don't say anything," he said. "I already knew about Sophia. The important thing here is that Condor knows about it and doesn't take too kindly to it." He diverted his eyes for a second then looked back. "We both knew your dick was going to get you in trouble sooner or later. It was just a matter of time."

Teffinger exhaled.

"Now what?"

"I don't have a choice Nick," he said. "I love you like a son. You know that, but this time my hands are tied. I have no option but to suspend you pending an investigation. That's the protocol and there's nothing I can do about it."

101

The tight little beauty from the club last night turned out to be a New York model named ReVelle Sunn. Yardley woke up to the woman in bed with her Saturday morning and studied her curves as she headed for the shower.

Things were unraveling.

Cave was still drawing air in and out of his lungs, un-killable.

Death was everywhere.

It still wasn't a hundred percent clear if Marabella was friend or foe. The specter of being held captive by Ghost Wolf wouldn't leave Yardley alone.

Plus the whole operation had grown too big. Too many links were in the chain. It was only a matter of time before the weakest one snapped.

It was time to cut and run.

She'd made herself a promise at the very beginning that she wouldn't get sucked in past the safety point. Today she was keeping that promise.

Nobody would know.

She wouldn't tell Marabella.

She'd disappear without a trace, never to be seen or heard from again.

The shower door opened and ReVelle slipped in, naked, still groggy but smiling. She got behind Yardley and rubbed her shoulders.

"Thanks for last night."

Yardley turned and kissed her.

"Do you have a roommate?"

No.

She didn't.

"Do you want one?" Yardley asked.

"You?"

She nodded.

"In New York?"

"Right. I'm going to move."

"When?"

"Today."

The woman ran her eyes down Yardley's body as if seeing it for the first time, then did the same with her face. "We'll make you a model," she said. "I'll hook it up."

An hour later Yardley drove nonchalantly past the bookstore, saw no signs of Cave and parked behind in the alley next to the dumpster. With the gun ever within reach, she began the sanitizing process. Every single shred of her existence for years needed to be erased.

There could be no loose ends.

All physical and electronic footprints needed to be destroyed.

Documents got shredded.

All the cash went into a suitcase.

Fake driver's licenses, passports, birth certificates and credit cards went into her purse.

The desktop computer had carefully been used only for legitimate bookstore business purposes. Still, out of an abundance of caution, Yardley reset it to initial factory settings, removed the hard drive and stuck it in the suitcase.

The laptop went in there too, after resetting it. Later it would be smashed and hidden from the world where no one would stumble on it in a million years, the bottom of the ocean or something equivalent.

Most of the critical information was stored on five flash drives.

Yardley cut each one into thirds.

On the drive home, she tossed them out the window one at a time, aiming for gutters and shrubs and whatnot.

Outside the clouds built up. The sunshine got spotty and then disappeared altogether. The temperature dropped into the low 80s and the humidity increased. A stronger wind blew.

A storm was coming.

With big kissing and a smiling face, ReVelle headed back to New York in a private jet late in the afternoon with Yardley's suitcases in hand. There'd be no check-in or checkout of baggage. Since the flight started inside the United States, customs wouldn't be involved.

The cash wasn't an issue.

Even if ReVelle took it, which was unlikely, Yardley still had eight times that amount in offshore accounts.

She sanitized her apartment.

Tonight she'd make Cave pay for killing Deven.

She'd spend the night in a sleazy hotel, paying cash.

Tomorrow she'd fly to New York irrespective of what happened tonight. If she had to come back for Cave two or three months down the road, so be it.

Late in the afternoon she bought a Kawasaki dirt bike, street legal with turn signals, plus a helmet, all for cash, under a fake name, Samantha Seagull. She wasn't new to bikes. Her license had a motorcycle endorsement.

Cave would never expect her on a bike.

He'd be looking for a car.

102

Things weren't like the old days when a guy could get a little dirty and bounce back. Now everything was politically correct, by the book, with checks and balances and fifty thousand people involved. Teffinger knew that. He'd screwed up this time past the point of no return. Driving back home after the fateful meeting with the chief, he called Kelly and told her the bad news.

"I'm thinking about resigning before I get officially fired," he said.

"No, don't," she said. "Let me give it some thought."

"There's no thought to give it," he said. "I broke into an attorney's office and stole confidential files. The whole damn thing is on videotape. What's the defense to that? That I had a few beers? That I did it in the name of catching the bad guy? That I won't do it again?"

"Nick—"

"God, I can't believe I did this to myself."

"Calm down."

"How can I? That job was my life. I don't have anything else."

"You have me."

He exhaled.

"You know what I mean," he said. "The pisser is that Tanker's going to catch a lot of flak for this too. He's stood up for me every time I got close to the edge. All that will come out."

Silence.

"Like I said, let me think about it," Kelly said. "Let's meet later this afternoon, say 4:30. Not my office though. The rumors from your last visit are still flapping out of everyone's gossipy little gums."

Fine.

Whatever.

"Where?"

"How about in front of the Daniels & Fisher Tower?"

The Daniels & Fisher Tower.

That's where he screwed Sophia last night.

"I'll make it easy for you," he said. "How about right outside your building. We'll go somewhere and I'll buy you a glass of wine."

She laughed.

"What's so funny?"

"You just used the word I and the word buy in the same sentence," she said.

He smiled.

"See what stress will do to you?"

"I guess."

It was a long time until 4:30. Teffinger was good at a lot of things but filling empty time wasn't one of them. He didn't even know what empty time looked like until this second.

Now he knew.

It wasn't pretty.

He drove west through Golden and wound up Clear Creek Canyon with vertical rock on one side and the rapids on the other. Where the water was the wildest, he found a turnoff and climbed down to a boulder at the river's edge.

The roar of the water filled his ears.

It was so weird being here.

It was a workday.

He got up to leave, once, then twice, then three times, each failing when he couldn't think of where to go.

Sophia left a message.

She was okay, she was at work, she just wanted to thank him for last night, she still tingled between the legs, she wanted more.

He called Sydney.

She'd already heard the bad news and was en route back to Denver to take over the Jackie Lake case.

"I had a feeling this would happen some day," she said. "I just pictured it at least a few years off."

"I guess you were half wrong."

"Yeah, I guess," she said. "Oh, by the way, the attorney refused to meet with me again. We have a total strikeout on Northway."

"That's because that's the way my life works," Teffinger said. "One good thing. The department's going to save a lot of money on coffee with me gone."

Sydney laughed.

"Millions," she said. "You're not gone yet though. Be on speed dial. As far as I'm concerned, you're still running the Jackie Lake case."

"If you want."

"I want."

He was downtown in front of Kelly's building at 4:20, sitting on the sidewalk with his knees up and his back against the stone.

Someone walked by and tossed a dollar at him.

He looked up.

It was a man swinging a leather briefcase.

"Thanks," he said.

The man didn't respond.

He just kept walking.

Teffinger wasn't worth a look back.

The appointed time came and went.

Kelly didn't come out.

She must be stuck on the phone.

At 4:45 she still wasn't out.

Then 5:00 came and still no Kelly.

He called her cell.

She didn't answer.

He called the law firm receptionist and asked for her.

"She's been out all afternoon, then she had a 4:30 appointment out of the office. I don't expect her back today."

Okay.

Thanks.

He stood up and paced.

Half an hour went by. Now it was 5:30. Kelly was officially a full hour late.

He called her cell.

She didn't answer.

103

Saturday night after dark a mean thunderstorm fell out of an even meaner sky. Bolts of lightning ripped the blackness, one after another after another, igniting swirling clouds in their eerie wrath and slapping thunder across the front range. Dressed in all things black, Yardley took shelter from the weather in the rusty interior of a 1972 Camero, east of Cave's house, in Honest Ed's Junkyard.

She was locked in dark thoughts.

Tonight was made for killing.

It was built for it.

Cave would show up.

"This is for Deven."

Those would be the last words his twisted little ears would hear on earth.

He lived in an uneventful two-story wooden structure at the end of a hundred-yard gravel drive that fed off South Golden Road in Golden. The area was a mismatch of development. Cave's property was bounded on one side by the junkyard and on the other by the decaying infrastructure of what had once been a trailer park but was now a ghost town.

Yardley trained a pair of AutoFocus Bushnell binoculars on Cave's windows. They were exactly the same as when she got here two hours ago, dark and lifeless.

He'd come.

She could feel it.

Tonight was the night.

She'd kill him.

She'd never regret it, not in fifty years. When she was old, she'd look back on this night and smile. She'd do it again, even then, if she had to.

Come on, Cave.

Come on home.

It's safe.

Don't be afraid.

104

In the midst of a violent storm, Sophia parked her car a hundred feet down from Honest Ed's Junkyard and headed for Cave's house on foot. Ever since Teffinger showed her the man's driver's license, his James Dean face became clearer and clearer as the person she saw murder Jackie Lake.

She needed to get into his house.

She needed to see if Jackie Lake's ear was in there.

Teffinger didn't know what she was doing.

He'd try to prevent it.

If she insisted, he might even break in himself just so she wouldn't put herself at risk. She didn't want to force him into that position, particularly given the trouble he was already in.

The night was dark except for when the lightning jerked it apart.

She made her way one silent step at a time to the house.

The windows were dark.

No light came from inside.

There was no garage.

There was no vehicle in the driveway.

She tried the front doorknob to find it locked.

She knocked on the door, loudly, then ran thirty steps and ducked behind an old barrel. The front door didn't open. No lights turned on inside.

Cave wasn't home.

Either that or he was lying in wait.

She headed around to the back of the house, trying the windows as she did and finding them all locked. The rear door was also secured. She went to the other side of the house, busted a window and yelled in, "Anyone home?"

No one answered.

She climbed in.

Water dripped off her face and hair and clothes onto a carpet. She stood still and listened for the charging feet of someone who'd laid a trap.

No charge came.

She fired up a flashlight to find herself in a small bedroom. A quick scan showed nothing of interest, which is what she expected. If someone had souvenir ears of murder victims, they'd be well stashed. A main level bedroom wouldn't be the first choice.

She headed downstairs into the basement.

The planks creaked.

The musty odor of stale humidity hung in the air. If the place ever had French drains they must have clogged up twenty years ago. The ceiling was low, six foot or thereabout, probably initially built for storage rather than living. She could stand upright without hitting her head on the joists but not by much.

In the corner was an old furnace.

Next to it was a shiny water heater, recently installed.

The flicker of a pilot light danced eerily behind a shield. Crude wooden shelves lined a wall, filled with junk and cobwebs.

The splash of the flashlight was creepy.

A bare light bulb screwed into a crude ceiling fixture had a pull chain hanging from it. She was half-tempted to see if it worked but there was a small garden-level window that could give her away.

She stayed with the flashlight.

There were no rooms, doors or enclosures.

The only hidden space to speak of was the one under the stairs, jammed with boxes and junk. Given the dust and spider webs, no one had disturbed it for some time.

Then she noticed something.

Over in the corner against the wall there were several vertical two-by-fours running from the floor to the ceiling and serving as supports for water pipes and ductwork. One section of those studs had a wooden cover. On inspection, it was a piece of plywood with circular holes in the top corners, approximately one inch in diameter. Those holes fit over nails, which supported the wood.

She lifted the wood off and set it on the ground.

What she saw she could hardly believe.

Between the studs were a number of horizontal, two-by-four shelves.

On those shelves were ten or more mismatched jars filled with some kind of yellowish liquid.

Inside each jar, sunk down at the bottom, was a human ear.

Cave's face jumped into Sophia's brain.

It was his face that she saw at Jackie Lake's.

It was his face that she saw when he chased her out the door that fateful night. It was his face that she saw right before he grabbed her foot and sent her flying into the fire hydrant.

It was his face.

There was no question.

This wasn't a dream.

It wasn't a trick of the night.

It was a memory.

105

Kelly was nowhere. She never showed up for the 4:30 meeting, never went back to the firm, never answered her phone and never called Teffinger. He swung past her house three times and her car wasn't in the driveway.

She was gone.

A dark thought emerged.

Maybe the gladiator took her to mess with Teffinger.

Maybe that's why the man didn't kill Teffinger last night. Maybe he was going to entice Teffinger to rescue his little squeeze and then murder her in front of his eyes.

It was night.

A nasty thunderstorm beat down on Denver.

Teffinger swung over to Kelly's house for the fourth time. Everything was the same as before. There was no car in the driveway. No interior or exterior lights shined. No one was home.

Still, Teffinger pulled into the driveway and killed the engine.

When he stepped out the weather assaulted him.

The rain was almost horizontal.

The front door was locked. He pounded on it, hard, and mashed the doorbell in again and again and again. No one came.

He went around to the back.

To his surprise, the back door was wide open and the kitchen floor was drenched with rain. Kelly's purse was sitting on the granite countertop. Inside were her wallet, keys and cell phone.

Then he spotted blood on the floor.

"Kelly!"

No one answered.

He searched the house.

She wasn't there.

Her car was in the garage.

Teffinger raced out to the Tundra, fired the engine and spun the back tires, heading for the gladiator's.

His stomach quivered.

His breath was short and rapid.

The beating of last night played with his brain.

Another trauma like it would be his death.

Halfway to the gladiator's, his cell rang. He answered hoping beyond hope that it was Kelly with some stupid explanation.

Instead Sophia's voice came through.

"Nick it's me," she said. "Listen carefully. Cave is the one who killed Jackie Lake. I'm at Cave's house right now. I broke in. I found the ears. They're in jars down in his basement. I remember him being at Jackie's. It's not a dream. It's a memory. I'm positive of it."

"You're at Cave's right now?"

"Yes."

"Where's Cave at?"

"I don't know," she said. "He's not here."

"Get the hell out of there right now!"

"It's okay. He's not here."

"Do it!"

"Teffinger, you don't have to yell—"

"Just do it! Go, go, go! Get out of there right now, this second."

"I'll bring a jar with me."

"Forget the jars. Just get out of there! Do you hear me? Do it now."

The line got silent.

"Are you there?"

No answer.

"Sophia, I said are you there?"

"Yes, I'm here. I think I heard something. I got to go."

The connection died.

Teffinger almost hit redial but had the presence of mind to consider that if the noise was Cave, the last thing Sophia needed was for her phone to ring.

Where to go?

The gladiator's?

Cave's?

He smacked his palm down on the dash.

Choose!

Choose!

Choose!

A bolt of lightning struck a telephone pole to his left and lit the night with a force that made his eyes shut. The thunder was so explosive and immediate that he instinctively jerked the wheel away from it.

106

Sophia flicked the flashlight off and stood perfectly still, frantic to not hear another strange sound, desperate to learn that what she heard before was simply a trick of the night. The storm pounded against the upper level, rattling the windows, loud but constant, with no jagged interruptions except for thunder.

Then something bad happened.

Glass shattered.

A door opened and then slammed shut.

Heavy footsteps walked almost directly above her.

She flicked the flashlight on just long enough to wedge into the junk under the stairs. No more than a second after she turned it off, the door above her opened and someone walked down, using a flashlight for a guide.

It was a man.

She could tell by his breathing.

Cave no doubt.

He didn't come at her when he got to the cement. Instead he shined the light at the corner where the jars were. Then he walked in that direction. Enough light splashed off the walls for Sophia to see that he was carrying a jar.

He set it on the shelf next to another one.

There was liquid inside the jar.

A human ear was in that liquid, sunk to the bottom.

Sophia gasped.

The flashlight jerked in her direction.

Then the man charged.

She scrambled back and raised her arms to protect her face.

The flashlight came down on the top of her skull.

Colors flashed in her brain.

She tried to stand but her legs wouldn't respond.

The flashlight stuck again.

Then everything went black.

107

From Honest Ed's Junkyard, Yardley saw something she didn't expect, namely a woman broke into the side window of Cave's house and disappeared inside. She didn't turn on any inside lights. A flicker of flashlight washed across the walls.

What was she doing?

Robbing the place?

Not more than five minutes later a man—Cave, no doubt—parked in front of the structure and entered from behind.

Strangely, he didn't turn the lights on.

Three or four minutes later he dragged a woman around the side of the house, put her in the trunk of his car and took off. Yardley hopped on the Kawasaki and followed with the headlight off.

The car was easy to keep in view; the right taillight was weaker than the left, as if there were two bulbs inside and one had burned out.

Vision was dangerous.

The storm built up too much on the helmet's faceplate to see through. She had to keep it raised. The rain stung her face with cold needles. She squinted but the occasional needle still got through to her eyeball.

East.

East.

East.

Forever east, that's where Cave was going. The traffic thinned then got almost non-existent. The sky was black and the road was equally so. She couldn't see it, not an inch. With the headlight off, she could only gauge where to go by the movement of the taillights ahead.

Half an hour passed, then five more minutes and then ten more.

Her face was so raw that it had to be bleeding.

Then something bad happened.

Her front tire hit something. The bike went down and slid out from under her. Her body skidded down the asphalt and then slammed into something hard and immobile.

The breath flew out of her chest.

She tried to stand.

Her knees buckled and her body crumbled.

108

Sophia regained consciousness to find she was tightly jammed into the trunk of a moving car. Her legs were tied at the ankles and knees, and her wrists were bound behind her back. The noise from a storm above and the road below was deafening.

Another person was inside the trunk with her.

It was Kelly Ravenfield, identically bound.

"See if you can get your hands by mine," Kelly said.

Sophia tried to shift her body.

There was no room.

There was hardly enough room to expend her chest to breath.

"I can't."

"Let me try."

She wiggled.

The wiggle did no good.

"He's going to kill us," Kelly said. "He already told me he was."

"Cave?"

"No, Michael Northway," Kelly said.

"That lawyer from New York?"

Yes.

Him.

"I don't get it."

"He killed Jackie Lake," Kelly said.

"No, Cave did."

"No, he did," she said.

Northway used to be a hotshot lawyer in Denver but he had a dark side and got himself mixed up with a serial killer. Bad things happened and he ended up on the run. He had a friend in Denver named Grayson Condor.

"From my firm?"

Right.

Him.

Condor got Northway a lawyer job in San Francisco under the name Rydell Rain. It was a complicated reciprocity scheme implemented by Condor's right-hand man, Marabella Amberbrook, who delegated almost everything to Yardley White.

"Jackie Lake was in San Francisco taking depositions," Kelly said. "She saw Northway on the street and knew who he was and the fact that he was on the run. She also knew that Northway had been a client of Condor's at one time. She called Condor to let him know she'd seen him. He talked her out of calling the police right away. He said he'd go with her to the police station tomorrow morning. They'd play it up and make sure they got lots of kudos in exchange. She didn't see the harm in it. She had a status conference set for the morning and sent you a text to see if you'd cover for her."

That was true.

"How do you know all this?"

"Northway told me," Kelly said.

"Why?"

"Because he's going to kill me."

"Why?"

"Because it was all the investigation I did initially that ended up bringing him down and forcing him on the run," she said. "Then I was the one who saw him in New York and called

Teffinger about it."

After Jackie Lake called Condor, he called Northway to let him know he'd been spotted. Northway wanted Condor to kill the woman. Condor tried. He called Yardley to set it up. She called Cave; she couldn't get a hold of him but left him a message. When she didn't get a call back she let Condor know it didn't look like the kill could be arranged before the morning. Condor called Northway back and gave him the bad news.

So Northway flew out and did it himself.

He made it look like Cave's work.

"You mean cutting off the ear?"

Right.

The ear.

The rape.

The strangulation.

Cave did that sick shit on the side for his own personal enjoyment. No one knew about it for a long time, then Condor found out about it one day when he had lunch with an attorney named September Tadge, who got calls from a man telling her about these murders he committed. Condor had a suspicion it might be Cave. He dug into it and confirmed the suspicion. That's when he met with Marabella and they decided that Cave was too sick to be part of the organization. They set him up to be hit down in Florida but it didn't go as planned. They've been trying to kill him ever since.

"Anyway, Northway flew to Denver and killed Jackie Lake," Kelly said. "As he was heading down the street, he spotted Cave sneaking into the woman's place. A few minutes later you showed up. You saw Cave at the body. You figured he was the killer and ran. He chased you and you ended up slamming into a fire hydrant." A beat then, "Here's the ironic part. Cave was going to kill you right then and there but Northway chased him off. Northway was the guy with the long hair that Teffinger could never find."

Suddenly what happened at Cave's house made sense.

Northway had Jackie Lake's ear in a jar.

He was planting it at Cave's.

He was framing the man.

The vehicle slowed and turned right onto a bumpy road.

"I think we're near to where Northway's taking us," Kelly said.

Sophia pulled at the rope.

It didn't budge.

"We have to do something."

"What?"

"I don't know," she said. "We have to talk him out of it somehow."

"He's too smart for that."

"Let's do this," she said. "Let's tell him to let us have a fight to the death. The winner goes free."

"Why would he do that?"

"To watch," she said.

"But he won't let one of us go free."

"Yeah but he'll lie about it and let us fight, thinking that he'll just kill the other one after he gets his jollies watching." A beat then, "One of us needs to get our hands on something deadly. Keep a look out. When one of us makes a move the other one needs to jump in immediately."

"Okay."

"Kill him," she said. "Don't get second thoughts."

"Trust me, I won't."

109

The car stopped, the trunk opened and Northway pulled Sophia out and laid her on the ground in the mud. He bent down with his knee on her chest, held a knife in front of her face and said, "Do something stupid and I'll gouge your eyes out. Do you understand?"

"Yes."

"Say it!"

"I understand."

"You better."

He checked the ropes on her wrists, found them secure then unfastened the rope on her ankles, rearranging it so there was a two or three foot gap, enough to walk in small steps but not enough to run. Then he removed the rope from her knees and wrapped it around her neck like a leash.

Kelly Ravenfield got pulled out next and treated the same way.

He held the leashes, got behind the women and said, "Walk."

They obeyed.

He took them past a small dark house and dilapidated barn, out into the terrain. The storm raged down. Lightning arced and thunder clapped.

"This is technically owned by the Apaches," he said. "Condor funded the purchase. There are a lot of people buried out here. Did you know that?"

"Look," Kelly said. "Give at least one of us a chance. Let us fight each other to the death, like gladiators. The weaker one will die. Let the stronger one go."

Northway laughed.

"That's the best trick you can think of? I'm disappointed. Keep walking."

"But—"

He punched her in the back.

"Shut up. Keep walking."

Ten minutes into it he powered up a powerful flashlight and swept it across the field. A hundred yards away an orange reflector lit up.

"Head for that," he said.

The light went out.

They walked in darkness.

The orange light turned out to be a bicycle reflector taped to a stick.

Next to it was a hole three feet or so in diameter, six or seven feet deep.

Northway stood the women face-to-face and then wrapped them together with rope. He wrapped even more rope around their arms behind them and then gagged their mouths with rope.

They were immobile.

They couldn't talk.

They couldn't scream.

He walked them to the hole and forced them in, feet first, standing up. They fought but it did no good.

"This was dug just for Kelly, so sorry if it's a little bit of a tight fit," he said.

Their heads were a foot below surface level.

They were looking directly into each other's eyes.

"There's a man who uses this place by the name of Ghost Wolf," he said. "This is how he buries all his people. It's weird how people develop these little quirks, wouldn't you say? You have to wonder sometimes how they get started on them. Anyway, it will look like his work."

With a shovel, Northway filled the hole past the women's stomachs, to just below their breasts.

"That's it," he said. "If I put any more in the compaction will keep your chests restricted and you won't be able to breathe." A beat then, "This way you'll be able to last for as long as you last. What will happen after you die is that the walls will eventually cave in and cover you up, then the weeds will grow and the butterflies will fly. Pretty neat, huh?"

He scattered the remaining dirt.

Then he bent down.

"I don't know exactly how it is you'll die," he said. "I don't know if the coyotes will find you and chew your heads, or whether the insects will eat you, or whether the sun will bake you to death or whether you'll just last a really long time and eventually starve to death. It's interesting to think about though, wouldn't you say?"

He was gone.

Ten seconds later he returned.

"Oh, and there's one I didn't think of," he said. "Maybe the rain will just fill the hole and you'll go gulp, gulp, gulp. It wouldn't be pretty but it's still probably better than the other ways."

Then he was gone.

He didn't come back.

110

Yardley had no idea how long she was unconscious. The storm was still plummeting down. Her helmet was partially filled with water. It took her a while to locate the Kawasaki but when she did it fired up. The taillight didn't work. The headlight did. With it, she located the gun and stuffed it back in her belt.

Then she headed east.

If her suspicion was right, Cave was headed to where Ghost Wolf took her yesterday. It made sense not only because this was the exact way there, but also because Cave and Ghost Wolf did the same work. They must have crossed paths and talked at some point, or talked to a mutual acquaintance.

The storm slowed her.

The front wheel wobbled.

Still, now able to use the headlight, she kept the pace up and got to the cutoff in half an hour. There she turned off the headlight and worked the bike through the pitch-blackness and the mud and the ruts.

When she got near the end where the old house was, the headlights and taillights of a parked car suddenly sprang to life.

The right taillight was weaker than the left.

It was Cave's car.

There was no question.

It turned around and headed her way, a hundred yards off, leaving.

She got the Kawasaki off the road and laid it down.

Then she waited at the edge of the road, nestled into a rabbit brush, with the gun in her hand and the safety off.

The vehicle was approaching steadily but slowly, keeping the momentum up enough to not get stuck while not going so fast as to lose control.

She'd have plenty of time to fire.

When the car got to her, she pointed at the driver's window and pulled the trigger three times.

The vehicle slowed and coasted off the road.

She approached slowly, one careful step at a time.

She opened the door and the interior lights shot on. Cave was slumped face first into the wheel.

The side of his head was a bloody mess.

At least two of the bullets landed there.

She pulled him back.

He wasn't Cave.

He was someone else.

Her chest tightened.

She popped the trunk to see if the woman was in there.

It was empty.

She got on the bike, turned on the headlight and headed for the house. No one was there, not in the barn either. The woman who got taken from Cave's house was undoubtedly dead and buried out in the north forty.

She got on the bike and pointed the headlight towards Denver.

It was time to get to New York and leave all this shit behind.

She'd come back for Cave in a month or two. For right now, enough was enough.

DAY
SEVEN

July 24
Sunday

111

Sunday was hell in the making. The manhunt for Cave continued to turn up nothing; whatever rock the little asshole slithered under, it was a big one. Sophia and Kelly both remained missing. Teffinger was subconsciously preparing himself for the worst. The gladiator had a solid alibi and had been ruled out.

Out of desperation, Teffinger drove over to September Tadge's house.

"Look," he said. "I don't care that you turned me in. That's not what I'm here about. Cave has Sophia. Every minute's critical. I need to see your notes on him and I need to see them now."

She hesitated, deciding.

Then she said, "Let me get my purse."

Teffinger drove.

On the way to the woman's office he learned a few things.

For one, September never told Condor to communicate with the department or the chief in any way, much less give them the videotape.

"Well he did," Teffinger said. "My career's shot."

September stared out the window.

Then she turned.

"After I give you the notes, I want to talk to the chief," she said. "I'm going to tell him that Condor was mistaken. He had no authority to speak to anyone on my behalf. More importantly, he was mistaken about the videotape. You were helping me install a security system. What you did was just a test to see if it was working the way it should. It was done with my full permission." She patted his hand, "When I tell him that, I need you to back me up."

Teffinger nodded.

He said, "Thanks," but his mind was on the notes.

There had to be something there to indicate where Cave might be hiding.

Ten minutes later he had the notes in front of him.

They were handwritten.

September deciphered them as necessary.

After the first pass through, Teffinger had nothing of use.

They went through them again.

Still there was nothing of use.

"Do you remember anything that he said or did, anything at all?"

She looked blank.

"I'm sorry."

DAY
EIGHT

July 25
Monday

112

Monday was a dismal endless repeat of Sunday, meaning no Cave, no Kelly and no Sophia. Teffinger was officially reinstated given September's words on his behalf, but he really didn't care much about it one way or the other.

That evening it rained.

He got a cold blue can from the fridge and sat on the front porch in the weather.

The women had been gone for 48-hours.

That was the unofficial dividing line.

The water matted his hair and soaked through his clothes.

He didn't care.

Then his phone rang.

It was September Tadge.

"I went over the notes again, twice actually, and remembered something that I never wrote down," she said. "He mentioned once that he buried one of his victims on some land owned by the Apaches, forty or fifty miles east of Denver. I checked the public records and found that there really is such a place. Do you want the directions?"

He did.

He did indeed.

Two minutes later he was in the Tundra heading east.

The storm thickened.

When he got to the location, he found something he didn't expect. A car was in the brush off the road. A man's body was slumped over the steering wheel. The left side of his head had been shot twice.

The smell of death was putrid.

He'd been dead at least a day, maybe two or three.

Teffinger pulled him back and looked at his face.

It was Michael Northway.

The trunk was popped open.

He took a look and spotted dried blood.

Kelly's?

He got in the Tundra, headed up the road and found an old house. Inside there were signs of recent activity but no one present.

"Kelly!"

No answer.

"Sophia!"

No answer.

A dilapidated barn out back was similarly empty.

Twilight was thick. It would be night in another half hour.

He shifted the truck into four-wheel drive and headed into the field, dodging rocks and yucca, looking for signs of a recent burial. Twenty minutes later he saw fresh dirt to the left and jerked the wheel over to it.

There he found a hole.

Inside about a foot down were two heads, infested with bugs. They were slumped to the side, motionless.

He shook them.

Neither one responded.

He spotted a shovel and started digging.

Don't be dead.

Don't be dead.
Don't be dead.
Don't you dare be dead!

ONE
MONTH
LATER

August 25
Thursday

113

With a little too much wine in her gut, Sophia flashed her legs at a passing LoDo cabbie who jerked to a stop, then got her home just as the twilight morphed into night. She locked the front door behind her and slithered out of a short black dress as she headed for the bedroom. En route a text came from Kelly—Lunch tomorrow?

She replied—Sounds good—then tossed the phone on the bed and checked her body in the mirror.

It was perfect.

It was built for sex.

She got the shower up to temperature but left the bathroom lights off, opting for the softer ambient light that filtered in from the bedroom.

She liked it dark.

The dark felt good after a scorching day.

In the shower, she put her head under the spray and let the sweet, sweet water soak through to her scalp and cascade over her face.

Then she lathered up.

It felt nice.

It felt right.

She turned her back to the spray, put her soapy hand between her thighs and moved her fingers. Her body tingled. She ran the index finger of her other hand in light circles over her right nipple.

Yeah.

That was nice.

That's what she needed since she got up this morning.

She closed her eyes.

She spread her feet and increased the tempo.

Little sparks of lightning shot through her veins.

Her mouth opened.

Her head rocked back and forth.

The pressure in her thighs grew stronger. When she came it would be a good one, it would be one of those mind-charging bolts of ecstasy that she'd still be feeling in the middle of the night.

She opened her eyes, just a tad.

A man was standing in front of her, a huge powerful man, right there in the shower with her.

He was holding a knife in front of her face.

He was the gladiator.

He grabbed her by the throat and said, "Don't make a sound."

She froze.

"Don't kill me," she said. "I'll do whatever you want."

He pushed the tip of the knife into her stomach enough to dent her skin without breaking through.

"Does that feel good?"

Her heart pounded.

"What do you want?"

"Want? Nothing," he said. "I came here to tell you something. You didn't kill Chiara de Correggio. I did."

"Chiara?"

Right.

Chiara.

"Chiara from California?"

"Yes," he said. "I was hired by Marabella to kill her. She drank wine every night. I laced it with roofies. You were there that night. I watched through binoculars until you both passed out in the living room. Then I came in and did my job. You were moving a little and may have opened your eyes. I didn't know if you saw me or not. Before I left I put the knife in your hand. I was hoping you'd believe you were the one who killed her. After all, you and her had a vicious fight not more than two hours before that."

"Why are you telling me this?"

"Because I want you to know," he said. "You actually believed the setup and went on the run. Marabella felt sorry for you. She tracked you down and gave you a new identity and a job. I knew she'd done that but I didn't know you were in Denver."

"So I didn't kill Chiara?"

"No," he said. "You threw her body off a cliff but you weren't the one who killed her. That was my one and only job. I didn't like doing it and Marabella didn't like that I got someone else involved." A beat then, "I spotted you on the street. The question I had was whether you would remember me if you saw me. I eventually arranged to bump into you, which was that night down at the Tequila Rose. You didn't remember me. That was good because if you had I probably would have killed you."

He ran the tip of the knife up her stomach drawing a thin line of blood.

"You see what I'm doing right now?"

Yes.

She did.

"Let it scar and look at it every now and then," he said. "Use it as a reminder that you're not to ever tell anyone what I just told you; no one, ever. If you do, you're going to get my touch again, only this time it won't be so nice. Do we have an understanding?"

"Yes."

"Good."

He slid the door open and stepped out.

Then he was gone.

Sophia stood there in the spray, alone and shaking.

Then she ran out.

The gladiator was walking through the bedroom, almost at the door.

"Hey," she said.

The man stopped and turned.

"Thanks for telling me."

He stared at her for a heartbeat.

Then he said, "You're welcome," and left.

ABOUT THE AUTHOR

Formerly a longstanding trial attorney before taking the big leap and devoting his fulltime attention to writing, RJ Jagger (that's a penname, by the way) is the author of over twenty hard-edged mystery and suspense thrillers. In addition to his own books, Jagger also ghostwrites for a popular, bestselling thriller author. He is a member of the International Thriller Writers and the Mystery Writers of America. All of Jagger's books are independent of one another and complete within their own four corners. Read them in any order.

RJJAGGER.com

CPSIA information can be obtained
at www.ICGtesting.com
Printed in the USA
BVHW030152170520
579803BV00006B/29/J